J. F. Shew & Co.

J. F. Shew & Co.

inventors, manufacturers and patentees of specialities in photographic apparatus

and dealers in every description of photographic materials and apparatus

J. F. Shew & Co.

J. F. Shew & Co.

inventors, manufacturers and patentees of specialities in photographic apparatus and dealers in every description of photographic materials and apparatus

ISBN/EAN: 9783337361310

Printed in Europe, USA, Canada, Australia, Japan

Cover: Foto ©Andreas Hilbeck / pixelio.de

More available books at **www.hansebooks.com**

J. F. SHEW & CO.,

ESTABLISHED 1849.

INVENTORS, MANUFACTURERS AND PATENTEES

OF

Specialities in Photographic Apparatus,

AND

DEALERS IN EVERY DESCRIPTION OF

Photographic Materials and Apparatus,

87 & 88, NEWMAN STREET,

(Four Doors from Oxford Street),

LONDON, W

TELEGRAMS—"DEVELOPER, LONDON."

A

IN introducing this Twenty-Sixth Edition of our Catalogue to the Photographic world we are assured that it will meet with the same approval as has been extended to our previous editions since 1849, and that it will be found by any one interested in Photography to repay them for perusal.

Since the issue of our last edition in 1888, the most noteworthy change in the manufacture of apparatus has been that caused by the growth of the use of the Hand Camera, which has so extended since our introduction, in 1885, of the system of working at fixed focus, that Hand, or " Fixed Focus " Apparatus, is now a recognized necessity in the Photographic world.

We are pleased to be able to state that having given almost exclusive attention to the perfecting of apparatus for this system of working, we have been enabled to manufacture successively increasing sizes, until we are now making our " Eclipse " Apparatus for working plates 8½ × 6½, and for Continental use 24 × 18 centimetres.

We have from time to time added to the original form of 1885, extra movements, as they were suggested to us until the " Eclipse " with the adjuncts of the present date is a complete apparatus for Hand Camera Work, as well as for Focussing and other purposes, in fact, we are enabled to state that out of the nine points mentioned recently by one of our writers on the subject, as essential to render a Hand Camera perfect, we already combine eight in ours; and we feel sure that in the near future we shall make still further improvements to extend the usefulness of this kind of apparatus, and so lead to the adoption of this system of Photography in a wider field than has hitherto been thought possible.

We still give special attention to all forms of Portable Apparatus, the simplifying of operations and reduction of bulk and weight being our first consideration, and we would draw the special attention of intending purchasers to our New Cameras for 1891, and feel sure that their quality and simplicity of design combined with portability and moderation in price will recommend them; our long experience in designing apparatus convinces us the more simple the apparatus the greater the facility of successful manipulation.

We beg to tender our sincere thanks for the largely increased support we have received during the past few years, and to assure our numerous patrons that we shall continue, as heretofore, to use every endeavour to deserve the continuance of their favors. We much regret to have been compelled to somewhat delay the output of our specialities during the past two years, owing to the unprecedented demand and the inevitable hindrance caused by the building of our New Premises; but we can only say that being now enabled to manufacture in increased quantities, we can promise that for the future the demand shall be better met.

INDEX.

SHEW'S 1891 CAMERA.

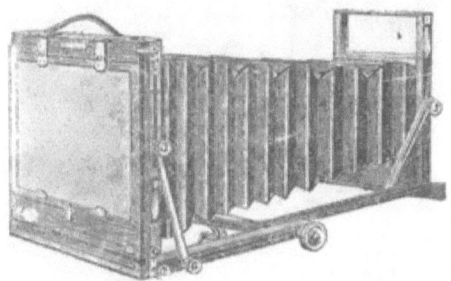

1891. OPEN.

1891. CLOSED.

OPEN FOR WIDE ANGLE WORK.

OF first-class quality and workmanship, combining every latest improvement with the greatest portability and compactness, every part being so constructed as to be perfectly rigid, although so light. The back part of the Camera sliding up close to the front when required, it is equally suitable for the short focus wide angle, and for the long focus landscape lenses, with double extension vertical and horizontal swing-back, rising and falling front, instantly adjustable by a patent lever fixing attachment, thus avoiding any loose screws. Rack-work focussing arrangement, and new patent turn-table top, fitted in base-board with patent lever fixing.

The above Camera for 8½ by 6½, weighs 4½ lbs., and measures when closed 11 by 10½ by 2.

Price, with three double backs of best manufacture, with new patent hinges and springs to shutters, and three-fold sliding tripod stand fitting in the turn-table top, complete.—

For Plates.	Length of Focus.	Price.	Brass Binding Camera and Three Backs.	Solid Leather Traveling Case
6½ × 4¾	16 inches	£8 17 6	£1 5 0	£1 5 0
7½ ,, 5	17½ ,,	9 13 6	1 7 6	1 7 6
8½ ,, 6½	19 ,,	10 15 0	1 10 0	1 10 0
10 ,, 8	22 ,,	13 17 6	1 15 0	2 0 0
12 ,,10	27 ,,	15 15 0	2 5 0	2 5 0
15 ,,12	33 ,,	19 15 0	2 15 0	3 3 0

B

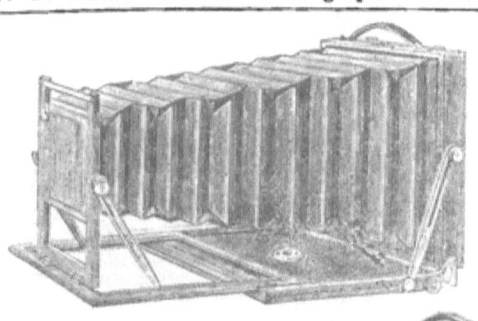

SHEW'S "MEDIUM" CAMERA.

A first-class Camera, at a moderate price. Double extension, rack-work focussing, the back arranged to slide forward to the front for use with wide angle lenses, rising and falling front, with new racking arrangement, automatically fixing the same in position. With three double backs of best manufacture.

For Plates.	Length of Focus.	Price.	Strong Waterproof Travelling Case.
6½ × 4¾	16-in.	£5 10 0	17/6
8½ ,, 6½	19 ,,	6 15 0	21/-
10 ,, 8	22 ,,	8 15 0	25/-
12 ,, 10	27 ,,	11 5 0	30/-

SHEW'S SIMPLE CAMERA.

OF similar construction to the above. Double extension, rising front, swing back, and three double backs.

Plates	Price.		For Plates.	Price.
4¼ × 3¼	£3 3 0		8½ × 6½	£5 15 0
5 ,, 4	3 7 6		10 ,, 8	7 15 0
6½ ,, 4¾	4 10 0		12 ,, 10	9 15 0

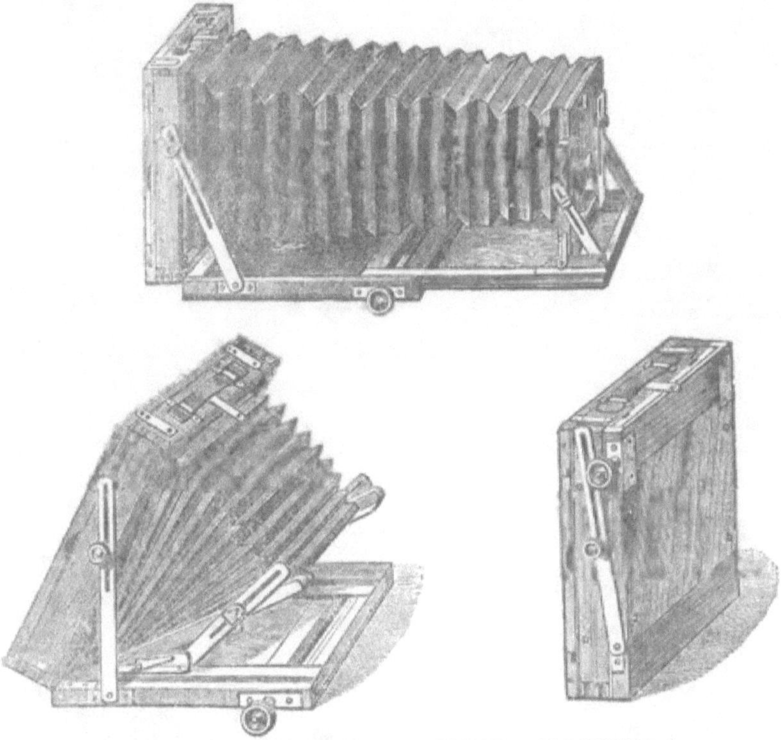

SHEW'S COMBINATION CAMERA.

(BROWN'S PATENT).

We are now selling the remainder of our stock of this well-known Camera at the following reduced prices, from which no further abatement can be made. Although heavier in construction than those of present date, it has much to recommend it to those to whom weight is not of great importance.

For Plates.	Weight.	Focal Length.	Size Closed.	Camera and Back.	Extra Backs, each.
6½ × 4¾	3½ lbs.	18½ in.	8¾ × 8¾ × 2½	£5 17 6	£0 15 0
7½ ,, 5	4½ lbs.	20 in.	9¾ ,, 9¾ ,, 2½	6 10 0	0 17 6
8½ ,, 6½	5½ lbs.	22 in.	10¾ ,, 10¾ ,, 2¾	7 10 0	1 0 0
10 ,, 8	7 lbs.	24 in.	12¼ ,, 12¼ ,, 3	8 10 0	1 4 0
12 ,, 10	12 lbs.	28 in.	14¼ ,, 14¼ ,, 3½	9 5 0	1 10 0

EASTMAN ROLL HOLDER

(For 48 Exposures).

FITTED TO ANY OF THE PRECEDING CAMERAS.

For pictures	4¼ × 3¼	£2 0 0	7½ × 5	£3 7 6
,,	5 ,, 4	2 10 0	8½ ,, 6½	4 5 0
,,	6½ ,, 4¾	3 0 0	10 ,, 8	5 0 0

Fitting up to 8½ × 6½ 5/-. Fitting up to 10 × 8 7/6.

See also Page 29.

SHEW'S LONG FOCUS CAMERA.

STUDIO OR FIELD.

THIS well-known Camera is still the best form yet constructed for all-round work, being equally suitable for studio or field. Of Spanish mahogany, with best leather bellows, double extension, suitable for the longest focus lenses, for copying, etc., with arrangement for racking-up to the front when required for use with short focus wide angle lenses. Double action front with an extra long cross front for stereoscopic work, in the two smallest sizes only. Double swing back, reversing frame for landscape or portrait work; best make of double backs with hinged divisions and patent springs to shutters, part brass-bound, and two carriers for smaller-sized plates. This camera is recommended by us for general work on account of its extreme simplicity of construction, strength and perfect rigidity when extended in any case where weight and bulk is not considered of the first importance.

For Plates.	Price, including three Double Backs.	Extra Double Backs, each	Second Quality Double Backs.	Brass Binding Camera & 3 Backs.
6½ × 4¾	£8 12 0	17/6	12/6	25/-
8½ ,, 6½	10 5 6	20/-	14/6	30/-
10 ,, 8	11 15 0	25/-	20/-	35/-
12 ,, 10	14 10 0	32/-	25/6	40/-
15 ,, 12	18 0 0	42/-	35/-	45/-
18 ,, 16	28 15 0			
20 ,, 16	32 0 0			
22 ,, 18	39 10 0			
24 ,, 20	43 10 0			

This camera is of the finest quality and manufacture in every detail.

A cheaper form of the above camera, Honduras mahogany, second quality backs, etc.

For Plates.	Price, including three Double Backs.	For Plates,	Price, including three Double Backs.
6½ × 4¾	£6 5 0	12 × 10	£10 10 0
8½ ,, 6½	7 12 6	15 ,, 12	12 15 0
10 ,, 8	8 10 0		

SHEW'S CHEAP STUDIO AND FIELD CAMERA.

A third quality of the preceding form, including three double slides.

For Plates.

$6\frac{1}{2} \times 4\frac{3}{4}$	£6 10 0
$8\frac{1}{2}$,, $6\frac{1}{2}$	8 0 0

For Plates.

10 × 8	£9 5 0
12 ,, 10	11 2 6

SHEW'S "MODEL" TOURIST CAMERA.

OF first-class manufacture only, square, with reversing frame, to take portrait or landscape pictures without turning the camera, finest mahogany best leather bellows body, double swing back, hinged focussing frame rackwork arrangements for focussing, one double back for dry plates, with new improved folding shutters, two inner frames for smaller plates, side wing, double action front, and extra front.

This camera is equally adapted for studio or field work.

For Plates.		Extra Double Backs, each.	Brass Binding for Hot Climates.	For Plates.		Extra Double Backs, each.	Brass Binding for Hot Climates.
5 ×4	£4 4 0	12/6	15/-	$8\frac{1}{2} \times 6\frac{1}{2}$	£5 10 0	20/-	20/-
$6\frac{1}{2}$,, $4\frac{3}{4}$	4 10 0	17/6	15/-	10 ,, 8	6 10 0	25/-	25/-
$7\frac{1}{2}$,, 5	4 17 6	18/6	17/6	12 ,, 10	7 10 0	32/-	30/-

EXTRA DOUBLE BACKS OR DARK SLIDES
FOR CAMERAS.

For Plates.	Our Best Make, with flexible shutters, automatic spring fastenings, hinged divisions, &c.	Second Quality.	Brass Binding extra.	Improved Make, with draw-out Shutters
4¼ × 3¼	12/6	9/6	3/6	6/9
5 ,, 4	13/6	10/6	3/6	7/9
6½ ,, 4¾	17/6	12/6	3/6	12/-
7½ ,, 5	18/6	14 6	3/6	—
8½ ,, 6½	20/-	16/6	4/-	14/6
10 ,, 8	24/-	—	4/6	—
12 ,, 10	28/6	—	5/-	
15 ,, 12	38/-	—	5/6	—
18 ,, 16	55/-	—	6/-	—
20 ,, 16	60/-	—	6/-	—
22 ,, 18	75/-	—	7/-	—

If made square, for Cameras without Reversing Frame, one-fourth extra.

CONTINENTAL SIZES.
Of best manufacture only.

12 × 9 centimetres, 13/6   16 × 12 cent. 17/6   18 × 13-cent. 18/6
21 × 15 cent. 25/-   24 × 18 cent. 28/6-

CARRIERS OR INNER FRAMES.

For carrying plates of smaller sizes than that from which the double-back is made.

Size outside of frame, or for double back—

5 × 4	6½ × 4¾	7½ × 5	8½ × 6½	10 × 8	12 × 10	15 × 12
1/6	1/6	1/6	1/9	2/6	2/9	3/6

CAMERA CASES

Of solid leather, with patent spring lock, handle, and sling, to contain Camera and three double backs, with divisions, compartment for lenses, &c.

For Modern Cameras, 6½ × 4¾, £1 7 6   10 × 8, £2 2 0
7½ ,, 5   1 10 0   12 ,, 10   2 7 6
8½ ,, 6½   1 15 0   15 ,, 12   3 3 0

Ditto, ditto, of second quality, leather not solid, for

6½ × 4¾ £0 17 6   10 × 8, £1 10 0
7½ ,, 5   0 16 6   12 ,, 10   1 13 6
8½ ,, 6½ 1 2 6   15 ,, 12   2 5 0

CASES FOR TRIPOD STANDS.
Of Solid Leather.

¼ plate, 11/6   1/1 plate, 12/6   10 × 8, 17/6   12 × 10, 22/6

WATERPROOF CANVAS CASES.

	Limp.	Stiff, with Locker's Key
For 6½ × 4¾	£0 9 6	£0 15 6
,, 8½ ,, 6½	0 12 6	1 1 0
,, 10 ,, 8	0 17 6	1 7 6

WATERPROOF CANVAS BAGS FOR TRIPODS
From 3/6.

SHEW'S STEREOSCOPIC CAMERAS.

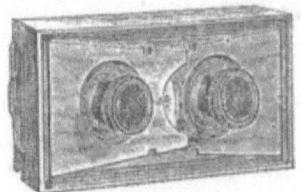

STEREOSCOPIC "ECLIPSE" CAMERA (Patent).

THIS camera, which we have made in response to numerous requests from users of our universally-known "Eclipse" (fully described on pages 13, &c., is fitted with rising front, folding bottom board, instantly detachable, enabling the operator to work time, instantaneous, or hand exposures with equal facility. Our 'Eclipse" lenses, accurately paired for stereoscopic work, and roller shutter working behind the lenses, with three double backs of our best make with folding shutters, hinged division, and patent spring fastenings.

For plates, 6¾ × 3¼.   Price, complete, £12 12 0.

Extra double backs, each, 17/6; or three for £2   5   0

COMBINATION STEREOSCOPIC CAMERA.

For plates, 6½ × 4¾, reversible for ½-plate portraits or views, double action front and large front with extra rise and fall to take a pair of lenses, removable division for stereoscopic work, etc., etc., with one double back of best make, folding shutters, hinge divisions and spring fastenings £3 17   6

Extra double backs, each, 17/6; or three for   2   5   0

THE SIMPLE STEREOSCOPIC CAMERA.

Of best Honduras mahogany, leather bellows, body with rack-work focussing adjustment, extra large rising front and three double backs £3   3   0

SHEW'S LANTERN SLIDE CAMERAS.

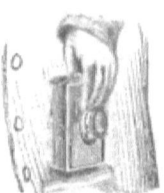

The "Eclipse," folded for
the pocket.
Weight .. 10 oz.

The "Eclipse," on Pocket Camera
Rest for time exposures.

SHEW'S LANTERN SLIDE "ECLIPSE" APPARATUS.

THIS apparatus is identical with our "Eclipse" Cameras, now so well known and in use all over the world, (see special pamphlet and further particulars at pages 13, &c.), and we can confidently assert that more work is shewn at lantern demonstrations in all parts, done with the "Eclipse" than with any other apparatus on the market.

Numerous medals have been awarded in open competition for Lantern Slides and for Enlargements, the greatest test for the quality and definition of the work of this Lens.

The Lantern "Eclipse" being 3¼in. square is the most compact form for carrying in the pocket, although in many cases the usual 4¼ × 3¼ is preferred even for lantern work, the larger plate giving greater facility for selection of subject in making the lantern slide, which is done at more leisure than is possible in so many cases in exposing the negative.

The apparatus complete consists of "Eclipse" Camera, Lens, Rotating Shutter and Stop Plate (patent) working between the lenses, one double back best make with folding shutters, hinged division and spring fastening   ..   ..   .. Price   £4 0   0

Double swing back extension to the above, with rackwork focussing arrangement and extra length of focus, enabling the operator to use long focus as well as the "Eclipse" or wide angle lenses ..   .. Price   2   2   0

SHEW'S POCKET CAMERA REST (Patent).

Easily carried in the pocket. Weight only 2½ ounces. For working the "Eclipse" for time exposures where a stand is not available   ..   .. Price   0   3   0

Shew's Bamboo Walking Stick and other Tripods for the "Eclipse" see page

SHEW'S LONG FOCUS LANTERN SLIDE CAMERA.

This is a most compact form of Camera for working with Lenses of various foci, with Swing Back, Rack Focussing, Sliding Front, &c., range of focus from 3 to 8 inches, folding up to measure only 4½ × 4½ × 2, including 1 Double Back, and weighing only 12 oz. Fitted with Patent Eclipse Lens and Shutter £5 15 0

Fitted with a single Landscape Lens of 5 in. focus, with rotary shutter 3 15 0

The Camera alone fitted with one Double Back as above 2 15 0

Extra Double Backs   ..   .. each 5/6, 6/9 and   0 12 6

Or in sets of 3 only   ..   ..   ..   per set 15/9; 19/6 and   1 13 0

SHEW'S NEW BOX CAMERA.

Introduced June, 1890 (see "The Optical Lantern Journal," July 1st, 1890).

THIS is the most useful form of Box Camera yet introduced, being equally suitable for hand or for time exposures, strongly made, with rackwork adjustment for focussing, measuring closed 5½ × 5½ × 5, and weighing only 1 lb. 11 oz.; with universal fitting to carry Double Backs for plates or for films, changing back, or roll holder, without alteration.

The Box Camera as above, neatly covered in morocco £1 10 0

Double Backs for plates or films..   ..   ..   .. 5/6, 6/9 and   0 12 6

Eastman Rollholder for 48 exposures fitted to the above 2 5 0

Patent Changing Back to carry 12 plates 2 2 0

CAMERAS

of any other maker supplied at their lowest advertised prices.

UNIVERSAL STUDIO CAMERA.

For plates, $6\frac{1}{2} \times 4\frac{3}{4}$, for one Cabinet or two Cartes de Visites on a $\frac{1}{2}$-plate, rack focussing, swing back, etc., etc. £4 4 0

For plates, $8\frac{1}{2} \times 6\frac{1}{2}$, Promenade, two Cabinets on a plate, $8\frac{1}{2} \times 6\frac{1}{2}$, two Cartes de Visites on a plate, $6\frac{1}{2} \times 4\frac{3}{4}$, and a single Carte de Visite on $4\frac{1}{4} \times 3\frac{1}{4}$, with double repeating back, bellows body, rack and pinion adjustment for focussing, two fronts, swing back, etc., etc. 5 5 0

For plates 10 × 8 and under 7 5 0

Extra double backs, square, to take plates either way, $8\frac{1}{2} \times 6\frac{1}{2}$, 27/- ;
10 × 8 ..   ..   1 11 6

SHEW'S IMPROVED STUDIO CAMERAS.
OF FIRST-CLASS MANUFACTURE ONLY.

OF the finest Spanish mahogany, thoroughly well-seasoned, best leather bellows, with extra extension giving great range of focus, strong screw adjustment for focussing, swing back, double repeating back, part brass bound, etc., etc., for taking two pictures on one plate, and carriers for the smaller-sized plates.

No. 1.—For $\frac{1}{2}$-plate or Cabinet, or for two Cartes de Visites on a $\frac{1}{2}$-plate £6 5 0

No. 2.—For 1/1 plate, 2 Promenades, 2 Cabinets or 2 Cartes de Visites on a $\frac{1}{2}$-plate 7 10 0

No. 3.—10 × 8, 2 Boudoirs, 2 Cabinets, or 2 Cartes de Visites on a $\frac{1}{2}$-plate 9 0 0

No. 4.—For 12 × 10, 10 × 8, Boudoir, Cabinet, and Carte de Visite   11 5 0

No. 5.—For 15 × 12, and two smaller sizes 13 15 0

No. 6.—For 18 × 16, and two smaller sizes 18 15 0

No. 7.—For 20 × 16, and two smaller sizes 22 0 0

No. 8.—For 24 × 18, and two smaller sizes 26 10 0

Double swing back, extra.

Up to $8\frac{1}{2} \times 6\frac{1}{2}$ .. 18/-.   12 × 10 .. 22/6.   15 × 12 .. 27/-.

The above represents a 10 × 8 Adapter on a Camera 8½ × 6½.

SHEW'S PATENT CAMERA ADAPTER.

THIS Invention has for its object the means of enabling the operator to work a plate of one or two sizes larger than that for which his Camera is constructed, thus by employing the Adapter with ½-plate Camera it is at once converted into a 1-1 plate, or 9 × 7, a 1-1 plate into 10 × 8 or 12 × 10, and other sizes in proportion. Every modern Camera will take an Adapter that will work plates of the next two sizes larger.

The Adapter is of the simplest form, fitting, as shown above, in the place of the Camera reversing frame, it is available for pictures horizontal or vertical. The weight is only about half that of a Camera of an equivalent size, it remains perfectly rigid and steady when fixed, and enables the Photographer by using the single Combination only of his Rectilinear or doublet lens (as well as with short focus lenses) to take pictures the next one or two sizes larger, at a very small outlay, with the extra advantage of being able to take away and dispense with the Adapter and use his Camera as usual when desirable, the Camera being in no way altered. Price, with one double back, and hinged focussing screen :—

For plates, 6½ × 4¾, 27/6; 8½ × 6½, 29/6; 10 × 8, 33/-; 12 × 10, 50/-
Extra double backs, each, 11/6;   13/6;   17/6;   25/-

A small charge for fitting to Camera from 1/6.

ENLARGING OR REDUCING
EXTENSION FRONT.

A sliding body addition, easily attached to any camera, enabling the operator to enlarge from ¼ or other small negatives, and also to reduce from large negatives to ¼ or lantern size, or to copy prints, etc. for the "Lantern," with sliding adjustment from 5½ to 10 inches, and with removable carrier for ¼-plate or 3¼ × 3¼ negatives .. .. Price £0 9 6

Double back, ¼-plate for reducing, with ground glass for focussing extra 0 5 9

Enlarging extension only, for enlarging from negatives, 6½ × 4¾, with sliding adjustment from 6 to 12 inches 0 9 6

Inner frames or carriers for smaller negatives, extra 0 1 0

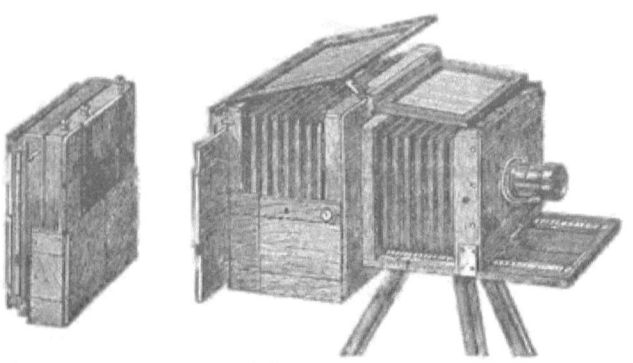

The above represents a 12 × 10 Adapter on a whole plate or 8½ × 6½ Camera.

SHEW'S PATENT CAMERA ADAPTER
WITH EXTENSION.

This form, with bellows extension, will be found useful in all cases where extra length is required for copying, enlarging, or for any short focus cameras.

Price, with one double back and hinged focussing screen :—

For Plates 6½ × 4¾, 32/6; 8½ × 6½, 35/6; 10 × 8, 45/-; 12 × 10, 63/-.

Ditto, ditto, of superior make, with double swing back, extra :—

For Plates 6½ × 4¾, 17/6; 8½ × 6½, 21/-; 10 × 8, 25/-; 12 × 10, 30/-.

SHEW'S NEW EXTENSION FRONT,
OR LENGTHENING BODY.

Bellows body, perfectly rigid when extended. Fitted on any camera at a slight charge, from 1/-.

7 inch, for 7½ × 5 or ½-plate camera					17/6
9 ,,	8½ ,, 6½	..	..	..	21/-
10½ ,,	10 ,, 8	..	..	..	27/6
12 ,,	12 ,, 10	..	..	..	32/6

Best leather bellows, 2/6, 3/6, 4/6, and 5/6 extra.

The above prices include plain front. Runners to take purchaser's sliding front, extra, 7 and 9 inch, 1/6; 10 and 12 inch, 2/6.

ENLARGING CAMERAS (See page 35).

REDUCING CAMERAS (See page 37).

HAND CAMERAS.

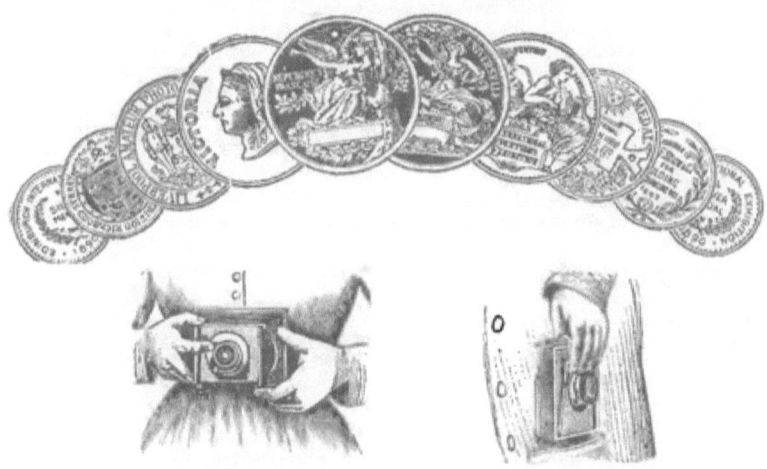

SHEW'S "ECLIPSE" HAND CAMERA AND FIXED FOCUS LENS (PATENT).

Now made in all sizes, English and French. Equally suitable for time exposures. Largely used by Artists at home and abroad, perfect pictures being taken with this little instrument, which, with the ordinary apparatus, it would be impossible to obtain.

Many Medals have been awarded for work done with the "ECLIPSE," Lantern Slides of Figures in Motion, Mountainous Views, Street Scenes, &c. Enlargements of Foreign Scenery, &c., in competition with the work of every other description of apparatus.

Highest Award, Paris Universal Exhibition, 1889; International Inventions Exhibition, 1885; Liverpool; Richmond; Edinburgh, &c., &c.

See the "Eclipse" Pamphlet (in English and French) free on application.

SINCE the advent of the modern Dry plate, Photographic processes and apparatus have undergone an entire change, subjects which it were deemed impossible to re-produce by the aid of the Camera are now of every day accomplishment.

There had long been felt the necessity of getting rid of the cumbersome impedimenta of the old collodion days, and for the past ten years we have given special attention to the invention and manufacture of many appliances of practical utility, the object of each being the simplifying of Photographic operations.

With this object still in view we, in 1885, first introduced the then unknown system of photographing without preliminary focussing, in other words, working with a fixed focus lens, which resulted in the creation of the now universally known "Eclipse" Hand Apparatus (patent), so justly described as the parent of all Hand Cameras in this country.

THE LENS.—A Rapid Rectilinear of the best quality, specially manufactured for working at fixed focus. It possesses great depth of definition, combined with remarkable brilliancy and crispness of image. No focussing is required, as all objects beyond a distance of 15 to 20 feet from the camera are always sharp. It is supplied with a revolving diaphragm-plate, with apertures $F/10$, $F/15$, $F/20$, $F/40$, these having been found most suitable for all purposes.

Mounted between the combinations of the lens in front of the diaphragm-plate and revolving on the same axis, is the patent shutter, which is circular in shape; with it is supplied a simple means of regulating it, and an efficient release.

Every lens is carefully tested and examined, the focus of each one being carefully determined by experiment previous to its being sent out from our manufactory.

This lens is the outcome of long and varied experiments, resulting in the production of an instrument superior in its working for this purpose, to any similar lens since made, as fully proved by the fact that at every high-class lantern demonstration, at home and abroad, the work of "The Eclipse" is shewn, and admitted to be equal—and in many cases superior—to that of any other class of apparatus, speaking volumes for the high-class quality we claim for this lens.

THE CAMERA consists of the usual bellows body, with mahogany front and back, the front being held in position by two wings, which, when not in use, fold over it, forming a compact article, measuring only $6 \times 4\frac{3}{4} \times 1\frac{3}{4}$. The double backs are of the best book form, with flexible folding shutters. The strictest attention is paid to the quality and manufacture of these slides, in order to ensure their being perfectly light-tight, a most important point in slides which must be worked in the open light without covering, to avoid the disappointment so often resulting from badly-fitting parts inseparable from cheap work. We are now making light film backs to contain cut films, six of which can easily be carried in the pocket, or for those who prefer the power of taking a large number of pictures without changing, we fit the Eastman Roll Holder, which, with the "Eclipse" Camera, forms a complete apparatus for taking 48 pictures, $4\frac{1}{4} \times 3\frac{1}{4}$, easily carried in the pocket.

In this apparatus we still claim to have produced the most compact and efficient hand-camera possible to design. This is proved by the fact that, in spite of the very numerous forms of hand or detective cameras introduced to the photographic world since ours of 1885, none have yet equalled it for compactness, portability, simplicity of operation, and perfection of results.

We have no hesitation in stating that it still eclipses any apparatus known in giving perfect pictures $4\frac{1}{4} \times 3\frac{1}{4}$ (without the preliminary focussing which so often results in the loss of the subject most desired), with a camera which is instantly set up, which weighs only 12 ounces, which folds up to measure only $6 \times 4\frac{5}{8} \times 2\frac{1}{2}$, and is easily carried in the pocket.

We would call special attention to the great advantages this apparatus possesses of compactness and the extreme rapidity with which it can be brought into use; also to the fact that glass or film can be used for the production of negatives, without having to use adapters of any kind.

The camera is taken from the pocket, and by a simple operation it is extended, the shutter drawn, and the exposure made, the whole operation occupying a few seconds and attracting no notice from passers-by.

UNSOLICITED TESTIMONY TO THE EFFICIENCY OF SHEW'S "ECLIPSE" HAND APPARATUS.

It is the fact that out of the magnificent selection of Lantern Slides shown in competition at the Crystal Palace Exhibition, TWO OUT OF THE SIX MEDALS were awarded for pictures taken with the "Eclipse," viz.:—

Foreign Views (Class 2), by W. A. GREENE, Esq.
Figures in Motion (Class 7), by H. LITTLE, Esq.

The Swiss Scenery shown by Mr. GREENE, proving without doubt that "The Eclipse" is The Apparatus for Touring in Mountainous Countries; and the much-admired series of Sporting subjects, shown by Mr. LITTLE, are conclusive proof of the advantage of this little apparatus in following up and (without any preparation being requisite) obtaining these subjects instantly at the will of the operator.

We append a few extracts from letters we are constantly receiving with reference to this apparatus:—

July 26, 1887.

I am very much pleased with your lens of a permanent focus, and think it a *decided advance*.   Yours truly,   HORACE DAY, M.D.

61, EASTCHEAP, E.C.

I have got so fond of the "Eclipse" that I have used my other cameras very little since I bought your "Little Wonder."   Yours truly,   T. J. WALKER.

34, PRIMROSE TERRACE, EDINBURGH.

GENTLEMEN,—The camera arrived safely, and I am much pleased with it. I have already done some good work in the way of skating and curling scenes.   Faithfully yours,   R. HENSLEIGH WALTER.

CHARTERHOUSE, GODALMING.

You will be glad to hear that though the day seemed unfavorable, I had two shots, both instantaneous; I got in each case a very clear sharp photo, with plenty of detail and density, speaking volumes for the excellent quality of the lens.   T. G. VYVYAN.

12, COVERDALE, RICHMOND, SURREY.

GENTLEMEN,—It may interest you to know that I made the enlargement, to which the Silver Medal has been awarded at the Birmingham Exhibition, from a negative which I took with one of your Eclipse Hand Cameras, the lens working at full aperture. . . . Five out of the six slides I sent up to the Crystal Palace Show were made from negatives taken with the ¼-plate Eclipse Camera I had from you. This makes the third medal I have taken for work done with your very handy little camera; and seeing that in each case it has been in competition with the work of fixed cameras, the utility of a hand camera seems pretty well established.   Yours truly   W. ASBURY GREENE.

February 5th, 1891.

The Camera which you sent me has proved most satisfactory, and of course it is quite superfluous to speak of the merits of the "Eclipse" which I also have.   Yours faithfully,   R. M. PHILPOTT.

THE "ACADEMY" ECLIPSE.

WE have long since seen the uselessness of the additional bulk in portable Apparatus, necessitated by the very square proportions of our commercial sized plates, which in no way add to the merit or artistic effect of the picture, so many having passed through our hands that would otherwise have been artistic, being spoiled by having either too much foreground or too much sky.

In order to meet the want of a plate or picture of more artistic or symmetrical form, as well as to dispense with the additional and unnecessary weight and bulk produced in carrying camera and backs for the square forms of plate now in use, we are now making our "Eclipse" apparatus in a size which possesses the advantage of having the length of a 5×4 plate, and is no larger than a $\frac{1}{4}$-plate in the other dimensions, viz., $5 \times 3\frac{1}{4}$.

This, it will readily be seen, is a much more pleasing size for Landscape as well as for figure work, and as we are making it, it will still have the advantage of being, as in the usual $\frac{1}{4}$-plate, easily carried in the pocket on tour.

The objection which at first sight appears, as to frames, dishes, &c., &c., not being made of this size, is fully met by the fact that anything made for 5×4 will really answer the purpose, and we feel assured that from our previous experience of the support we have received from our extensive clientéle, we shall be induced to make every requisite for the Academy plate at no very distant date.

So sure are we of this, that we are already manufacturing plates as well as films of the Academy size and in these days of Parcel post and cheap small parcels conveyance, we experience no difficulty in sending supplies of either to any part of the world.

For those who prefer to work a larger size of similar proportions, we supply the "Eclipse" for pictures, $7\frac{1}{2} \times 5$, which we have sold with great success during the past year.

THE "ECLIPSE" IN LARGE SIZES.

1/1-PLATE "ECLIPSE" for Portraiture. Time or Instantaneous.

1/1-PLATE "ECLIPSE" for Architecture. Time or Instantaneous.

1/1-pl. "ECLIPSE" for Landscape.

1/1-PLATE "ECLIPSE' ON TOUR.

In order to meet the wishes of a great number of our customers, we have continued to manufacture the "Eclipse" in increasing sizes until we are now making the 8½ × 6½ size, embodying all the advantages of the smaller patterns, with the addition of double-action rising front as well as extra arrangement for working within a short range as may required for large figures, &c., &c. or, if preferred, the power of focussing by means of our patent focussing flange, which entails no increase in bulk and gives the same power of adjustment as in an ordinary racking lens, without in any way detracting from its portability and compactness when closed.

The "Eclipse" lens being found suitable for any other work requiring a rectilinear lens of high class qualities, particularly for interiors and any dimly lighted subject requiring long exposure, we have added to the "Eclipse" apparatus a folding bottom board, instantly adjustable, which firmly supports the camera either in a vertical or horizontal position, see above, and when not in use takes less room than a double back, we are now making them for all sizes, see page 47. For prices see page 21.

SHEW'S ECLIPSE HAND APPARATUS.

For Plates or Paper.	Complete with 1 Double Back.	Extra Backs 1 or 2 each.	Set of 3 extra Backs.	Apparatus complete without Backs.
3¼ × 3¼	£4 4 0	0 12 6	1 13 0	3 17 6
4¼ ,, 3¼	4 9 0	0 12 6	1 13 0	4 0 0
5 ,, 4	5 0 0	0 13 6	1 13 9	4 10 0
6½ ,, 4¾	6 0 0	0 17 6	2 5 0	5 10 0
7½ ,, 5	6 15 0	0 18 6	2 10 0	6 5 0

CONTINENTAL SIZES-

12 × 9	£5 5 0	0 13 6	1 19 0	4 15 0
16 ,, 12	6 0 0	0 17 6	2 5 0	5 10 0
18 ,, 13	6 10 0	0 18 6	2 10 0	6 0 0

Fitted with Roll Holder for 48 Pictures.

			Centimeters.	
4¼ × 3¼	£6 5 0		12 × 9	£7 10 0
5 ,, 4	7 5 0		16 ,, 12	8 15 0
6½ ,, 4¾	8 15 0		18 ,, 13	9 12 6
7½ ,, 5	9 17 6		—	.

Fitted with Shew's Automatic Changing Back, for 1 dozen Plates.

4¼ × 3¼	£6 2 0		6½ × 4¾	£8 13 0
5 ,, 4	6 15 0		—	

BRASS BINDING FOR TROPICAL CLIMATES.

Size Centimeters.	Apparatus and 1 double back.	Extra Double backs, each.	Apparatus and Roll Holder.
4¼ × 3¼	£0 7 6	0 3 6	0 9 6
5 ,, 4 or 12 × 9	0 7 6	0 3 6	0 10 6
6½ ,, 4¾ or 16 ,, 12	0 9 6	0 3 6	0 12 6
7½ ,, 5 or 18 ,, 13	0 10 6	0 4 0	0 13 6

DIMENSIONS AND WEIGHT OF ECLIPSE APPARATUS.

For Plates or Films.	Complete with 1 Back. Size.	Weight.	3 Extra Backs. Size.	Weight.	With Roll Holder for 48 Pictures. Size.	Weight.
3¼ × 3¼	4¾ × 4⅝ × 2⅜	13 oz.	4¾ × 4¼ × 2	13 oz.	—	—
4¼ ,, 3¼	6 ,, 4½ ,, 2½	18 ,,	5¼ ,, 4¼ ,, 1⅞	15 ,,	6½ × 4¼ × 4	28 oz.
5 ,, 4	6¾ ,, 5¼ ,, 2¼	19 ,,	6½ ,, 5 ,, 2	21 ,,	7 ,, 5¼ ,, 5	24 ,,
6½ ,, 4¾	8¼ ,, 6¼ ,, 3½	2 lbs.	8¼ ,, 5¾ ,, 2	29 ,,	8½ ,, 6¼ ,, 5	2lb. 14oz.
7½ ,, 5	9½ ,, 6½ ,, 3¼	2½ ,,	9½ ,, 6½ ,, 2¼	—	9¾ ,, 6¼ ,, 5¼	3¼ lbs.

Centimeters.

12 × 9	6¾ × 4¾ × 2½	6 × 4 × 2	20 oz.	6¾ × 5 × 5	22 oz.	
16 ,, 12	8¼ ,, 6¼ ,, 3½	8¼ ,, 5¾ ,, 2	29 ,,	6¼ ,, 4½ ,, 5	2½ lbs.	
18 ,, 13	9¼ ,, 6½ ,, 3¼	9 ,, 6½ ,, 2¼	2 lbs.	9½ ,, 6½ ,, 5¼	3¼ ,,	

ACCESSORIES TO THE ECLIPSE APPARATUS.

AUTOMATIC CHANGING BACK.

SHEW'S PRIZE MEDAL PATENT.

CONSISTING of two boxes sliding one in the other, the outer box taking the place of the double back, being readily fitted to any camera. This receives the plate to be exposed, after which it is rapidly transferred back to the inner case from which it was taken, the two boxes forming part of one box a little larger than the plate contains.

THE CAMERA, Feb. 1, 1889.

The other silver medal has gone to a new form of Changing Box invented by Messrs. Shew.

This is a most ingenious contrivance, and one which is sure to meet with the approval of tourist photographers, for in a box which takes up no more space than two double slides there are contained one dozen plates, each one of which can be brought under command of the lens by a most simple movement.

PHOTOGRAPHY, Jan. 17, 1889.

J. F. Shew & Co., 88, Newman Street, London. This firm had several novelties of real value. They secured the silver medal with a new changing box, one of the most ingenious things we have ever seen in this direction. It will hold twelve plates, which can be exposed in succession by simply pulling out the slide and returning it, and it is most compact in form and size.

THE AMATEUR PHOTOGRAPHER, Jan. 18, 1889.

Messrs. Shew & Co. had a very excellent exhibit, including one novelty which deservedly earned a silver medal. This is a new form of changing back, which will hold one dozen plates, each one of which is, by a simple movement, brought to the front for exposure. We venture to think that this back will be found very useful.

SHEW'S AUTOMATIC CHANGING BACK.

Fitted to the Eclipse Cameras.

$4\frac{1}{4} \times 3\frac{1}{4}$	£2 2 0	$6\frac{1}{2} \times 4\frac{3}{4}$	£3 3 0
5 ,, 4	2 5 0		

$\frac{1}{4}$ plate weighing under 15 ounces. The inner case or refill weighing under $6\frac{1}{2}$ ounces and carrying 12 plates without sheaths, the refill closing automatically and enabling an exchange of 12 plates to be made in the field.

Inner Cases or Refills.

$4\frac{1}{4} \times 3\frac{1}{4}$	£0 16 6	$6\frac{1}{2} \times 4\frac{3}{4}$	£1 1 0
5 ,, 4	0 18 6	—	—

BRASS BINDING FOR TROPICAL CLIMATES.

Changing Backs, complete.

$\frac{1}{4}$ plate	14/6	5×4 18/6		$\frac{1}{2}$ plate	25/6

Binding extra refills, each.

$\frac{1}{4}$ plate	7/-	5×4 8/6		$\frac{1}{2}$ plate	10/6

AUTOMATIC CHANGING **BACK**. **The Eureka**. Carrying 12 plates or films in sheaths, with a simple arrangement for changing by lifting the plate into position through a bag permanently attached, which folds into a very small space in the lid of the box.

Outside Dimension $6 \times 4\frac{1}{4} \times 2\frac{1}{2}$.   Weight 18 ounces.
Fitted to $\frac{1}{4}$ Eclipse for £2 10 0.
$\frac{1}{4}$ plate only kept in stock, fitted to the Eclipse.   Other sizes to order.

BOTTOM BOARD. We have lately designed a folding bottom board for the Eclipse which is instantly attached to the Camera when required for time exposures, firmly supporting it in either horizontal or vertical position, and serving also, when not in use, as a sheath for keeping the interior of the camera and lens free from dust, &c., on tour, by being grooved at the edges to run in, in the place of the roll holder or double back.

For $\frac{1}{4}$ plate Academy or 4×5 Eclipse fitted with screw and plate for tripod stand 5/6
    $\frac{1}{2}$ plate 6/6 $7\frac{1}{2} \times 5$ 7/6 $8\frac{1}{2} \times 6\frac{1}{2}$ 8/6

CAPS. Extra caps to Eclipse Lenses each
    $\frac{1}{4}$ plate 1/3 $\frac{1}{2}$ plate 1/6 $7\frac{1}{2} \times 5$ 1/6   1-1 plate 1/9

EXTRA SETTING. We are now arranging an extra setting for working at short distances for figures without in any way altering the original setting.
The Camera and Lens must be sent for this arrangement, the price of which is 3/6.

FILM SLIDES. A very light form of double back fitted to the Eclipse for carrying cut films.

For films.	One.	Three for	Six for
$4\frac{1}{4} \times 3\frac{1}{4}$	5/6	15/9	30/-
5 ,, 4	7/6	21/-	39/-
$6\frac{1}{2}$,, $4\frac{3}{4}$	8/9	25/6	48/-

Three $4\frac{1}{4} \times 3\frac{1}{4}$ measure only $5\frac{1}{2} \times 4\frac{1}{4} \times 2\frac{1}{2}$ ins.   Weight 11 ozs,

FINDER. Shew's Eclipse. For hand cameras with reflector and shade, the lenses manufactured with our Eclipse lenses of the same angle in order to give a true miniature of the picture. Price 7/6

FLANGES For Eclipse Lenses.
    $\frac{1}{4}$ plate 2/3 $\frac{1}{2}$ plate 2/6   1-1 plate 3/-

FOCUSSING FLANGE. Shew's Patent. A simple device for enabling the operator, when desirable, to focus between the fixed focus points—in no way increasing bulk—and giving the same power of fine focussing as on a racking lens without disturbing the original setting. Price, including flange and lever indicator   ¼ plate 12/6   ½ plate 15/-   1-1 plate 21/-

FOCUSSING SCREENS. We stock these to fit the Eclipse.
¼ plate 2/9   5 × 4 3/-   ½ plate 3/6   7½ × 5 3/6   1-1 plate 4/9

SCREWS. Two screw plates fitted to cameras for horizontal and vertical rise on tripod and screw for same, extra 2/-

SPRINGS. Extra springs for Lens shutter   each 9d. or fitted ..   1/6

SWING BACK.—We are now making (to order) a double swing back extension to the "Eclipse" Camera, with rack-work focussing arrangement, enabling the operator to use the camera for any work requiring long, as well as short focus lenses, and in no way interfering with its original use as a fixed focus camera.
     Price ..   ¼ to ½-plate, 42/-.   7½ × 5 and 1-1 plate, 50/-.

SWING FRONT.—We are now manufacturing for the "Eclipse," a gimbal or swing flange, enabling the operator to move the lens in every direction and instantly adjust same at any point by a single movement. This is said to advantageously replace the swing back (which necessarily entails extra length and bulk in the camera), without in any way detracting from the portability and compactness of the apparatus as it takes very little more room than an ordinary flange. See page 59.

RISING FRONT.—Fitted to "Eclipse" Cameras, vertical and horizontal.
     If ordered at the time of purchase, ¼ to ½-plate, 7/6 ; 7½ × 5, 8/6.
     If added to finished cameras which necessitates reduction of side wings and resetting lens, any size up to 7½ × 5, 10/6.

LEVELS.—Shew's "Eclipse" level, of oblong tube form, fitting easily in sockets attached to the camera for horizontal or vertical work, complete with two
sockets 2/6
Circular levels..   ..   .. from   1/6
Shew's Duplex Level of T form 3/6

THE ECLIPSE FOR PLATES, 8½ × 6½.

·Consisting of Eclipse Camera, partly brass bound, patent Lens and instantaneous shutter, with patent focussing flange and rising front, one double back, and focussing screen, complete £11 11 0

EXTRA DOUBLE BACKS, each 1 0 0

BRASS BINDING, DOUBLE BACKS, each 0 4 0

EASTMAN ROLL HOLDER for carrying sufficient film for 48 transparent film negatives, fitted to the Eclipse for 4 12 6
     For prices of Spools of film, see page 146.

·**CASE OF SOLID LEATHER** to contain the Eclipse Apparatus, three double backs or roll holder, focussing screen and folding bottom board, of best make, with sling, strap and handle, and double action lock 1 5 0

WATERPROOF CANVAS ditto, ditto..   ..   .. 0 17 6

CASES FOR THE ECLIPSE APPARATUS.

THE FIELD GLASS CASE.

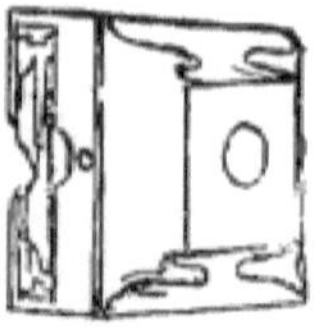

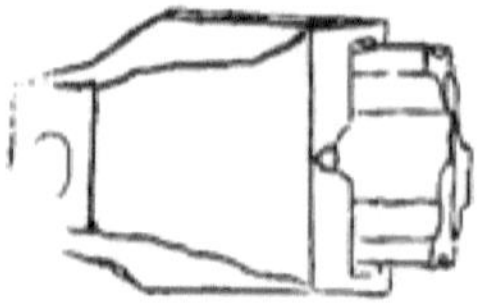

A COLLAPSIBLE leather case, in which the apparatus can be carried either open or closed, enabling the operator to draw out and replace the dark slide or roll holder without opening the case. The shutter and stops also being worked from the outside.

	Size folded.	Weight.	Price.
$4\frac{1}{4} \times 3\frac{1}{4}$	$6 \times 5\frac{1}{4} \times 2\frac{1}{4}$	9 oz.	17/6
5 ,, 4	7 ,, $5\frac{1}{4}$,, $2\frac{1}{4}$	10 ,,	19/6
$6\frac{1}{2}$,, $4\frac{3}{4}$	$8\frac{1}{2}$,, $6\frac{3}{4}$,, $2\frac{1}{2}$	13 ,,	22/6

THE LADIES' CASE.

A neat hand bag of Gladstone shape, to contain Camera and three backs, roll holder or changing back.

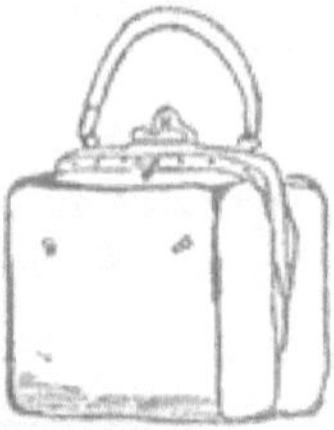

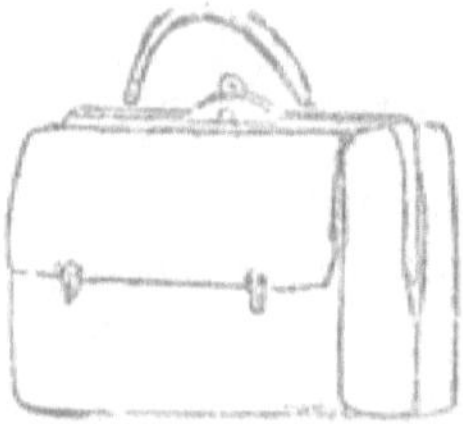

	Size.	Weight.	Price
$4\frac{1}{4} \times 3\frac{1}{4}$	$8 \times 6\frac{1}{4} \times 3\frac{3}{4}$	13 oz.	11/6
5 ,, 4	9 ,, $6\frac{1}{2}$,, 4	15 oz.	13/6
$6\frac{1}{2}$,, $4\frac{3}{4}$	10 ,, 7 ,, $4\frac{1}{2}$	18 oz.	14/6

THE TOURIST CASE.

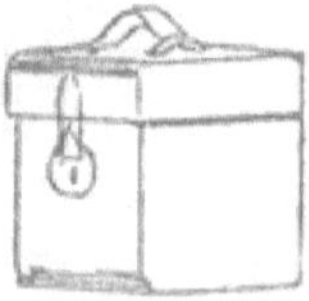

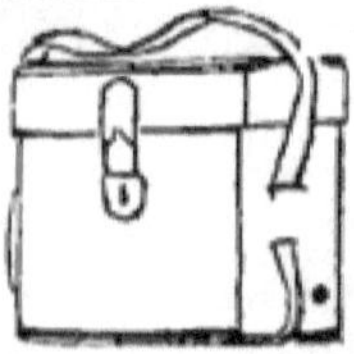

Of solid leather, with spring lock and handle, either black or brown.

For Cameras.	With 3 Backs or Roll Holder.	For 6 Backs, or 3 Backs and Roll Holder.
$4\frac{1}{4} \times 3\frac{1}{4}$	11/6	15/6
5 ,, 4	12/6	17/6
$6\frac{1}{2}$,, $4\frac{3}{4}$	14/6	21/0
$7\frac{1}{2}$,, 5	16/6	25/0

Sling strap to the above, 1/9 to 2/6 extra.

THE DETECTIVE CASE.

A strongly made box, fitted with two finders for horizontal and vertical pictures, to contain apparatus open ready for use (the shutter being worked from the outside), and three double backs for glass plates, or cut films or roll holder for 48 film negatives; covered in morocco leather with good snap fastening and cross handle, as in above.

Size.		Weight.	Price
4¼ × 3¼	8 × 5½ × 7	2 lbs. 3 oz.	25/-
6½ „ 4¾	11 „ 7 „ 9½	4¼ lbs.	30/-

THE 1891 CASE, Registered.

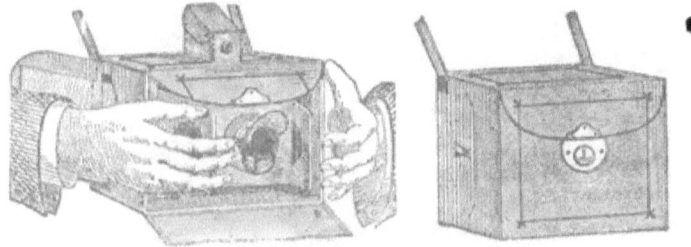

FOR carrying the Camera closed, or open for operating without removal from the case; made to carry 3 double backs, changing back, or roll holder for 48 exposures, with sling, and lock

4¼ × 3¼, 21/-; 5 × 4, 25/-; 6½ × 4¾, 27/6; 7½ × 5, 30/-.

DETECTIVE OR BOX CAMERAS.
SHEW'S COMBINATION HAND CAMERA.

To carry 12 plates in automatic changing back, and with sliding inner body adjustable to different lenses.

To carry 12 plates, 4¼ × 3¼, measuring only 7 × 5¾ × 4 .. .. .. £2 15 0
Ditto, ditto, fitted with Eastman roll holder, for 48 film exposures   3 15 0
Our Eclipse lens and shutter, fitted to either of the above for .. 3 10 0
Adjusting purchaser's own lens and shutter, testing focus, setting, etc. from 0 15 0

THE "ECLIPSE" DETECTIVE APPARATUS.

OF box form, with patent automatic changing back to carry 12 plates. Ebonized and all fittings blacked; fitted with Shew's "Eclipse" Lens and Instantaneous Shutter, patent, the whole (for 12 plates, 4¼ × 3¼) measuring only 6¾ × 5¼ × 4¼.

This Camera is well suited for time or stand exposures, for which a screw plate is fitted on the bottom board. Price, complete   ..   £5 10 0

The above fitted with a good landscape lens, mounted in sliding tube for adjustment to different distances, or for focussing when desired, and fitted with stops and instantaneous shutter 3 10 0

For 12 plates, 5 × 4, measuring only 7 × 6½ × 5, with Shew's "Eclipse" Lens and Shutter, patent 6 10 0

   Ditto, ditto, fitted with landscape lens, etc., as above 4 0 0

For 12 plates, 6½ × 4¾, measuring only 9½ × 5¾ × × 8, and fitted with Eclipse lens and shutter, patent 7 10 0

   Ditto, ditto, with landscape lens, as above 5 0 0

SHEW'S NEW BOX CAMERA,

(See "The Optical Lantern Journal," July 1st, 1890).

THIS is the most useful form of Box Camera yet introduced, being equally suitable for hand or for time exposures, strongly made, with rackwork adjustment for focussing, measuring closed 5½ × 5½ × 5, and weighing only 1 lb. 11 oz.; with universal fitting to carry Double Backs for plates or for films, changing back or roll holder, without alteration.

The Box Camera as above, neatly covered in morocco £1 10 0

Double Backs for plates or films ..   .. 5/6, 6/9 and   0 12 6

Eastman Rollholder, for 48 exposures, fitted to the above 2 5 0

Patent Changing Back to carry 12 plates 2 2 0

Our Eclipse Lens, fitted for 3 10 0

Landscape Lens and Instantaneous Shutter, fitted for 1 10 0

Adjusting Purchaser's own Lens and Shutter, from 0 15 0

THE "DIAMOND" DETECTIVE CAMERA.

With changing back for 12 pictures, 2¾ × 3¼, on ordinary dry plates, in sheaths. The size of the instrument is 6 × 3 × 3½. It is fitted with a rapid rectilinear lens, always in focus, a finder, and a shutter for time or instantaneous pictures £1 8 0

THE "GUINEA" DETECTIVE OR HAND CAMERA.

Contains Three Double Slides.

In appearance resembles a small sample case. Covered with waterproof cloth.

£1   1   0

Size, 8 × 6½ × 5.

Weighing under 3 lbs.

THE "ITAKIT."

A CHEAP CAMERA FOR CYCLISTS'.

The Lens is achromatic. The shutter is ever-set (instantaneous or time), and plates are changed by two movements. Price, 12/6.

Extra magazines for 24 plates, 3/6.

Shoulder Strap, 1/- extra.

Leather cases for holding the "Itakit" for travelling and when in use, 8/6 each extra.

Size, 5½ × 4½ × 4. Weight, 3½ lbs. including plates. Capacity, 24 plates 3¼ × 3¼.

THE "SOVEREIGN ITAKIT."

The "Sovereign Itakit," has in addition a finder and focussing screen the full size of the plate, and is the most complete, the most durable, and the most simple Hand Camera ever produced for the price.

The "Sovereign Itakit," 20/. Extra magazines for 24 plates, 3/6. Shoulder strap, 1/- extra. Leather case, 8/6 extra.

Being made entirely of metal, the "Itakits" are specially suited for Cyclists.

THE "KINEMATIC,"

THE "KINEMATIC" is a superior magazine camera, carrying twelve quarter plates, 4¼ × 3¼, is self-contained, has no loose backs, and does not require either hand-bag or plate-changing box, one simple movement only being necessary to change the plate from the magazine or store, and place it in focus opposite the lens.

It is fitted with a patent central opening and self-registering exposure shutter which cannot possibly be accidentally opened or shut by vibration or any other cause. This shutter is unique and is the only one that registers the number of exposures taken, and can be used for either instantaneous or time exposures.

Neatly finished in leather, and altogether of superior finish. Price, £3 3 0 Size, 9 × 9 × 3¾ ins. Weight complete, including plates, 4½ lbs. Capacity, 12 quarter-plates. Fitted with rapid achromatic 'ens and view finder.

THE KODAK.

THE NO. 1 KODAK.

For Round Pictures 2½ inches in diameter, fixed focus—Rectilinear lens, with self-capping shutter.

Capacity, 100 exposures without necessity of re-loading.

Size of Camera, 3¼ × 3¾ × 6 inches—73 cubic inches.

Weight 1 lb. 8 ozs.

Price loaded with 100 exposures, including leather Carrying Case and Instruction Book £5 5 0

THE NO. 2 KODAK.

For Round Pictures 3½ inches diameter, fixed focus—Rectilinear lens with 3 stops, self-capping shutter, and finder for centreing the View.

Capacity, 100 exposures without necessity of re-loading.

Size of Camera, 4½ × 5 × 9 inches—202 cubic inches.

Weight loaded, 2 lbs. 12 ozs.

Price loaded with 60 exposures, including leather Carrying Case and Instruction Book £7 0 0

THE NO. 3 KODAK, "Regular."

For Rectangular Pictures 3¼ × 4¼ inches, adjustable focus, with graduated focussing device—Rectilinear lens with 3 stops, self-capping shutter, with adjustable speed.

Fitted with sockets for tripod.

Capacity, 100 exposures without necessity for re-loading, 2 finders for centreing the View.

Size of Camera, 4¼ × 5½ × 11½—268½ cubic inches.

Weight loaded, 4 lbs.

Price loaded with 60 films, including leather Carrying Case and Instruction Book £8 7 6

NOTE.—The price includes spool for 60 exposures only, but the Camera is capable of receiving spool for 100 exposures.

THE NO. 3 KODAK "Junior."

This Camera is a modification of the No. 3 Regular. It makes the same size picture, and has the same adjustments.

It is fitted with sockets for tripod.   Capacity 60 exposures.

Price loaded with 60 exposures, including leather Carrying Case and
Instruction Book £8   7   6

THE NO. 4 KODAK.

This is an entirely new style of Kodak, embodying the Kodak principle but folding up into about two-thirds the space. It is self contained when closed, and can be opened and closed in two motions. It is the most compact and simple folding Camera ever made, and can be used either for tripod or detective work.

Size of picture, 4 × 5 inches.

Rectilinear lens, special self-capping shutter, rotating stops, adjustable speed, reversible finder, 2 sockets for tripod, screw and graduated focussing index,

The Camera forms its own carrying case—See cut above.

Capacity, 48 exposures without the necessity of re-loading.

Size of Camera (folded), 7 × 5 × 5½ inches—192½ cubic inches.

Weight loaded, 3 pounds 9 ounces.

Price, including Shoulder-Strap and Instruction Book, loaded for
48 exposures £10   7   6

GENERAL KODAK PRICE LIST.

SIZE OF PICTURE.	2⅝ in. diameter. Circular.	3½ in. diameter. Circular.	3¼ in. × 4¼ in.	
Description.	Fixed Focus.	Fixed Focus; 3 Stops and Finder.	Adjustable Focus; 3 Stops; 2 Finders.	
Capacity of Exposures	100	100	100	60
Length of Spool ..	2¾ in. No. 1.	3¾ in. No. 2.	4¼ in. No. 3. Regular.	3¼ in. No. 3 Junior
Price complete ..	£5 5 0	7 0 0	8 7 6	8 7 6
Loaded for Exposures	100	60	60	60
Reloading, Developing and Printing ..	£2 2 0	2 2 0	2 2 0	2 2 0
*Developing, Printing and Mounting, without Reloading ..	£1 10 0	1 14 0	1 14 0	1 14 0
†Spool for Reloading — Exposures	100	60	60	60
†Spool for Reloading — Price ..	£0 10 6	0 10 6	0 10 6	0 10 6
Spool for Reloading — Exposures	..	100	100	..
Spool for Reloading — Price ..	..	0 17 6	0 17 6	..
‡Developing only, each	£0 0 2	0 0 3	0 0 3	0 0 3
‡Printing only, each (Mounted)	£0 0 2½	0 0 3½	0 0 3½	0 0 3½
‡Developing and Printing only, each ..	£0 0 3½	0 0 5½	0 0 5½	0 0 5½

SIZE OF PICTURE. Description.	4 in. × 5 in. Adjustable Focus; 3 Stops; 2 Finders.		
Capacity of Exposures ..	100	48	48
Length of Spool	5 in. No. 4. Regular.	4 in. No. 4. Junior.	4 in. No. 4. Folding.
Price complete	£10 7 6	10 7 6	10 7 6
Loaded for Exposures	48	48	48
Reloading, Developing and Printing ..	2 2 0	2 2 0	2 2 0
*Developing, Printing and Mounting, without Reloading	1 10 0	1 10 0	1 10 0
†Spool for Reloading — Exposures ..	48	48	48
†Spool for Reloading — Price	0 12 6	0 12 6	0 12 6
Spool for Reloading — Exposures ..	100	..	..
Spool for Reloading — Price ..	1 6 0	..	..
‡Developing only, each	0 0 4	0 0 4	0 0 4
‡Printing only, each (Mounted) ..	0 0 5	0 0 5	0 0 5
‡Developing and Printing only, each .	0 0 7½	0 0 7½	0 0 7½

*This price is for full Spools only.

☞ †In ordering Spools always state whether for Regular, Junior, or Folding, as the length of Spool is thereby determined; and also give the number of exposures required.

‡NOTE.—On orders for less than two-fifths of the Developing or Printing of an entire Spool, an addition of 25 per cent. will be made on the prices charged "per each," in order to cover extra working expenses.

Prices of loaded Cameras and Separate Spools include carriage to any part of the United Kingdom.

THE EASTMAN-WALKER ROLL HOLDER.

For Transparent Film Negatives on Celluloid Film.

Fig. 1.

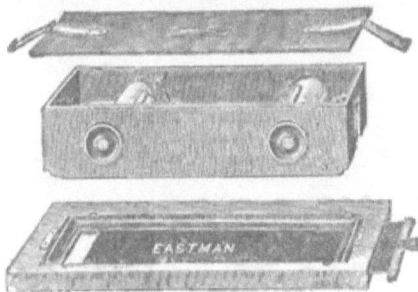

Fig. 2.

LATEST MODEL 1889.

The most important features of the model of 1889 Roll Holder are:

The Automatic Tension.
Whereby the film is kept stretched flat and smooth and in focus under varying conditions.

The Removable Mechanism.
Which enables the operator to change the spool of film with a minimum amount of labour.

The Interchangeable Spools and Reels.
Which permit the re-loading of the exposed film and the insertion of a fresh spool without unwinding the film.

The Side Guards.
For holding down in focus the side edges of the film.

The Audible and Visible Indicator.
Indicating by sight and sound the complete change of film.

The Automatic Perforator.
(Of which the intermittent marker is the latest form) for marking the divisions between the exposures, so that they can be separated without danger of cutting into the picture.

Fig. 1 represents the complete instrument, showing the winding key at the upper left hand, and the indicator and the audible alarum at the upper right-hand corner.

Fig. 2 represents the instrument divided into three parts, the upper portion being the back removed from the central portion or case in which is seen the rolls or spools of film in position.

ROLL HOLDERS.

PRICES—   CAPACITY 48 EXPOSURES.

Size of picture	Weight of holder	
3¼ × 4¼	1¼ lbs.	£2 0 0
4 ,, 5	1¼ ,,	2 10 0
6½ ,, 4¾	1½ ,,	3 0 0
4½ ,, 7¼	1½ ,,	3 7 6
5 ,, 7	2 ,,	3 7 6
5 ,, 7½	2 ,,	3 7 6
5 ,, 8	2 ,,	3 7 6
6½ ,, 8½	2¼ ,,	4 5 0
8 ,, 10	3 ,,	5 0 0
10 ,, 12	3¾ ,,	6 10 0
11 ,, 14	5¼ ,,	8 10 0
9 ,, 12 centimetres	1¼ ,,	2 10 0
13 ,, 11 ,,	2 ,,	3 7 6
18 ,, 24 ,,	2½ ,,	4 15 0
21 ,, 27 ,,	3¼ ,,	5 0 0

EXTRA CLAMPING REELS.

The above shows the Clamping Reel upon which the exposed film is wound by the roller slide mechanism. This Reel and its exposed film may be removed from the roller slide *with the exposed film upon it*, and in this condition may be sent by post to any part of the world for development. Therefore by having extra Clamping Reels a tourist may obviate the necessity of unwinding hid exposed films.

Size.	Price.	Size.	Price.	Size.	Price.
3¼ ins.	3/-	4½ ins.	3/-	5 ins.	3/-
4 ,,	3/-	4¾ ,,	3/-	6½ ,,	3/-
				8 ,,	3/6

NOTE.—We keep the Roll Holder in stock already fitted to our "Eclipse" apparatus in all sizes up to 8½ × 6½.

For fitting to other Cameras we require the reversing frame of the camera only.

Price for Fitting—

Up to and including 8½ × 6½	..	..	5
From 8½ × 6½ to 12 × 10 ..	..	..	7/5

LANCASTER'S
CHEAP SETS FOR AMATEURS.
THE 1891 "LE MERVEILLEUX" PATENT.

Each Set consists of Camera,
Lens, and Stand.

		£	s	d
For ¼-plate		1	1	0
,,	5 × 4 plate	1	15	0
,,	½ plate	2	2	0
,,	7½ × 5 plate	2	15	0
,,	1-1 plate	3	3	0

Extra Slides.

	Double Dry Slides.			Carriers.		
¼	£0	5	6	—		
½	0	10	6	£0	1	6
1-1	0	18	0	0	2	6

THE 1891 "LE MERITOIRE" PATENT.

Each Set consists of Camera,
Lens, and Stand.

		£	s	d
For ¼ plates		1	11	6
,,	5 × 4 plate	2	12	6
,,	½ plates	3	3	0
,,	7½ × 5 plates	4	0	0
,,	1-1 plates	4	10	0

Extra Slides

	Double Dry Slides.			Carriers		
¼	£0	5	6			
½	0	10	6	£0	1	6
1-1	0	18	0	0	2	6

THE 1891 "INSTANTOGRAPH" PATENT.

Each Set consists of Camera, Lens, Slide and Stand.
Price complete for ¼-plate   £2 2 0   ½-plate   £4 4 0
1-1-plate   £6 6 0

THE 1891 "INTERNATIONAL."

Price complete—

¼ (4¼ × 3¼)	£2 10 0	½ (6½ × 4¾)	£5 0 0
5 × 4	5 0 0	7½ × 5	6 6 0
1-1 (8½ × 6½)	£7 10 0		

Fitted with Rectigraph Lens and New Patent Shutter, in place of Instantaneous Lens and Shutter.

¼ (4¼ × 3¼)	£3 12 6	½ (6½ × 4¾)	£6 17 6
5 × 4	4 0 0	7½ × 5	8 8 0
1-1 (8½ × 6½)	£9 17 6		

THE LADIES' CAMERA.

This apparatus consists of Camera Lens rack mount, and triple folding tripod. Price complete—

¼-plate	£1 15 0	1-1-plate	£4 5 0
½ "	3 0 0	10 × 8 "	5 15 0

LANCASTER'S CAMERAS ONLY.

Le Merveilleux.

	¼	½	1-1	10 × 8	12 × 10	15 × 12
Camera and Slide	1[illegible]/-	25/-	42/-	56/-	70/-	84/-
Extra Slides ..	5/9	10/6	16/-	25/-	35/-	40/-

Le Meritoire.

	¼	½	1-1	10 × 8	12 × 10	15 × 12
Camera and Slide	21/-	42/-	63/-	84/-	100/-	120/-
Extra Slides ..	5/6	10/6	18/-	25/-	35/-	40/-

The Instantograph.

	¼	½	1 1	10 × 8	12 × 10	15 × 12
Camera and Slide	25/-	50/-	75/	100/-	120/-	160/-
Extra Slides ..	7/6	12/6	20/	28/-	40/-	45/

The International.

	¼	½	1-1	10 × 8	12 × 10	15 × 12
Camera and Slide	32/6	63/-	95/-	115/-	140/-	165/-
Extra Slides ..	7/6	12/6	20/-	28/-	40/-	45/-

The Ladies'.

	¼	½	1-1	10 × 8	12 × 10	15 × 12
Camera and Slide	22/6	42/-	63/-	84/-	100/-	120/-
Extra Slides ..	5/6	10/6	18/-	25/-	35/-	42/-

Sliding Body Wet Plate Cameras.

	¼	½	1-1	10 × 8	12 × 10	15 × 12
Camera and Slide	15/-	21/-	35/-	45/-	63/-	—
Extra Slides ..	6/6	10/6	16/-	21/-	25/-	—

CHEAP AMATEUR SET.

THE
"CONTINENTAL."

MAHOGANY, leather bellows rack and pinion movement, sliding front, reversable back, self-adjusting focussing screen, swing back, with 3 double dark slides, rigid threefold tripod stand with fixed top screw.

Camera and stand in separate carrying cases with shoulder strap all complete.

				London made, Rapid Rectilinear Lens.		
¼ plate	£3	10	0	£1	1	0
½ ,,	3	17	6	1	5	0
1-1 ,,	5	5	0	2	5	0

c

SHEW'S AMATEUR SETS.

No. 1.—Consisting of a Portable Folding Camera of mahogany, bellows body, reversing frames and double back. Rapid rectilinear lens of English manufacture for portraits, landscape or architectural work. Folding tripod stand, portable dark room lamp, dry plates, developing and fixing dishes and chemicals. For printing—frames, paper, dishes and chemicals for toning and fixing   Complete in travelling box for pictures 4¼ × 3¼ 2 10 0

No. 2.—The whole apparatus, as above, for plates 6½ × 4¾ and 4¼ × 3¼   4 10 0

No. 3.—Shew's Simple Camera, with double extension rack work focussing arrangement, rising front, reversing frame, hinged focussing screen and 3 double backs for plates or films, superior mahogany sliding tripod and lens as above, with developing and printing materials, complete for pictures, 4¼ × 3¼ 5 5 0

No. 4.—Ditto,   ditto   for pictures, 5 × 4   ..   ..   ..   5 15 0

No. 5.—Ditto,   ditto   for pictures 6½ × 4¾ and 4¼ × 3¼ 8 5 3

SHEW'S SPECIAL OUTFIT.

CONSISTING of our 1890 Camera (see page 1), with 3 double backs of latest improved make, with patent light proof hinges and springs to shutters; patent turntable top, and folding and sliding tripod, our extra rapid rectilinear lens, and the Eclipse repeat shutter, self setting for time or instantaneous work.   Best solid leather case for camera, lens, &c.

For plates 6½ × 4¾ and 4¼ × 3¼ ..	..	..	..	..£14 17 6
„ 7½ „ 5 „ 5 „ 4 ..	..	..	..	.. 15 15 0
„ 8½ „ 6½ „ 6½ „ 4¾ ..	..	..	..	.. 18 10 0
„ 10 „ 8 „ 6½ „ 4¾ ..	..	..	..	.. 23 10 0
„ 12 „ 10 „ 8½ „ 6½ ..	..	..	..	.. 29 10 0

COMPLETE OUTFITS.
THE ECLIPSE SETS.
For Pictures, 4¼ × 3¼.

CONSISTING of the Eclipse apparatus (see page 13). 4¼ × 3¼ with three double backs for plates or films, fitted with finder and folding bottom board for occasional time exposures, with extra setting to lens for interiors or near figures

The apparatus, in best solid leather case, and the developing materials, plates, etc., enclosed in a neat chemical case, with lock and key, complete £8 8 0

Ditto, ditto for pictures 5 × 4 or Academy (the new pocket size)..   9 15 0

Ditto, ditto for pictures 6½ × 4¾ and 4¼ × 3¼, including 2 dozen plates for each size 11 10 0

Ditto, ditto for pictures 7½ × 5 and 5 × 4, including 2 dozen plates for each size 12 15 0

Ditto. ditto for plates 8½ × 6½ and 6½ × 4¾ 18 10 0

PRINTING MATERIALS FOR ABOVE.

Printing frames, papers, dishes. toning and fixing baths, blotting book, &c., extra.

For pictures, 4¼ × 3¼	..	..	..	..£0 12 6
„ 5 „ 4 or 5 × 3¼ (Academy)		..	..	0 17 6
„ 6½ „ 4¾	..	..	..	.. 1 1 0
„ 7½ „ 5	..	..	..	.. 1 5 0
„ 8½ „ 6½	..	..	..	.. 1 10 0

THE ECLIPSE YACHTSMEN'S SETS.

CONSISTING of the Eclipse Apparatus for pictures $8\frac{1}{2} \times 6\frac{1}{2}$, fitted with our patent focussing flange for instantly altering the focus for near as well as distant objects, and when required, for finely focussing between the fixed distances, an extra speed arrangement to the shutter of lens for snap shots of near vessels passing at great speed, folding bottom board for occasional time exposures, focussing screen, one double back for plates or films, and Eastman roll holder for 48 transparent film exposures.

The whole in strong solid leather travelling case, with 1 dozen plates, $8\frac{1}{2} \times 6\frac{1}{2}$, and Eastman film for 48 pictures, complete £19 10 0

CHEMICAL CHESTS.

STRONGLY made travelling cases with hinged lid in front as well as at top, and strong carrying strap, containing portable dark room lamp, glass measures, scales and weights, 3 dishes for developing and 2 for printing, with necessary solutions for developing and fixing. Frames and paper for printing with toning and fixing solutions, dusting brush, blotting book, &c.

Complete for pictures	$6\frac{1}{2} \times 4\frac{3}{4}$	..		..	..	..	..	£2 10	0
,,	,,	$8\frac{1}{2}$,, $6\frac{1}{2}$	..		..	..	..	..	3 3	0
,,	,,	10 ,, 8	..		..	..	..	..	4 4	0
,,	,,	12 ,, 10	..		..	..	..	..	5 5	0

ENLARGING AND REDUCING CAMERAS.

A simple addition to
any large Camera.

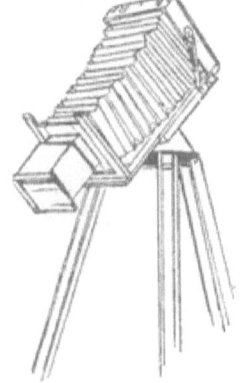

FOR ENLARGING.   FOR REDUCING.

SHEW'S ECLIPSE ENLARGING or REDUCING APPARATUS.

THIS apparatus forms a simple means of enlarging or reducing with any form of large camera available, using for the purpose the same lens as that with which the original was taken (where practicable). It consists of two small square bodies of polished mahogany, one sliding within the other with a fixing screw to hold them in position, and a tilting table to screw on to the tripod or to stand on a table by which the large camera can be tilted at any angle in order to face the light employed. The end of the sliding body is then screwed to a spare front of the large camera.

Full particulars for use accompany each apparatus.

C 2

THE COMBINATION
ENLARGING CAMERA AND LANTERN.

A bellows camera with rack work focussing, on solid base board, carrying also a Russian iron lantern with 5-in. condensor and 3 wick patent lamp, a double combination Lens with rack and pinion complete £6 6 0

MORGAN'S DAYLIGHT ENLARGING CAMERA

A bellows body camera with sliding front, and negative frame with carriers.

For negatives, ¼, 5,4 and ½ plate £1 15 0

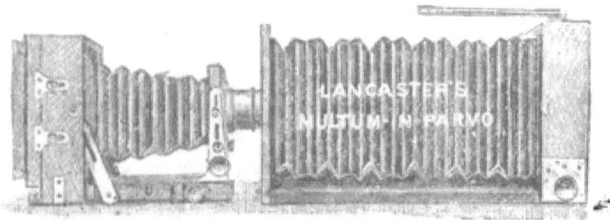

LANCASTER'S MULTUM-IN-PARVO CAMERA

(For Enlarging and Reducing.)

THE MULTUM-IN-PARVO CAMERA can be used with any ordinary Camera, and may be used, for enlarging, copying same size, or reducing. Also for Lantern Transparencies.

A capital daylight enlarging apparatus.

FOR ENLARGING.—The Negative must be placed in the Dark Slide of the ordinary Camera, and the enlargement taken in Multum-in-Parvo, the plate going into the end of the Camera.

FOR COPYING same size, the two Cameras must be opened out equally to about twice the length of focus of Lens used.

FOR REDUCING.—The Negative must be placed in Multum-in-Parvo Camera, and plate put into Dark Slide of ordinary Camera.

PRICES.

To enlarge up to	¼ plate	£0 10 6	To enlarge up to	18 × 15 plate	£3 0 0
,,	,,	½ ,,	0 15 0	,,	,,	20 ,, 18 ,,	3 15 0
,,	,,	1/1 ,,	1 1 0	,,	,,	24 ,, 20 ,,	4 4 0
,,	,,	10 × 8 plate	1 5 0	,,	,,	30 ,, 24 ,,	5 5 0
,,	,,	12 ,,10 ,,	1 10 0	,,	,,	36 ,, 30 ,,	8 8 0
,,	,,	15 ,,12 ,,	2 0 0				

Extra Slides, ¼, 5/-; ½, 7/6; 1/1, 12/6; 10 × 8, 16/-; 12 × 10, 20/-; 15 × 12, 25/-

The dark slide will hold either a dry plate or bromide paper, and can have carriers for any smaller sized plate.

SHEW'S ENLARGING OR REDUCING
EXTENSION.

(See page 11).

Attached to the above Camera, works very successfully without requiring removal.

LANCASTER'S
COMBINATION MULTUM-IN-PARVO.

With double bellows, the front part detachable, so that Camera and Lens may be used for ordinary work. The Lens is an Achromatic one, specially constructed for enlarging and reducing. Each set consists of Camera, Dark Slide, and Achromatic Lens.

1/1 Combination Multum-in-Parvo, 35/-; 10 × 8, 42/-; 12 × 10, 50/-; 15 × 12, 63/-; 18 × 16, 105/-; 24 × 20, 126/-

EXTRA SLIDES.

1/1 plate, 10/-; 10 × 8, 13/6; 12 × 10, 16/-; 15 × 12, 20/-; 18 × 16, 30/-; 24 × 20, 35/-

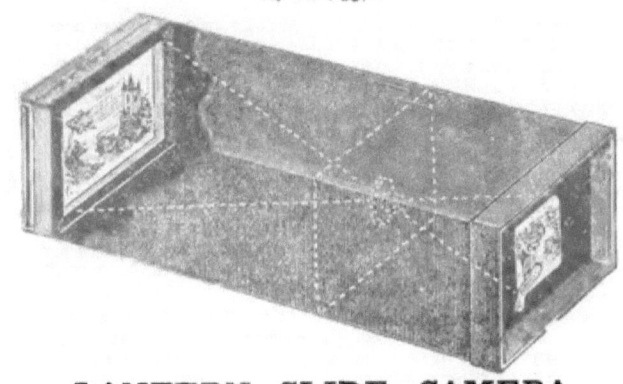

LANTERN SLIDE CAMERA.

For making Lantern Slides from larger negatives without focussing.

	Square Corner.	Oblong.
To carry negatives 6¼ × 4¼	12/6	14/6
„ „ 8½ „ 6½	15/-	17/6

LANCASTER'S
LANTERN SLIDE MULTUM-IN-PARVO.

Camera Lens and shutter for reducing from 4¼ × 3¼ plate   ..   £1 1 0
Adapters to attach to the Camera to reduce from larger negatives
6½ × 4¾ 3/-   8½ × 6½ 4/-

PEARSON & DENHAM'S
PATENT REDUCING CAMERAS FOR LANTERN SLIDES.

THIS is now acknowledged to be the most successful arrangement for the purpose. Any Lens from 5 to 8 inch back focus can be used, and any part of the negative reduced.

Price without Lens, including one Dark Slide.

<table>
<tr><td></td><td></td><td></td><td>Rack and pinion
focussing extra.</td></tr>
<tr><td>For Negatives</td><td>$6\frac{1}{2} \times 4\frac{3}{4}$</td><td>£1 15 0</td><td>6/-</td></tr>
<tr><td>,,</td><td>$8\frac{1}{2}$,, $6\frac{1}{2}$</td><td>2   2 0</td><td>6/-</td></tr>
<tr><td>,,</td><td>10 ,, 8</td><td>2 10 0</td><td>6/-</td></tr>
</table>

Extra Dark Slides, each 5/6.

ENLARGING LANTERNS.

Russian iron lantern with patent triple wick lamp and reflectors, giving brilliant light with the slightest possible amount of heat.

Double combination lens, 1 plate, 4 inch compound plane convex condenser, including portable case, forming a stand for the apparatus, which serves admirably as an exhibition lantern, complete with case £3 15 0

Ditto, ditto with new patent 4 inch slanting lamp, $\frac{1}{2}$ plate double combination lens and 6 inch compound condenser, without case   5 15 0

SHENSTONE'S ENLARGING LANTERN AND STAND.

An enlarging Lantern with lamp, &c., with platform for the camera and lens and measured bottom board with screen or easel attached, to carry the sensitive paper.

By a simple movement a magnesium lantern replaces an oil lantern offering convenience for focussing. Enlargements can be made with it of any size up to 24 × 24, and any sized picture can be easily repeated. Price complete £5 10 0

ENLARGING EASELS.

For holding the paper for enlargement. Sliding and easily adjustable.

Each 24 × 18, 13/6.   26 × 22, 15/6.   30 × 25, 21/-

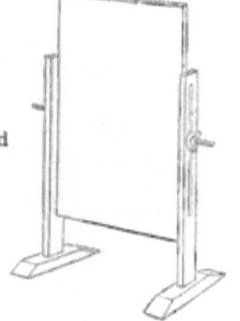

HUGHES BIJOU ENLARGING LANTERNS.

The above are fitted with the patent rectangular condensers, in japanned lantern, with patent Pamphengos Lamp, sliding bellows camera extension and double combination lens, with rack and pinion focussing. These condensers are equivalent to 6 inch ..   £6 10 0
Or if without front lens 5 15 6
The same Lantern as above, with condensers equal to $7\frac{1}{2}$ inch, and good front lens 7 15 6
If without front lens 6 10 0
The same Lantern for $\frac{1}{2}$ plate, with condensers equivalent to 9 inch 14 10 0
If without front lens 12 0 0

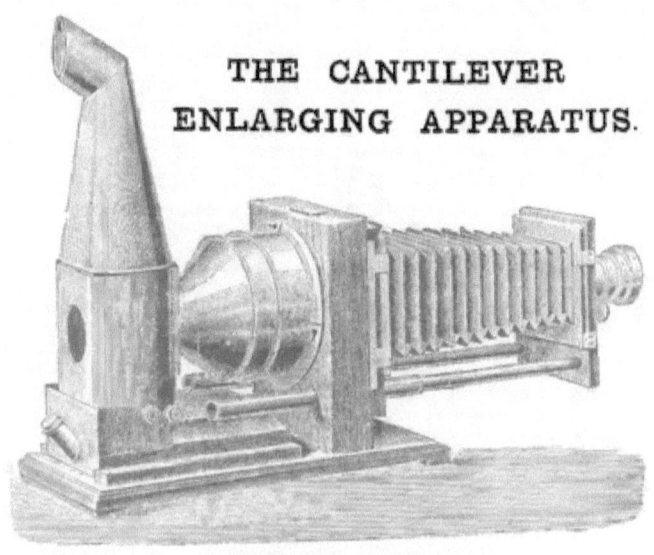

THE CANTILEVER ENLARGING APPARATUS.

QUARTER PLATE.

(Stage admits plates up to 8½ × 6½.)

5½ inch Condensers without objective £4 15 0
Ditto complete with enlarging objective, having Rack, U.R. Stops,
    and yellow glass cap 6 10 0
    Packing case, 20 × 11 × 14 inches outside, 1/6, weight about 34 lbs. packed.

This size furnishes a strong plea for the use of small plates in the field, and will be appreciated by all who employ Hand, Detective, or good ¼ plate Cameras.

HALF PLATE.

(Stage admits plates up to 10 × 8.)

8½ inch Condensers without objective £8 10 0
Ditto complete with enlarging objective, as above 11 15 0

    Packing Case, 34 × 15 × 17 inches, 2/6, weight about 72 lbs. packed,

THE NINE INCH SIZE.

(Stage admits plates up to 12 × 10.)

9 inch Condensers with objective £10 10 0
Ditto complete with enlarging objective, as above 16 10 0
    Packing Case, 34 × 16 × 20 inches, 3/-, weight about 96 lbs. packed.

THE TEN INCH SIZE.

(Stage admits plates up 11 inches.)

10 inch Condensers without objective £12
Ditto complete with enlarging objective   19
    Packing Case, 36 × 17 × 21 inches, 4/-, weight about 112 lbs. packed.

THE ELEVEN INCH SIZE.

11 inch Condenser without objective £15 15
Ditto with enlarging objective 22 10 0
Fine screw motion for use with non-racking lenses 0 10 6

Fitting customer's own lenses when suitable, per quotation. Charge includes fitting, centring, testing, wood centre, spare flange, yellow glass cap, and when necessary, cone adapter.

EXTRA CARRIERS.

With any size opening frame will admit.

For stage of   5½   8¼   9   10 inch Lanterns.
3/-   4/-   5/-   5/- each.

Extra Circular Wooden Fronts, Spanish Mahogany, for fitting on additional Lenses, 1/6 and 2/-

Extra chimneys, for ¼ 6d., larger, 9d. each.

Full directions for working accompany each instrument.

THE "NIMROD" ENLARGER.

THE "NIMROD" though manufactured with the same regard for accurate workmanship which characterizes the "Cantilever," is a simpler and less expensive apparatus of more limited range, though including most of required sizes and yielding good results within its scope.

The centre Wood Block is employed both as the seat for the Condenser and for the Stage. The negative carrier is square, reversing and masking, and as it is placed quite close to the Condensers the full benefit is obtained.

The Condensers have been specially made full aperture 5 and 8 inches diameter respectively.

The one rod on which the front is mounted is square, lending itself well to fine focussing even in the absence of rack on the objective, by grasping it firmly in one hand, using the thumb as a brake to prevent jerk, by placing it partly on the rod and partly on the outer tube.

The lamp is mounted on the axis of the apparatus, with flames flat side to the Condenser, and with a ruby window at the back. The bellows are made of stout tough cloth and are not removable.

PRICES.

Quarter-plate 5 inch Condenser without objective £3 5 0
Do.   with objective, having rack, ordinary stops, and yellow
cap 4 6 0
Half-plate 8 inch Condenser 6 10 0
Do.   with objective, as above 8 10 0

Customers own Lenses when suitable in focus, about 5 and 7 inches respectively, will be fitted on, subject to a charge for mounting, testing, extra flange, yellow cap, and when necessary, a lengthening cone.

OPTICAL
LANTERNS FOR DEMONSTRATIONS.

See special Circular.

CONDENSERS.

For enlarging by artificial light. Two plane convex lenses of best quality Mounted in double metal frame.

Diameter 5½ in.   £1 4 0   Diameter 10 in.   £5 0 0
"   6 "   1 10 0   "   11 "   6 15 0
"   8 "   2 14 0   "   12 "   8 5 0
"   9 "   3 15 0

RECTANGULAR CONDENSERS (PATENT).

8½ × 6½ £7 10 0   6½ × 4¾ £5 5 0   4¾ × 3¼ £2 15 6

LENSES.

PORTRAIT LENSES.

THE J. F. S. PORTRAIT LENSES have now been in use for the last forty years, and have obtained a world-wide reputation for high-class quality, combined with moderate prices.   They are manufactured for us by the celebrated DARLOT of Paris, selected and marked "J. F. S." without which mark none are sent out.

	Diameter.	Focus.						
Carte-de-Visite	1¾-in.	5-in.	with waterhouse diaphragms	£1	15	0
Extra Rapid do.	2¼-in.	6-in.	,,	,,	,,	3	5	0
Cabinet	2¾-in.	6-in.	,,	,,	,,	5	10	0
Extra Rapid do.	3¼-in.	8-in.	,,	,,	,,	7	10	0
Promenade and 8½×6½	4¼-in.	13-in.	,,	,,	,,	18	10	0

FOREIGN PORTRAIT LENSES

OF good quality. selected, double combination racking adjustments, warehouse diaphragms.

¼-plate ..		..		..	£0 15 0
½-plate ..		..		..	1 15 0

ROSS' IMPROVED PORTRAIT LENSES.

THESE Lenses are constructed to give all the sharpness that can be optically obtained, and enlargements from small negatives may be produced with them which will favourably compare with others of the same size taken direct with a large lens.   This is the most severe test for the defining power of a Portrait Combination, and one which no *diffusion-of-focus* lens will stand.

Nos.	3	3A	4	5	6
Focus	10-in.	12-in.	15-in.	20-in.	24-in.
Plate	6½ × 4¾	8½ × 6½	10 × 8	15 × 12	18 × 16
Prices	£17 10 0	£27 0 0	£38 0 0	£42 10 0	£54 0 0

These Lenses are admirably adapted for Vignette, Half Length and Sitting Figures, but for Full Lengths the Cabinet and Carte series are preferable, having a flatter field.

QUICK-ACTING C.-D.-V. LENSES.

These Lenses give very rapid results, with brilliancy and exquisite definition.

Nos.	1	2	3
Focus	4½-in.	4¾-in.	6-in.
Prices	£5 15 0	£6 10 0	£11 10 0

BRILLIANT DEFINITION AND GREAT RAPIDITY.

ROSS' 'CARTE' LENSES differ from ordinary Portrait Lenses in being constructed with as flat a field as is consistent with good marginal definition. They are invaluable for the production of either standing or sitting figures with full aperture, and give very rapid results with brilliancy and exquisite defining power.

ROSS' RAPID "CABINET" LENSES.

These Lenses have all the sharpness and good qualities of the Portrait Lenses, but having a flatter field, give better marginal definition.

Nos.	1	2	3
Focus	6-in.	8-in.	10-in.
Prices	£13 0 0	£17 10 0	£19 10 0

BRILLIANT DEFINITION AND GREAT RAPIDITY.

IN all cases where the length of Studio exceeds twenty feet it is desirable, to obtain the best results, to use the No. 3 C.-D.-V. Lens, in consequence of the pleasing pictures and correct perspective obtained ; for short Studios (less than twenty feet) the No. 2, or even No. 1, will be found to give excellent results ; but it is recommended that a Diaphragm be used, and care be taken that the Camera is placed at a proper elevation.

ROSS' UNIVERSAL LENSES.

FOR GROUPS, PORTRAITS OR STUDIES IN THE STUDIO, INTERIORS, COPYING, &c.

THE "UNIVERSAL" Lenses have great freedom from flare, with sharpness, depth of focus, and flatness of field—qualities so necessary in producing first-rate Negatives for direct Printing or Enlargements.

Nos.	1	2	3	4	5
Focus	8½-in.	10¾-in.	13½-in.	16½-in.	20-in.
Views	8½×6½	10×8	12×10	15×12	18×16
Groups	7½×4½	8½×6½	10×8	12×10	15×12
Prices	£7 10 0	£9 0 0	£12 10 0	£16 10 0	£25 0 0

Larger sizes to order.

The "Universals" are not designed to compete with the Rapid Portrait Lenses, which have about twice their intensity when used with full aperture, but on account of their excellent covering qualities and moderate cost, they will be much appreciated for taking large Portraits, Busts, and Groups in the open air or in well-lighted studios, when the expense of a large Portrait Lens is an objection.

DALLMEYER'S PORTRAIT LENSES.

No. 1 A*.—Patent Lens, with rack and pinion movement, Diameter of front and back combinations, 2¾ and 2⅝-in. respectively, and 6½-in. back focus; for pictures 5×4 inches £13 0 0

No. 2. A*.—ditto, ditto, Diameter [of front and back combinations, 3½ and 3¼ in. respectively; 10 in. back focus; for pictures 6½×4¾ inches. 18 0 0

No. 3 A*.—ditto, ditto, Diameter of Lenses 4 in., and 12 in. back focus; for pictures 8½×6½ in. and Promenades, and Cabinets.. .. 27 5 0

No 4 A.—ditto, ditto, Diameter of Lenses 4½ in., and 14 in. back focus; for pictures 10×8 in., and under 38 10 0

No. 5 A.—In rigid mount, Diameter of Lenses 5 in., and 18 in. back focus; for pictures 15×13 in., and under 50 0 0

No. 6 A.—ditto, ditto, Diameter of Lenses 6 in., and 22 in. back focus; for pictures 20×16 in., and under 60 0 0

* These Lenses are well adapted for the Cabinet Portraits, according to length of gallery.—Thus, No. 1 A requires a distance of 14 feet between subject and lens (not recommended if a longer focus lens can be used). No. 2 A, 20 feet, and No. 3 A, 24 feet.

No. 1 B.—Carte de Visite Lens, with rack and pinion movement, the Lenses 2 in. diameter, and 4½in. back focus; for portraits 4½×3¾ £6 5 0

No. 1 B.—(Long), with rack and pinion movement, the Lenses 2½ in., diameter, and 4¾ in. back focus* 6 15 0

This Lens is constructed to meet the requirements of Photographers who desire to use a longer focus Lens than No. 1 B, but who have not sufficient length of gallery for No. 2 B.

No. 2 B.—Carte de Visite Lens, with rack and pinion movement, the Lenses 2¾ in. diameter, and 6 in. back focus ; for portraits 5 × 4 in. £12 16 0

DESCRIPTION.—These Lenses work, full aperture, at an intensity ¼. The distance between subject and lens being for the No. 1 B, 12 to 13 ft.; for No. 1 B (Long), 14 to 15 ft.; for No. 2 B, 18 to 19 ft. With full aperture Nos. 1 B and 2 B require the same exposure. Since, however, No. 2 B covers a larger plate, it can be used with a larger aperture for standing figures, card size. Hence, for this purpose, it becomes practically the quicker acting Lens. The increased distance also between the Object and Lens tends to better perspective in the resulting picture. The 1 B (Long) is a little slower in action than the 1 B, but for standing figures it produces better results.

DALLMEYER'S PATENT PORTRAIT LENSES (B).

No. 2 B.—Patent Lens, with rack and pinion movement. Diameter of Lenses, 2¾ in., and back focus 6 in. Especially constructed for Carte de Visite Portraits. *Distance between subject and lens for a standing figure,* 18 ft. £13 5 0

No. 3 B.—ditto, ditto. Diameter of Lenses 3½ in., and back focus 8 in. Especially constructed for the Cabinet Portraits. *Distance between subject and lens for a standing figure,* 18 ft. *For Carte de Visite, distance* 25 ft. 20 0 0

No. 4 B.—ditto, ditto. Diameter of Lenses, 4½ in., and back focus 12 in., for pictures 8½ × 6½ in., and under. *Distance for a Cabinet Portrait (standing figure)* 25 ft. 40 0 0

DALLMEYER'S "EXTRA" QUICK-ACTING PORTRAIT LENSES.

No. 2 C.—Portrait Lens, with rack and pinion movement, the Lenses 2¾ in. diameter and 4½ in. focal length from the back glass ; for pictures on plates 4¼ × 3¼ in., and under £15 15 0

No. 3 C.—Portrait Lens, 3½ in. diameter, 6 in. back focus, with rack and pinion, &c., as above, for pictures 5 × 4 in. and under ..   26 5 0

Miniature Lens.—do., do., the Lenses 1¼ in. and 1⅜ in. diameter respectively, and 2 in. focus from the back glass ; for pictures on plates 2 in. × 2 in., and when used with stops for 3¼ in. × 2¾ in. 5 15 0

Medallion Lens.—Diameter of combinations ¾ in., back focus 1 in., in a rigid mount, without stops 2 10 0

DESCRIPTION.—No. 2 C and No. 3 C are perhaps the quickest acting Lenses extant, working full aperture at an intensity of ½ nearly.

They possess double the rapidity of Nos. 1 B and 2 B Lenses respectively, and are especially suitable for quick portraits of children, or for portraits in the dull light of winter.

When required for *standing* figures, card size, a stop must be used to obtain sufficient flatness of field. In this condition their performance, as regards time of exposure, definition, and distance from subject, is about equal to that of Nos. 1 B and 2 B Lenses.

The Miniature Lens, suitable for locket portraits, vignette heads, &c., works in about the same time as No. 2 C Lens.

DALLMEYER'S PATENT PORTRAIT AND GROUP LENSES (D).

With the exception of No. 3 D, these Lenses are mounted in rigid settings, *i.e.*, without rack and pinion movement.

	Diam. of Lenses.	Back Focus.	Size of Group.	Size of View.	£	s.	d.
No. 3 D*	Patent $2\frac{1}{8}$ in.	$10\frac{1}{2}$ in	$8\frac{1}{2} \times 6\frac{1}{2}$ in.	10 × 8 in.	9	10	0
No. 4 D	„ $2\frac{3}{8}$ „	13 „	10 „ 8 „	12 „ 10 „	13	10	0
No. 5 D	„ $3\frac{1}{4}$ „	16 „	12 „ 10 „	15 „ 12 „	17	10	0
No. 6 D	„ 4 „	$19\frac{1}{2}$ „	15 „ 12 „	18 „ 16 „	26	10	0
No. 7 D	„ 5 „	24 „	18 „ 16 „	22 „ 20 „	48	0	0
No. 8 D	„ 6 „	30 „	22 „ 20 „	25 „ 21 „	58	0	0

* *Distance for a Cabinet Portrait with No. 3 D 18 feet.*

In the above-mentioned Lenses where distances are given between subject and lens, about one half the distance would be required for head and bust pictures.

SHEW'S NEW RAPID WIDE-ANGLE RECTILINEAR.

Specially constructed for Architectural Photography—for Interiors, etc., in confined space.

No	Diameter.	Focus.	For Plates.	Price.		
1	$1\frac{1}{10}$ in.	$3\frac{3}{4}$ in.	$4\frac{1}{4} \times 3\frac{1}{4}$	£2	5	0
2	$1\frac{3}{8}$ „	$5\frac{1}{4}$ „	$6\frac{1}{2}$ „ $4\frac{3}{4}$	3	5	0
3	$1\frac{3}{4}$ „	$9\frac{1}{4}$ „	$8\frac{1}{2}$ „ $6\frac{1}{2}$	4	5	0

SHEW'S EXTRA-RAPID RECTILINEAR LENSES.

FOR INSTANTANEOUS WORK.

THESE Lenses are a new combination for views, groups in the open air and in the studio, and for architecture. They cover with brilliant definition to the margin, and work with much greater rapidity than Lenses of ordinary intensity, giving great depth of focus. For correctness of perspective they are unequalled.

No.	Diameter.	Focus.	For Plates.	Price.		
1	1 in.	$5\frac{1}{2}$ in	5 × 4	£2	5	0
2	$1\frac{1}{4}$ „	$7\frac{1}{2}$ „	$7\frac{1}{2}$ „ 5	3	5	0
3	$1\frac{1}{2}$ „	9 „	$8\frac{1}{2}$ „ $6\frac{1}{2}$	4	5	0
4	$1\frac{3}{4}$ „	$10\frac{1}{2}$ „	10 „ 8	5	5	0
5	2 „	$12\frac{1}{2}$ „	12 „ 10	6	5	0

IRIS DIAPHRAGMS.

Supplied to the above, Nos. 1 and 2 10/-, 3 and 4 12/6, No. 5 17/6, extra. Mounted in Aluminium instead of Brass, reducing the weight by two-thirds extra. Nos. 1 and 2, 20/-; 3 and 4, 30/-; 5, 40/-.

SHEW'S WIDE ANGLE PORTABLE PANORAMIC LENSES (Rectilinear).

OF extra short focus, specially manufactured for Panoramic views, interiors, and any Architectural work in confined situations, giving exquisite definition and perfectly flat field.

This Lens, although specially designed for the above work, is also, from remarkably small size, recommended for general tourist work and for out-door groups, &c.

No.	For Plates.	Focus.	Price.		
1	5 × 4	$3\frac{1}{4}$	£2	5	0
2	$7\frac{1}{2}$ „ 5	$4\frac{3}{4}$	3	0	0
3	10 „ 8	7	4	0	0
4	12 „ 10	$8\frac{3}{4}$	5	0	0
5	15 „ 12	11	6	5	0

J.F.S. VIEW LENSES.

LANDSCAPE Lenses, single combination achromatic, manufactured by DARLOT, and specially selected for us. These well-known Lenses have stood the test of nearly forty years competition, and are still acknowledged to be the best for purely landscape work yet made.

Diameter.	Focus.	For Pictures.	With Diaphragm.
1¼ in.	6 in.	4¼ × 3¼	£1 1 0
2 ,,	10 ,,	6½ ,, 4¾	1 10 0
2¼ ,,	12 ,,	8½ ,, 6½	1 15 0
2½ ,,	14 ,,	10 ,, 8	2 2 0
2¾ ,,	16 ,,	12 ,, 10	2 10 0
3 ,,	20 ,,	15 ,, 12	3 10

LANDSCAPE LENSES.

Of superior quality, with rotating diaphragms.

Diameter.	Focus.	For Plates.	Price.
1⅛ in.	4 in.	4¼ × 3¼	10/6
1¼ ,,	5½ ,,	5 ,, 4	12/6
1¾ ,,	8 ,,	6½ ,, 4¾	15/6
2¼ ,,	10 ,,	8½ ,, 6½	22/6

WIDE ANGLE DOUBLET.

Diameter.	Focus.	For Plates.	Price
1 in.	4½ in.	4¼ × 3¼	21/-
1¼ ,,	6 ,,	6½ ,, 4¾	25/-
1½ ,,	7¾ ,,	8½ ,, 6½	35/-
2 ,,	9 ,,	10 ,, 8	50/-

THE LONDON LENS.

Rapid Rectilinear, of good covering power for landscape, architecture, and instantaneous work.

To cover Plates	5 × 4	6½ × 4¾	8½ × 6½	10 × 8	12 × 10
Price	21/-	25/-	45/-	100/-	115/-

DARLOT LENSES.

UNIVERSAL LENS.

WITH this Lens a Photographer can take Landscapes, Interior or Exterior Work.

It gives Six Rectilinear Lenses, various foci, covering 18 inches to 5 inches, and 15 doublets, various foci (angle of 90 degrees), covering 12 inches to 3½ inches.

Set No. 2, in Leather-Covered, Velvet-Lined Case, with Waterhouse Diaphragms. Complete.. .. .. £10 10 0

DARLOT'S EXTRA RAPID RECTILINEAR LENS.

	For Plates.	Focus.	Price.
No. 1.	5 × 4	5½ in.	£3 10 0
2.	7¼ ,, 4½	9 ,,	5 10 0
3.	8½ ,, 6½	10½ ,,	7 0 0
No. 4.	10 × 8	14 in.	£9 0 0
5.	14 ,, 12	18 ,,	14 0 0
6.	18 ,, 16	21 ,,	16 0 0

DARLOT'S RAPID WIDE ANGLE HEMISPHERIC LENSES.

For Plates.	Focus.	Price.
4¼ × 3¼	2½ in.	£3 3 0
8½ ,, 6½	5 ,,	4 0 0
10 ,, 12	8 ,,	5 0 0
16 ,, 14	12 ,,	8 0 0
20 ,, 16	16 ,,	12 0 0

SHEW'S ECLIPSE LENS AND INSTAN-
TANEOUS SHUTTER PATENT.

THIS Lens manufactured specially for use in our well-known Eclipse Hand Camera, working at fixed focus, since its introduction by us in 1885, and further improvements in 1887, has met with such universal approval that having been for the last three years urged by our numerous *clientèle* to work the same Lens still larger, we are, after careful study and repeated trials, enabled to produce it of a size to cover 1/1 plate or 8½ × 6½, which is now used most successfully for snap-shots at a fixed focus, giving pictures of a size hitherto deemed impossible by this method.

We beg to draw particular attention to the fact, that although it has been stated on good authority to be impossible to make a Lens suitable for Hand Camera work of such dimensions, we have at considerable outlay continued our experiments in this direction, encouraged by the fact that such was the universal opinion in 1885, when we first introduced to the world the then unknown system of working at fixed focus (in ¼-plate), which, although opposed to the prescribed theory of optics, and for some time the subject of much adverse criticism has since, owing to the high class results obtained with this Lens of special and peculiar construction become universally adopted, and Hand or Fixed focus Cameras are now a recognized necessity in the Photographic world, with the result that owing to the great competition Hand or detective Cameras are to be obtained at such prices as to preclude the use of a Lens of any value.

Many manufacturers are now making Lenses on similar lines to ours, in small sizes, which we supply at advertised prices to order, but we cannot exchange these when once sent out.

We are pleased to be able to state that we have, after long and careful trials succeeded so far that the results we have obtained with our 1-1 plate Eclipse have much exceeded our expectations, and we are willing to send specimens of the work done with it or, when practicable, to lend an apparatus for trial to an intending purchaser.

The Eclipse is a Rapid Rectilinear of the highest class, possessing great depth of definition combined with remarkable brilliancy and crispness of image; it is supplied with a revolving diaphragm plate, and revolving on the same axis is the instantaneous shutter of circular form, with aperture of a crescent shape, supplied with a simple and very efficient release; the whole forming a most compact arrangement of Lens, Shutter and Stops complete, less in bulk than any Lens alone of similar capacity.

The Shutter as usually supplied gives exposures varying from 1/30 to 1/60 of a second, this we find sufficiently rapid for general Hand Camera work, but for special subjects which require greater speed any increase can be obtained by the additional of an extra spring, for which an attachment is provided on the Lens, for time exposures the shutter need only be opened and the Lens used in the ordinary way

This Lens, with the addition of our Patent Focussing Flange, is complete for time exposures, for focussing, as well as for the work for which it was originally designed.

FAC SIMILE OF WHOLE-PLATE LENS AND SHUTTER.

We are now stocking the above in all sizes at the following prices, including Diaphragms and Instantaneous Shutter :—

For Pictures.	Equiv. Focus.	Price.	For Pictures.	Equiv. Focus.	Price.
4¼ × 3¼	4½	£3 10 0	6½ × 4¾	7¼	£4 10 0
do.	4¾	3 10 0	7½ „ 5	7¼	5 0 0
5 × 4	5½	4 0 0	8½ „ 6½	9¼	6 10 0
do.	6½	4 10 0	—	—	—

ROSS' PORTABLE SYMMETRICAL LENSES.

FOR Landscapes, Architecture, and Copying. These Lenses give extraordinary definition and flatness of field, and are constructed in an exceedingly portable form, all fitting the same flange 7

Nos.	1.	2.	3.	4.	5.	6.	7.	8.	9	10.
Focus	3 in.	4 in	5 in.	6 in.	7 in.	8 in.	9 in	10 in.	12 in.	15 in.
Large Stop	3×3	4×3	5×4	7¼×4½	8×5	8½×6½	9×7	10×8	12×10	13×11
Price	60/-	65/-	70/-	80/-	100/-	120/-	140/-	160/-	180/-	200/-

ROSS' RAPID SYMMETRICAL LENSES.

FOR out-door Groups, Views, Interiors, Copying, and every kind of out-door Photography. The Rapid Symmetricals, being aplanatic, work with full aperture, and are, perhaps, the best and most useful Lens an Amateur or Professional Photographer can possess for general out-door purposes. They are invaluable for all kinds of architectural subjects, dimly-lighted interiors, copying, enlarging, etc.

View size	4×3	5×4	7¼×4½	8 ×5	8½×6½	9 ×7	12×10	13×11	15×12
Group size		4 ,, 3	5 ,, 4	7¼ ,, 4½	8 ,, 5	8½ ,, 6½	10 ,, 8	12 ,, 10	13 ,, 11
Focus	4½ in.	6 in.	7½ in.	9 in.	10½ in.	12 in.	16 in.	18 in.	20 in.
Price	80/-	85/-	105/-	115/-	130/-	150/-	210/-	230/-	290/-

ROSS' UNIVERSAL SYMMETRICAL LENSES.

(New Series, Extra Rapid).

For Landscapes, Portraits, Groups, and Instantaneous Pictures, and every description of out-door Photography.

U.S. Nos.	2	4	8	16	32	64	128	256
Ratio of Stops	$\frac{f}{5.657}$	$\frac{f}{8}$	$\frac{f}{11.3}$	$\frac{f}{16}$	$\frac{f}{22.6}$	$\frac{f}{32}$	$\frac{f}{45.2}$	$\frac{f}{64}$

THESE Lenses work with double the rapidity of the Rapid Symmetrical Series. They are the result of exhaustive calculations, and are constructed of Special Optical Glass, are perfectly aplanatic, give brilliant pictures with full aperture. They are very suitable for Studio work, and when stopped down to the same extent as the Rapid Symmetricals they are equally adapted for all kinds of out-door Photography, Copying, and Enlarging. Their great rapidity renders them specially suitable for obtaining fully exposed instantaneous pictures with rapid shutters, and the smaller sizes are invaluable for use in Detective Cameras.

Prices, Sizes, &c., of the Universal Symmetrical Lenses

View Size.	Group Size.	Equiv. Focus.	Price in Rigid Setting. With Waterhouse Diaphragm.	Price in Rigid Setting. With Iris Diaphragm.
4¼ × 3¼	3 × 3	4½ in.	£5 0 0	£5 10 0
5 ,, 4	4¼ ,, 3¼	6 ,,	6 10 0	7 2 6
6 ,, 5	5 ,, 4	7½ ,,	7 17 6	8 12 6
8 ,, 5	6 ,, 5	9 ,,	8 12 6	9 7 6
8½ ,, 6½	8 ,, 5	10½ ,,	9 15 0	10 12 6
9 ,, 7	8½ ,, 6½	12 ,,	11 10 0	—
10 ,, 8	9 ,, 7	14 ,,	14 0 0	—
12 ,, 10	10 ,, 8	16 ,,	16 16 0	—

ROSS' NEW SINGLE WIDE-ANGLE LANDSCAPE LENSES.

Size of Plate.	Diam. of Lens.	Equiv. Focus.	With Rotary Diaphragm.	With Iris Diaphragms.
5 × 4	1⅛ in.	5 in.	£3 0 0	£3 10 0
6½ „ 4¾	1¾ „	6½ „	3 10 0	4 0 0
8½ „ 6½	2 „	8 „	4 5 0	4 15 0
10 „ 8	2¼ „	10 „	5 10 0	6 2 6
12 „ 10	2½ „	12 „	6 10 0	7 2 6
15 „ 12	2¾ „	15 „	8 10 0	9 5 0
18 „ 16	3 „	18 „	10 0 0	10 15 0

DALLMEYR'S.
RAPID RECTILINEAR (Patent).

The best Lens for general use out of doors and for Copying.

Size of View or Landscape	Size of Group or Portrait.	Equivalent Focus.	Price, Rigid Setting.
4¼ × 3¼ in.	3¼ × 3¼ in.	4 in.	£3 15 0
5 „ 4 „	4¼ „ 3¼ „	6 „	4 10 0
6 „ 5 „	5 „ 4 „	8¼ „	5 10 0
8½ „ 6½ „	8 „ 5 „	11 „	7 0 0
10 „ 8 „	8½ „ 6½ „	13 „	9 0 0
12 „ 10 „	10 „ 8 „	16 „	11 0 0
13 „ 11 „	French size.	17½ „	12 0 0
15 „ 12 „	12 „ 10 „	19½ „	15 0 0
18 „ 16 „	15 „ 12 „	24 „	20 0 0
22 „ 20 „	18 „ 16 „	30 „	27 0 0
25 „ 21 „	22 „ 20 „	33 „	32 0 0

WIDE-ANGLE RECTILINEAR (Patent).

For Architectural Views in Confined Situations.

No.	Largest Dimensions of Plate.	Back Focus.	Equivalent Focus.	Price.
*1AA	7¼ × 4½	3½ in.	4 in.	£4 10 0
1A	8½ „ 6½	4⅝ „	5¼ „	5 10 0
1	12 „ 10	6¼ „	7 „	7 10 0
2	15 „ 12	7½ „	8½ „	10 10 0
3	18 „ 16	11 „	13 „	14 0 0
4	22 „ 20	14 „	15½ „	20 0 0
5	25 „ 21	17 „	19 „	30 0 0

* To be had in pairs for Stereoscopic Views.

WIDE-ANGLE LANDSCAPE LENS (Patent).

For Landscapes Pure and Simple.

No.	Size of Plate.	Equivalent Focus.	Price.
1A	5 × 4	5¼ in.	£3 5 0
1	7¼ „ 4½	7 „	3 15 0
2	8½ „ 6½	8½ „	4 10 0
3	10 „ 8	10 „	5 10 0
4	12 „ 10	12 „	7 0 0
5	15 „ 12	15 „	8 10 0
5A	15 „ 12	18 „	9 10 0
6	18 „ 16	18 „	10 10 0
7	22 „ 20	22 „	14 0 0
8	25 „ 21	25 „	19 0 0

DALLMEYER'S NEW RAPID LANDSCAPE LENS.

For Distant Objects and Views.

No.	Largest Dimensions of Plate.	Diameter of Lenses.	Equiv. Focus.	Price.
1	6½ × 4¾ in.	1·3 in.	9 in.	£4 10 0
2	8½ ,, 6½ ,,	1·6 ,,	12 ,,	5 15 0
3	10 ,, 8 ,,	2·125 ,,	15 ,,	7 10 0
4	12 ,, 10 ,,	2·6 ,,	18 ,,	9 10 0
5	15 ,, 12 ,,	3 ,,	22 ,,	11 10 0
6	18 ,, 16 ,,	3·5 ,,	25 ,,	14 0 0
7	22 ,, 20 ,,	4·25 ,,	30 ,,	17 10 0

NEW RECTILINEAR LANDSCAPE LENS (Patent).

No.	Largest Dimensions of Plate.	Diameter of Lenses.	Equiv. Focus.	Price.
1	6½ × 4¾ in	1¼ in.	8½ in.	£4 15 0
2	8½ ,, 6½ ,,	1¾ ,,	11½ ,,	6 0 0
3	10 ,, 8 ,,	2 ,,	13½ ,,	8 0 0
4	12 ,, 10 ,,	2¼ ,,	16½ ,,	10 0 0
5	15 ,, 12 ,,	2¾ ,,	20 ,,	12 10 0
6	18 ,, 16 ,,	3 ,,	25 ,,	16 0 0
7	22 ,, 20 ,,	3½ ,,	32 ,,	21 0 0

TAYLOR TAYLOR & HOBSON'S LENSES.

RAPID RECTILINEAR.

ANGLE OF VIEW, BETWEEN 40 AND 50 DEGREES.

	Size of Plate.	Approx. Equiv. Focus.	Diam. of Standard Screw.	Price with Waterhouse Diaphragms.	Price extra for Iris Diaphragm.
No. 1.	4¼ × 3¼	5 in.	1¼ in.	£2 10 0	£0 6 0
,, 2.	6½ ,, 4¾	7 ,,	1½ ,,	3 0 0	0 7 0
,, 3.	8 ,, 5	9 ,,	2 ,,	3 10 0	0 8 0
,, 4.	8½ ,, 6½	11 ,,	2 ,,	4 10 0	0 9 0
,, 5.	10 ,, 8	13 ,,	2½ ,,	6 0 0	0 10 0
,, 6.	12 ,, 10	16 ,,	3 ,,	8 0 0	0 13 0
,, 7.	15 ,, 12	18 ,,	3 ,,	9 10 0	0 15 0
,, 8.	18 ,, 16	24 ,,	4 ,,	16 0 0	0 17 0
,, 9.	22 ,, 20	30 ,,	5 ,,	22 0 0	0 19 0

RAPID VIEW LENSES.

	Size of Plate.	Approx. Equiv. Focus.	Diam. of Standard Screw.	Price with Waterhouse Diaphragms.	Price extra for Iris Diaphragm.
No. 1.	4¼ × 3¼	6 in.	1¼ in.	£1 8 0	£0 7 0
,, 2.	6½ ,, 4¾	8 ,,	8½ ,,	1 10 0	0 8 0
,, 3.	8 ,, 5	10½ ,,	2 ,,	2 2 0	0 9 0
,, 4.	8½ ,, 6½	12 ,,	2 ,,	2 10 0	0 10 0
,, 5.	10 ,, 8	15 ,,	2½ ,,	3 0 0	0 13 0
,, 6.	12 ,, 10	18 ,,	3 ,,	3 14 0	0 15 0
,, 7	15 ,, 12	22 ,,	3½ ,,	4 10 0	0 17 0
,, 8.	18 ,, 16	25 ,,	4 ,,	5 10 0	0 19 0
,, 9.	22 ,, 20	30 ,,	5 ,,	7 10 0	1 1 0

SWIFT'S

RAPID PARAGON LENSES

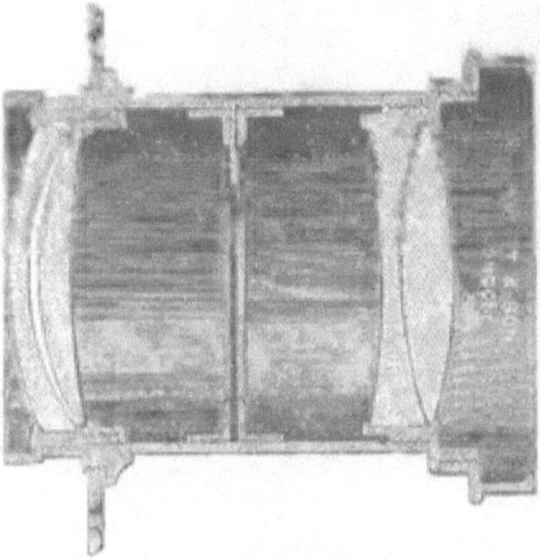

6½ x 5 Rapid Paragon fitted with Iris Diaphragm (actual size).

ARE composed of two symmetrically cemented combinations, which are aplantic, *i.e.*, they work with the full opening, thus importing considerably more light to the sensitive plate than any other rapid outdoor lens yet made, whether English or Foreign. Their superiority in all kinds of out-door pictures, whether for portraits, groups, instantaneous effects, landscapes, architectural subjects (giving straight lines to the edge of the plate) or dimly lighted interiors, they are unrivalled. For copying and enlarging purposes these Lenses are unique, and have been supplied to Home and Foreign Governments. With smaller stops, each Lens will cover the next or even two sizes larger plates than recorded, thus embracing angles of pictures from 60 to 80 degrees, and without any flare or central white spot.

Waterhouse diaphragms marked thus:—

U.S. Nos.	2	4	8	16	32	64	128	256
	f/5·657	*f*/8	*f*/11·314	*f*/16	*f*/22·627	*f*/32	*f*/45·255	*f*/64

Working Intensity.	Size of View.	Size of Group.	Diameter of Lenses.	Equivalent Focus.	Price in Rigid Settings and Waterhouse Diaphragms.	Price with Iris Diaphragm.
U.S. No. 2 *F*. 5·657	3 × 3	..	¾ in.	3 in.	£3 3 0	£3 18 0
,,	4 ,, 3	..	¾ ,,	4½ ,,	3 12 0	4 7 0
,,	5 ,, 4	4¼ × 3¼	1 ,,	6 ,,	3 16 0	4 11 0
U.S. No. 306 *F*. 7	6 ,, 5	5 ,, 4	1¼ ,,	7½ ,,	4 14 6	5 9 6
,,	8 ,, 5	7¼ ,, 4½	1⅜ ,,	9 ,,	5 3 6	5 18 6
U.S. No. 4 *F*. 8	8½ ,, 6½	8 ,, 5	1½ ,,	11 ,,	5 17 6	6 12 6
,,	9 ,, 7	8½ ,, 6½	1⅝ ,,	12 ,,	6 15 0	7 10 0
,,	10 ,, 8	8½ ,, 6½	1¾ ,,	14 ,,	7 12 0	8 7 0
,,	*12 ,, 10	10 ,, 8	2 ,,	13 ,,	9 9 0	10 9 0
,,	12 ,, 10	10 ,, 8	2 ,,	14 ,,	9 9 0	10 9 0
,,	12 ,, 10	10 ,, 8	2 ,,	16 ,,	9 9 0	10 9 0
,,	13 ,, 11	11 ,, 9	2¼ ,,	18 ,,	10 7 0	11 9 0
,,	15 ,, 12	13 ,, 11	2½ ,,	20 ,,	13 0 0	14 5 0
,,	18 ,, 16	15 ,, 12	3 ,,	24 ,,	16 13 0	18 5 0
,,	22 ,, 18	18 ,, 16	3½ ,,	30 ,,	22 10 0	24 5 0
,,	25 ,, 22	22 ,, 18	4 ,,	34 ,,	27 0 0	29 0 0
,,	28 ,, 24	25 ,, 20	4½ ,,	38 ,,	36 0 0	39 0 0
,,	32 ,, 28	28 ,, 24	5 ,,	44 ,,	51 0 0	55 0 0
,,	36 ,, 31	31 ,, 27	5½ ,,	52 ,,	67 0 0	71 0 0
,,	40 ,, 35	36 ,, 32	6 ,,	58 ,,	85 0 0	90 0 0

*Extensively used by Professional Photographers where position will not allow of the use of a 16 inch focus Lens. For general work J. S. and Son recommend the 12 × 10 16 in. focus.

SWIFT'S PORTRAIT PARAGONS.

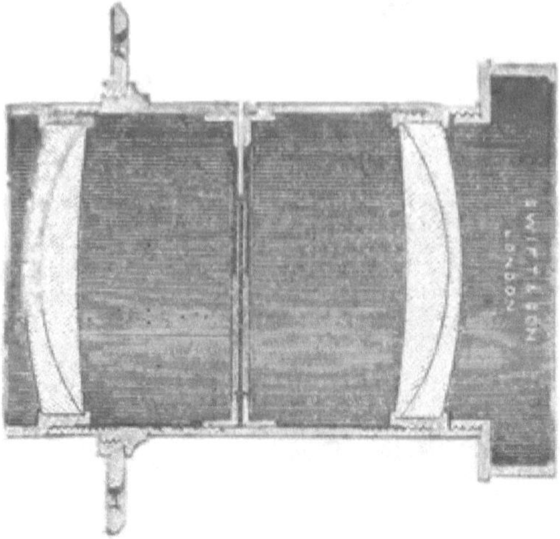

No.	Size of Plate	Diam. of Lenses.	Equiv. Focus.	Price in Rigid Settings with Waterhouse Dia.	Price with Iris Dia.
1	Stereo	1½	5¼	£4 10 0	£5 5 0
2	4¼ × 3¼	1¾	6½	5 8 0	6 3 0
3	5 ,, 4	2	7¾	6 6 0	7 1 0
4	6 ,, 5	2¼	8½	7 7 0	8 7 0
5	8 ,, 5	2¾	10	10 10 0	11 12 0
6	10 ,, 8	3¼	12½	16 0 0	17 5 0
7	12 ,, 10	3¾	15	21 10 0	23 2 0
8	15 ,, 12	4½	18	28 0 0	30 0 0
9	20 ,, 16	5½	24	51 0 0	54 0 0
10	23 ,, 18	6½	30	77 0 0	81 10 0

THE UNIVERSAL PARAGON.

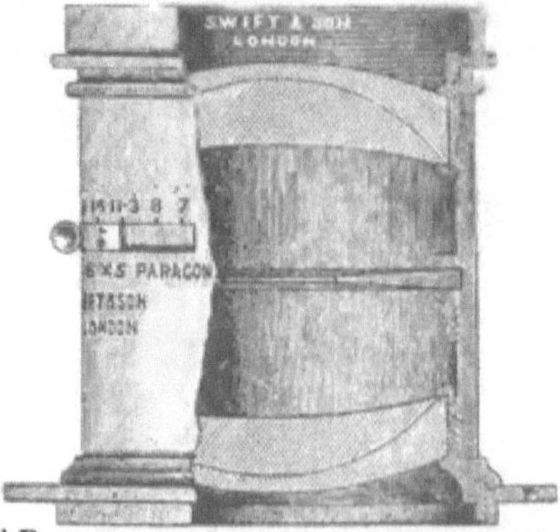

The Universal Paragon may be said to possess properties between the Portrait Lens and Rapid Paragon. Waterhouse Diaphragms marked as below.

U.S. Nos.	2	4	8	16	32	64	128
	f	f	f	f	f	f	f
	5·657	8	11·314	16	22·627	32	45·255

SWIFT'S UNIVERSAL PARAGON.

Working Intensity.	Nos.	View Size.	Group Size.	Diameter of Lenses.	Back focus.	Price in Rigid Mounts and Waterhouse Diaphragms.	Price with Iris Diaphragm.
U.S. No. 2, *F* 5·657	1	8½ × 6½	7¼ × 4½	2 ins.	8½ ins.	£6 15 0	£7 15 0
,,	2	10 ,, 8	8½ ,, 6½	2¼ ,,	10¾ ,,	8 2 0	9 2 0
,,	3	12 ,, 10	10 ,, 8	2¾ ,,	13½ ,,	11 5 0	12 10 0
,,	4	15 ,, 12	12 ,, 10	3¼ ,,	16½ ,,	14 17 0	15 12 0
,,	5	18 ,, 16	15 ,, 12	4 ,,	20 ,,	22 10 0	24 10 0
,,	6	22 ,, 18	18 ,, 16	5 ,,	24 ,,	40 10 0	43 10 0
,,	7	25 ,, 21	22 ,, 18	6 ,,	30 ,,	53 10 0	57 10 0
,,	8	28 ,, 24	25 ,, 20	7 ,,	36 ,,	72 0 0	79 0 0

PORTABLE PARAGON LENSES.

Giving either wide, medium, or ordinary angle, according to the stop used

To cover.	Equiv. Focus.	Price.	With Iris Diaph.
3 × 3	3 in.	£2 14 0	£3 9 0
4 ,, 3	4 ,,	2 18 6	3 13 6
5 ,, 4	5 ,,	3 3 0	3 18 0
7½ ,, 4½	6 ,,	3 12 0	4 7 0
8 ,, 5	7 ,,	4 10 0	5 5 0
8½ ,, 6½	8 ,,	5 8 0	6 3 0
9 ,, 7	9 ,,	6 6 0	7 1 0
10 ,, 8	10 ,,	7 4 0	7 19 0
12 ,, 10	12 ,,	8 2 0	8 17 0
13 ,, 11	15 ,,	9 0 0	9 18 0

WIDE ANGLE LANDSCAPE TRIPLE LENSES

(First Series.)

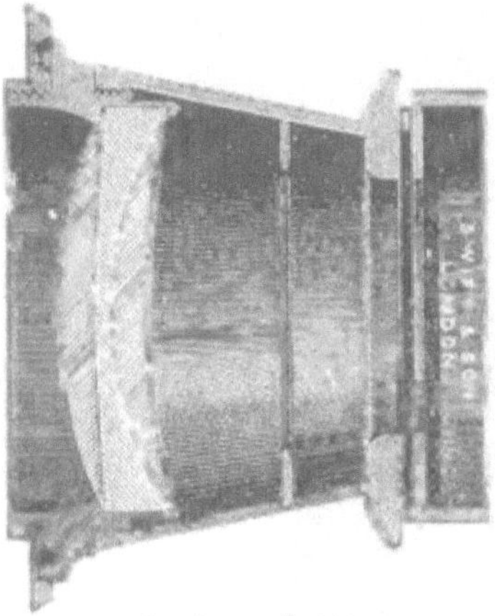

Landscape Lens
5 × 4 Wide Angle (Actual Size).

EACH of these Lenses is composed of three distinct single ones cemented together, producing brilliant negatives of Landscapes, pure and simple. This result is due to the fact of there being only two reflecting surfaces. Architectural subjects are not so satisfactorily rendered when taken with a single as with a double combination, such as the Rapid Paragon, it being impossible to correct single combinations so as to produce straight lines at the margin of the plate.

This First Series being composed of a triple combination gives finer pictures than the Second Series, which is formed of two Single Lenses only, it being a recognised fact that a triple or threefold combination produces a considerably flatter field than that consisting of but two.

U.S. Nos. ..	4	8	16	32	64	128	256
	f/8	f/11·314	f/16	f/22·627	f/32	f/45·255	f/64

Working Intensity	No.	Size of Plate	Diam. of Lenses.	Equiv. Focus.	Prices with Waterhouse Diaphragms.	Prices with Iris Diaphragms.
U.S. No. 4, *F*. 8	1	5 × 4 in.	1⅜ in.	5¼ in.	£2 19 0	£3 14 0
,,	2	6 ,, 5 ,,	1½ ,,	6 ,,	3 2 0	3 19 0
,,	3	7½ ,, 5 ,,	1¾ ,,	7 ,,	3 5 0	4 3 0
,,	4	8½ ,, 6½ ,,	1⅞ ,,	8½ ,,	4 1 0	4 19 0
,,	5	10 ,, 8 ,,	2⅛ ,,	10 ,,	4 19 0	5 14 0
,,	6	12 ,, 10 ,,	2½ ,,	12 ,,	6 6 0	7 2 0
,,	7	15 ,, 12 ,,	2⅝ ,,	15 ,,	7 19 0	8 14 0
,,	8	18 ,, 16 ,,	3 ,,	18 ,,	9 9 0	10 10 0

BECK'S "AUTOGRAPH" RAPID RECTILINEAR LENSES.

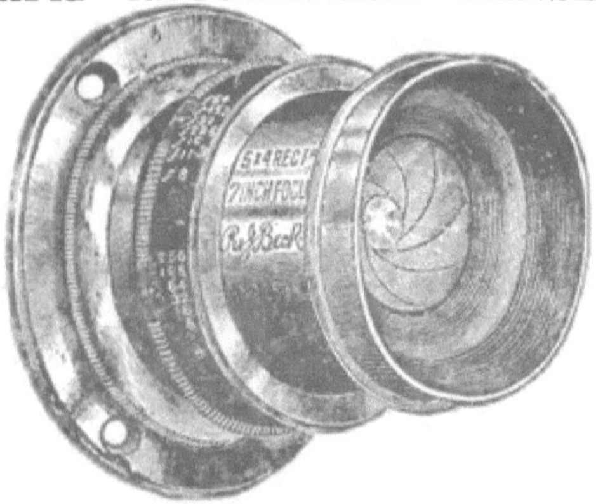

No.	Size of Plate.	Equivalent Focus.	Price with Set of Waterhouse Stops.	Price with Iris Diaphragm.	Price with Iris Diaphragm mounted Aluminium.
0	3¼ × 3¼	4¼ in.	£3 0 0	£3 7 6	£4 7 6
1	4¼ ,, 3¼	5 in.	3 3 0	3 10 6	4 14 6
2A	5 ,, 4	6 in.	3 3 0	3 10 6	5 0 0
2	5 ,, 4	7 in.	3 6 0	3 13 6	5 15 6
3	8 ,, 5	8¾ in.	3 19 0	4 6 6	7 15 0
4	8½ ,, 6½	11 in.	5 10 6	6 1 0	9 15 0
5	10 ,, 8	13 in.	7 2 0	7 12 6	13 13 0
6	12 ,, 10	16 in.	8 8 0	9 3 0	16 16 0
7	13 ,, 11	18 in.	10 0 0	10 17 6	24 10 0
8	17 ,, 14	24 in.	16 16 0	17 17 0	34 13 0

AUTOGRAPH EXTRA RAPID RECTILINEAR LENS.

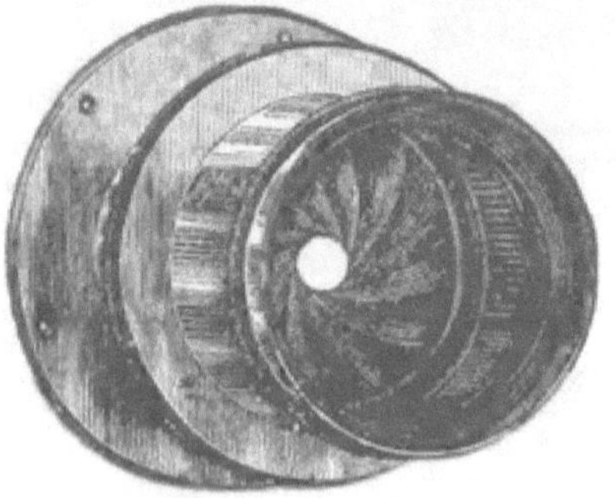

No.	Equiv. Focus.	For Portraits.	For Views.	Price with Iris Diaphragm.
2.	7½ in.	Cartes and Busts	5 × 4	£9 0 0
3.	9¾ in.	Cartes and Cabinets	6½ ,, 4¾	11 0 0
4.	11⅜ in.	Cabinets	8½ ,, 6½	16 10 0
5.	14 in.	Panel	10 ,, 8	22 0 0

BECK'S NEW SERIES OF LENSES.

THE AUTOGRAPH COMBINATION LENS.

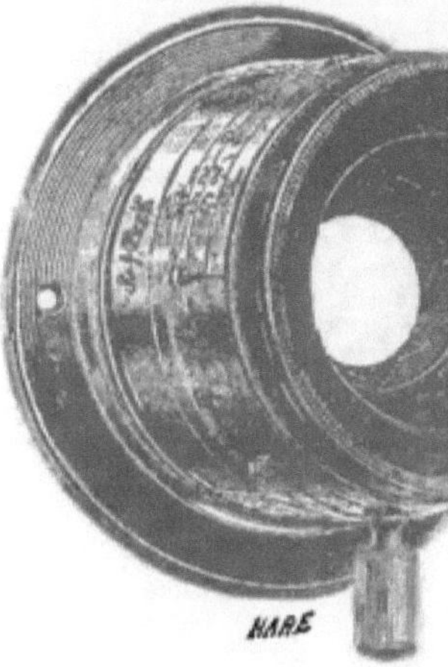

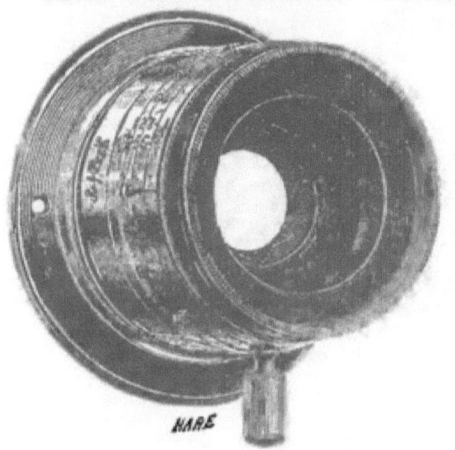

BY the introduction of this combination series of lenses, it has been the endeavour of the maker to construct a series which can be used for all purposes for which a lens is required, except for studio portraiture.

No.	SIZE OF PLATE Full Aperture.	Moderate Stop.	Small Stop.	Equivalent Focus.	Price with Iris Diaphragm.
1	3¼ × 3¼	4¼ × 3¼	5 × 4	3 in.	£3 0 0
2	4¼ ,, 3¼	5 ,, 4	6½ ,, 4¾	4 in.	3 5 0
3	5 ,, 4	6½ ,, 4¾	7½ ,, 5	5 in.	3 7 6
4	6½ ,, 4¾	7 ,, 5	8½ ,, 6½	6 in.	3 10 0
5	7¼ ,, 4½	8½ ,, 6½	9 ,, 7	7 in.	3 13 6
6	7½ ,, 5	9 ,, 7	10 ,, 8	8 in.	3 17 6
7	8 ,, 5	10 ,, 8	11 ,, 9	9 in.	4 5 0
8	8½ ,, 6½	11 ,, 9	12 ,, 10	11 in.	5 15 0
9	10 ,, 8	12 ,, 10	15 ,, 12	13 in.	7 0 0

BECK'S "AUTOGRAPH" COMBINATION LENSES.

In Sets.

No. 1 For ¼ plate Camera, set of Lenses Nos. 1, 3, 5, all fitting the same mount, giving foci of 3 in., 5 in., 7 in., 6 in., 10 in., 14 in. The mount provided with Iris diaphragm graduated with three scales of apertures. The whole packed in Morocco case .. £8 10 0

No. 2. For 5 × 4 Camera, set consisting of Lenses Nos. 2, 4, 6 .. 9 5 0

No. 3. For ½ plate Camera, set consisting of Lenses 3, 5, 7 .. 10 0 0

No. 4. For 1-1 plate Camera, set consisting of Nos. 4, 6, 8, .. 11 15 0

No. 5. For 10 × 8 Camera, set consisting of Nos. 5, 7, 9 .. 13 10 0

Full particulars accompany each lens.

WRAY'S NARROW ANGLE LANDSCAPE LENS.

To cover plate.	Diameter of Lens.	Focus.	Price.
5 × 4	1⅛ in.	7½ in.	£2 5 0
6½ ,, 5	1⅜ ,,	8¾ ,,	2 10 0
7½ ,, 5	1½ ,,	10 ,,	2 15 0
8½ ,, 6½	1¾ ,,	12 ,,	3 5 0
10 ,, 8	2 ,,	15 ,,	4 0 0
12 ,, 10	2 7/16 ,,	18 ,,	4 15 0
15 ,, 12	2¾ ,,	21 ,,	5 10 0
18 ,, 16	3¼ ,,	25 ,,	6 15 0

WRAY'S

RAPID RECTILINEAR with IRIS DIAPHRAGM.

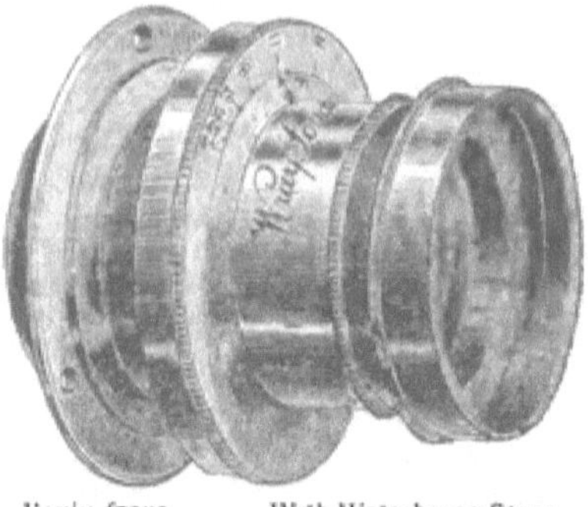

To cover plate.	Equiv focus	With Waterhouse Stops.	With Iris Diaphragm.
5 × 4	5½-in.	£2 10 0	£3 5 0
6½ „ 5	8¼ „	3 10 0	4 5 0
8 „ 5	9½ „	4 0 0	4 15 0
8½ „ 6½	11 „	4 10 0	5 5 0
10 „ 8	13 „	6 0 0	6 15 0
12 „ 10	16 „	8 0 0	9 0 0
15 „ 12	18 „	10 10 0	11 15 0
18 „ 16	23½ „	14 0 0	15 10 0

WIDE ANGLE
LANDSCAPE LENS with IRIS DIAPHRAGM.

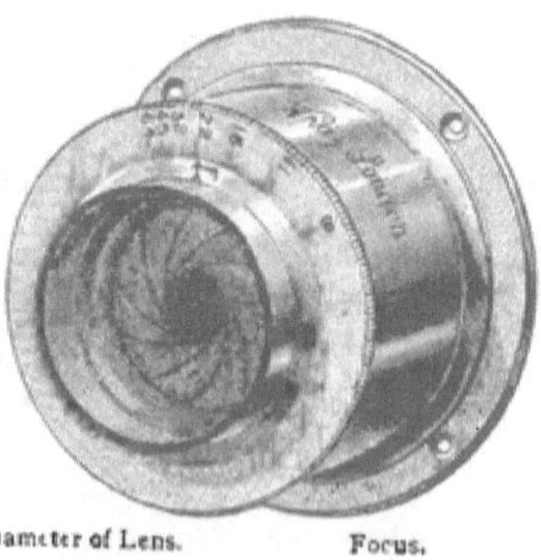

To cover plate.	Diameter of Lens.	Focus.	Price
5 × 4	1⅜-in	5-in	£2 10 0
6½ „ 5	1⅝ „	6½ „	3 0 0
7½ „ 5	1¾ „	7½ „	3 5 0
8½ „ 6½	2 „	8¾ „	3 15 0
10 „ 8	2 3/16 „	10 „	4 15 0
12 „ 10	2¼ „	12 „	5 5 0
15 „ 12	2¾ „	15 „	6 5 0
18 „ 16	3¼ „	18 „	7 15 0
22 „ 20	3⅜ „	21 „	9 15 0
25 „ 21	4¼ „	25 „	14 0 0

GRUBB'S

"RAPID" APLANTIC DOUBLET LENSES.

For Groups and Views.

Each Lens supplied with a Set of Waterhouse Diaphragms.

Size of Plate.	Diameter of Leuses.	Focus.	Price. Rigid Mount.
4¼ × 3¼ in.	¾ in.	4½ in.	£4 0 0
5 ,, 4 ,,	⅞ ,,	6 ,,	4 5 0
6½ ,, 4¾ ,,	1⅛ ,,	7½ ,,	5 5 0
8 ,, 5 ,,	1¼ ,,	8½ ,,	5 15 0
8½ ,, 6½ ,,	1½ ,,	11 ,,	6 10 0

NEW PORTABLE

LONG FOCUS LANDSCAPE LENSES.

Working Intensity.	No.	Size of Plate.	Diam. of Lenses.	Equivalent Focus.	Prices with Waterhouse Diaphragms.	Prices with Iris Diaphragms
U.S. No. 8. *F.* 11·314	1	5 × 4 in.	1⅛ in.	9 in.	£2 19 0	£3 14 0
,,	2	6 ,, 5 ,,	1⅜ ,,	11 ,,	3 5 0	4 0 0
				14 ,,	3 15 0	4 10 0
,,	3	8½ ,, 6½ ,,	1½ ,,	14 ,,	4 1 0	4 16 0
				16 ,,	4 10 0	5 5 0
,,	4	9 ,, 7 ,,	1¾ ,,	16 ,,	4 10 0	5 5 0
				18 ,,	4 15 0	5 10 0
,,	5	10 ,, 8 ,,	2 ,,	18 ,,	4 19 0	5 14 0
				20 ,,	5 9 0	6 4 0
,,	6	12 ,, 10 ,,	2⅛ ,,	20 ,,	6 6 0	7 1 0
				22 ,,	6 16 0	7 13 0
,,	7	13 ,, 11 ,,	2¼ ,,	22 ,,	7 0 0	7 17 0
,,	8	15 ,, 12 ,,	2½ ,,	25 ,,	7 19 0	8 19 0

Longer Focus Lenses to those mentioned in above List made to Order.

LENSES FOR DETECTIVE OR BOX CAMERAS.

SHEW'S ECLIPSE LENS.

(See page .)

FOREIGN DETECTIVE LENS.

Mounted in sliding tube for adjustment to different distances, with stops in front and fitted with instantaneous shutter complete.

To cover 5 × 4. Diameter 1¼. Focus 5 in. each £1 2 6

RECTILINEAR DETECTIVE LENS.

Extra Rapid of superior quality in rigid mount with Waterhouse Diaphragms.

To cover 5 × 4. Diameter 1 in., Focus 5½ in. £1 7 6

BURR'S NEW DETECTIVE DOUBLET.

Equiv. Focus, 5⅝. Diameter 1⅛. Working Aperture, F/6 .. .. £2 0 0

WRAY'S SPECIAL LENSES FOR DETECTIVE CAMERAS.

Largest working aperture, F/8.

Focus.	Waterhouse Stop.	Iris Diaphragm.
4½ in.	£2 5 0	.. £3 0 0
5 ,,	2 5 0	.. 3 0 0
5½ ,,	2 5 0	.. 3 0 0
6 ,,	2 10 0	.. 3 5 0

BECK'S RAPID AUTOGRAPH.

No.	Focus.	With Iris Diaphragm.	Iris Diaphragm Mounted in Aluminium.
0.	4½-in.	£3 7 6	£4 7 6
1.	5 ,,	3 10 6	5 14 6

SWIFT'S RAPID PARAGON.

To cover.	Focus.	With Waterhouse Diaphragms.	With Iris Diaphragms
4 × 3	4½ in.	£3 12 0	£4 7 0
5 × 4	6 ,,	3 16 0	4 11 0

ROSS'S UNIVERSAL SYMMETRICAL.

New Series Extra Rapid.

View Size.	Group Size.	Equiv. Focus.	With Waterhouse Diaphragm.	With Iris Diaphragm.
4¼ × 3¼	3 × 3	4½ inch	£5 0 0	£5 10 0
5 ,, 4	4¼ ,, 3¼	6 ,,	6 10 0	7 2 6
6 ,, 5	5 ,, 4	7½ ,,	7 17 6	8 12 6

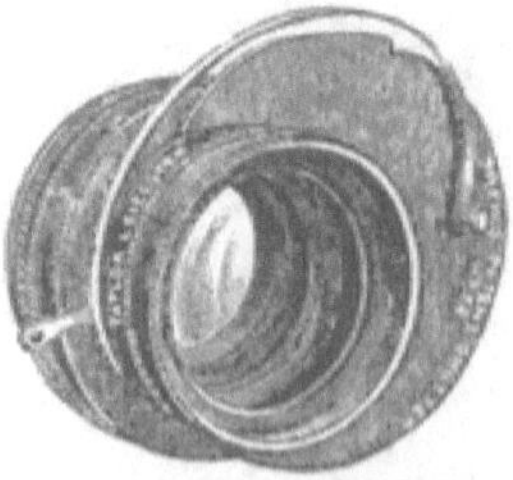

TAYLOR TAYLOR AND HOBSON'S.

No.	Approximate Equivalent Focus.	To Cover.	With Waterhouse Diaphragms.	Extra for Iris Diaphragms.	Extra for Patent Shutter.
0	3-in.	2½ × 2½	£2 10 0	7/-	18/-
1	4 ,,	3¼ ,, 3¼	3 0 0	7/-	18/-
2	5 ,,	4¼ ,, 3¼	3 10 0	7/-	20/-
3	6 ,,	4¼ ,, 3¼ or 5 ,, 4	3 10 0	7/-	20/-

SHEW'S PATENT FOCUSSING FLANGE.

WE have lately completed the above, a simple device adaptable to any make of Lens, enabling the operator to focus with much greater accuracy than with the racking lens or camera, and invaluable for all cameras now made for fixed focus or hand camera work.

The Patent Flange entails no extra bulk, and besides being capable of adjustment or setting at different distances or points for hand work, is easily used for fine focussing between these points by rotating a lever which causes the lens to advance or recede as desired.

It is admirably adapted to box cameras, as the lever may be actuated from the outside, serving also as a scale indicator. Price:—

$\frac{1}{4}$-plate, 12/6.　$\frac{1}{2}$-plate, 15/-　1-1 plate, 21/-

SHEW'S GIMBAL OR SWIVEL FLANGE.

WE are now manufacturing the above as a simple means of obtaining a swing front, said to advantageously replace the swing front It forms a swing for the lens in every direction; is easily fixed in any position by one movement, and takes up little more room than an ordinary flange.

THE UNIVERSAL LENS ADAPTER.

AN adapting flange which will hold with a firm grip any lens from the smallest to the largest in general use. It is formed on the principle of the Iris diaphragm, the blades being considerably stronger than is necessary when adapting such a diaphragm to a lens

SHEW'S 1885 ECLIPSE
INSTANTANEOUS SHUTTER
(PATENT).

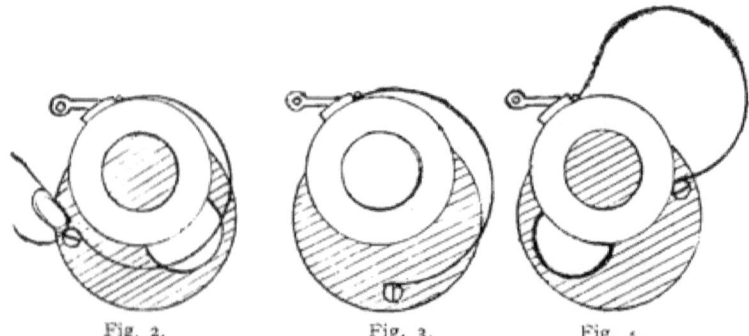

Fig. 2.	Fig. 3.	Fig. 4.
Closed.	Open, for time exposures.	Set, for exposure.

FOR hand or other small Cameras. This Shutter is mounted between the combinations of the Lens, is supplied with a simple means of regulating the exposure, and an efficient release.

This Shutter as usually sent out registers a speed of 1-60th of a second, and is considered by us to be sufficiently rapid for general snap-shot exposures. For special work the speed can be increased to any degree, by the addition of extra springs, for which an attachment is provided on the lens mount.

The above Shutter fitted to any lens from 15/-

SHEW'S ECLIPSE REPEATING SHUTTER
(PATENT).

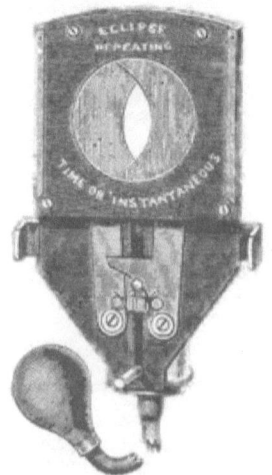

ADJUSTABLE to different lenses, and equally suited for time or instantaneous work. Never requires setting, and is the most compact form of the kind yet made. Specially suited for Detective Cameras, being silent in action, simple in construction, and moderate in price.

No. 1, for ¼ and ⅝ Lenses 17/6
No. 2   ,,   ½   ,,   1-1-plate ditto 18/6

SHEW'S 1890 ECLIPSE SHUTTER

(PATENT).   (System MATTIOLI).

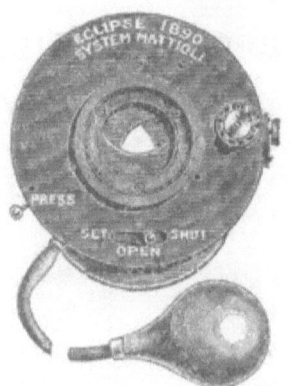

THIS Shutter recommends itself over all others yet introduced for the following advantages :—

1—It can be fitted in the centre of the lenses, at the back, or on the hood, as required.

2—It is of very high rate of speed, due to an entirely new system of propelling disc.

3—It can be adjusted to 8 different speeds, as well as for time exposures.

4—It is perfectly smooth and free from vibration in its action, whether at full speed or slow.

5—It is smaller and more compact than any shutter in the market, being at the same time very strong and not liable to be affected by any change of climate—a shutter uncovering a lens for 8 × 5, measuring only 3½-in diameter by half-inch thickness.

6—It is provided with a rotating diaphragm plate, corresponding with the stops of the lens.

7—Owing to an improved method of releasing valve, the ball or pear of the pneumatic release is considerably smaller than usual, and instantly refills itself.

8—It is provided with a trigger, which may be used in lieu of the pneumatic release, for Box Detective and other Hand Cameras.

9—The mode of manipulating the shutter is engraved on the face, thus dispensing with loose instructions.

10—Finally.—In addition to the many advantages possessed by this shutter over others, it is, for a shutter of this class, moderate in price.

To uncover lense.			Price.	To uncover lense.		Price.
1-inch	..	..	£1 10 0	1¾-inch	..	£2 15 0
1⅛ ,,	..	..	1 15 0	2 ,,	..	3 10 0
1½ ,,	..	..	2 0 0	2⅜ ,,	..	4 10 0

Mounting the shutter in the centre of the tube, 1 to 1½-in. 3/-; 1¾ to 2⅜-in. 5/6
The mounting can be done from 1 to 2 days from the receipt of the tube of the Lens.

INSTANTANEOUS AND OTHER SHUTTERS

SHEW S ECLIPSE INSTANTANEOUS SHUTTER.

THIS Shutter, invented by us November, 1880, is made on the concentric principle, thereby giving the greatest possible amount of light during exposure. It is simple in construction and perfect in action, with a screw adjustment, by which any length of exposure can be obtained, from instantaneous to 5 or 10 seconds, according to size, the "Eclipse Shutter" is acknowledged by all to be the most durable and most efficient of any yet made.

This Shutter has now been ten years before the public. We beg to call attention to the fact that we are the original inventors and sole makers of this form of shutter, of which the Adjustable Spring Break forms such an important feature, and that none are genuine unless they bear the name "Eclipse."

Price, including Extra Adjustment, for lengthening exposures :—No. 1. for 1-in. Lens and under, £1 9s 6d.; No. 1a, for 1½-in. Lens, and under, £1 15s. 6d.; No. 2, for 2-in. Lens and under, £2 5s.; No. 3, for 2½-in. Lens, and under, £2 14s

SARJEANT'S PATENT SHUTTER.

Giving rapid or prolonged exposures at will of the operator, the lightest and smallest Shutter made

Prices—Aperture	1	1¼	1⅜	1¾	1½	2	2¼	3	in.
	22/6	26/-	30/-	30/-	30 -	35/-	35/-	40/-	
Solid Leather { Cases extra {	2/-	2/-	2/6	3/-	3/-	3/6	3/6	5/-	

KERSHAW'S PATENT ROLLER
INSTANTANEOUS SHUTTER.

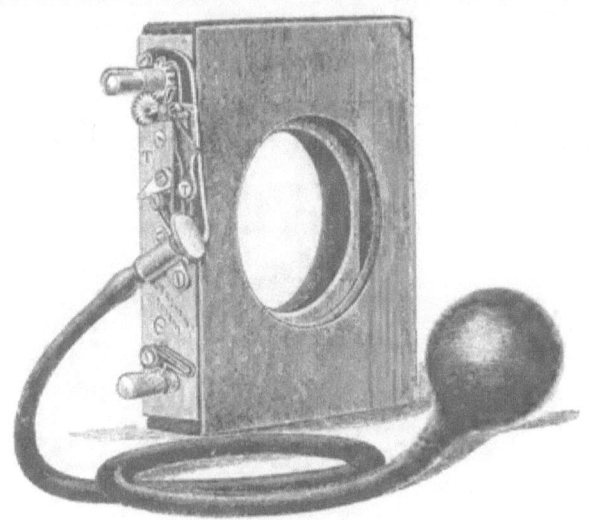

Price, complete, with Pneumatic Release :—

2-inch	..	..	18/-	3-inch	..	24/-
2½ ,,	..	..	21/-	3½ ,,	..	30/-
		4-inch	..	..	36/-	

THE THORNTON-PICKARD
PATENT "TIME" SHUTTER.

For prolonged or instantaneous exposures.   Adapted for all classes of work

Prices—For Lens having Hood up to

	Ins. 1½	2	2¼	2½	2¾ diam.
For "Time" and	18/6	20/6	22/6	23/6	25/-
"Instantaneous" ,, 3	27/6	3½ 32/6	4 37/6	4½ 42/6	5 ,, 47/6

THE THORNTON-PICKARD
INSTANTANEOUS ROLLER-BLIND SHUTTER.

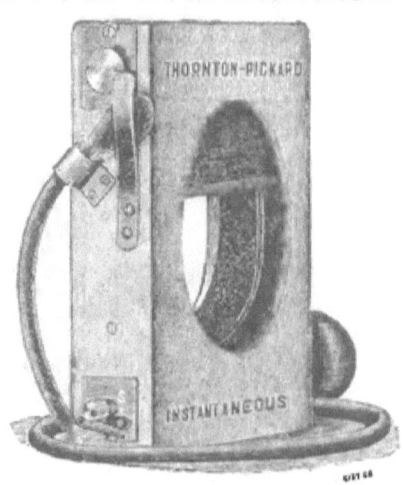

Prices—For Lens having Hood up to

	Ins. 1½	2	2¼	2½	2¾
For Instantaneous ,,	13/6	15/6	17/6	18/6	20/-
3	22/6	3½ 27/6	4 32/6	4½ 37/6	5 diam. 42/6

THE THORNTON-PICKARD
PATENT STEREOSCOPIC SHUTTER.

Prices—for a pair of Lenses having hoods up to

Inches	1½	2 diam.
For "Time" and "Instantaneous"	26/-	23/-
For "Instantaneous"	21/-	23/-

THE MARVEL DROP SHUTTER.
Very light, simple and effective.

Aperture 1¾ or under ..	..	..	..	..	..			2/3
,, 2¾ ,,	..	..	..	..	..			2/9

A slight charge for fitting to Lenses, from 9d.

THE AUTOMATIC SHUTTER.

A SELF-SETTING Shutter for time or for instantaneous exposures, easily regulated, opening from the centre and very smooth in action, adjustable for different lenses.

In three sizes, for lens ¼ to 10 × 8, each   ..   21/-

    India rubber adapters for smaller lenses, each ..   1/-

TYLAR'S "NORDERN" FLAP SHUTTER.

THIS Shutter is either used for time or instantaneous exposures.   Hand exposures are made by means of the milled head, the spring lever being discharged by means of the small catch at back of shutter.

Price, fitted with pneumatic release .

Up to 1½-inch	5/-
,, 2 ,, ...	6/6
,, 3 ,, ...	10/-

D

TYLAR'S SELF PORTRAIT SHUTTER.

Enables the operator to take his own portrait either in a group or otherwise.

No. 1, fit up to 2-in. hood 5/

,, 2   ,,   3   ,, ...   7/6

Larger sizes to order.

TYLARS "WINDOW" SHUTTER.

No. 1 fit up to 2-in. hood ..   ..   ..   : 3/6

,, 2   ,,   3   ,, ...   6/-

,, 3   ,,   4   ,, ...   8/6

Each has cork back, and can be fitted to lens by aid of a pen-knife.

LANCASTER'S NEW SHUTTERS.
THE CHRONOLUX, 1889.

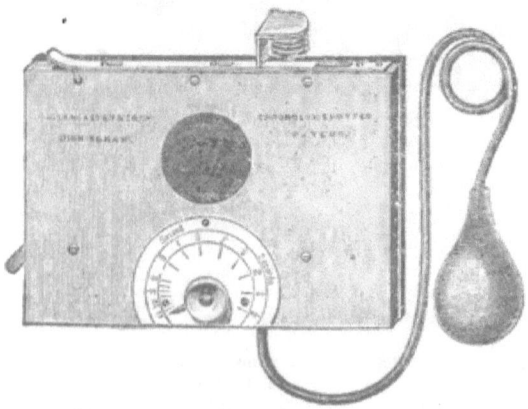

Giving any exposure from $\frac{1}{64}$th to 3 seconds.

Price with pneumatic release—$\frac{1}{4}$ plate, 21/· $\frac{1}{2}$-plate, 25/·   1/1-plate, 30/·

NEW MODEL CHRONOLUX, 1890.

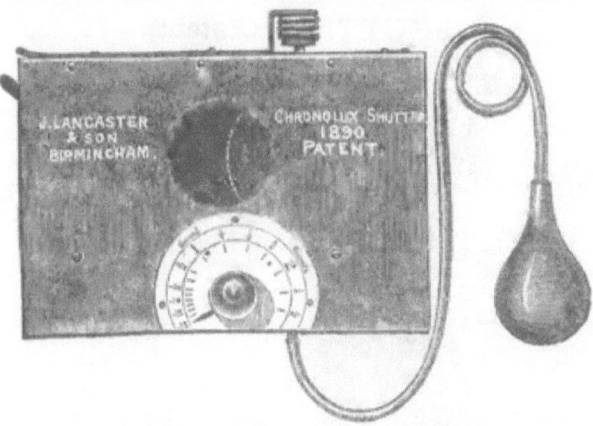

THIS has the same mechanical arrangement as the 1889 Chronolux, with the exception that both shutters move at the same instant in 1890, and not one after the other as in 1889 shutter.

The 1890 Chronolux opens and closes at the centre, and moves without the slightest vibration; it works from $\frac{1}{40}$ of a second to 3 seconds, and by moving the lever on left hand side and slide on top, any length of exposure may be obtained.

Prices—¼ plate, 25/-;   ½ plate, 30/-;   1/1 plate, 35/-

LANCASTER'S PNEUMATIC SHUTTER.

Giving either rapid or time exposure.

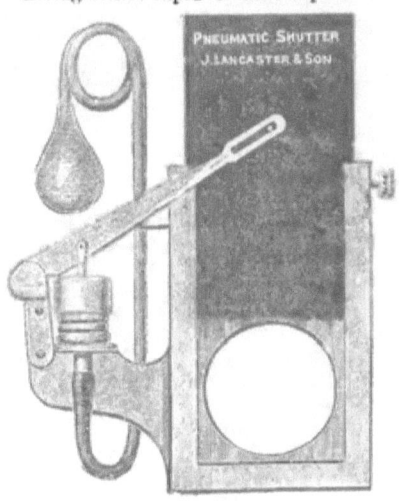

Prices—¼ plate, 7/6;   ½ plate, 10/6;   1/1 plate, 15/

Giving exposures from 1-20th of a second upwards.

D2

LANCASTER'S "PNEUMATIC SEE-SAW" SHUTTER (Patent).

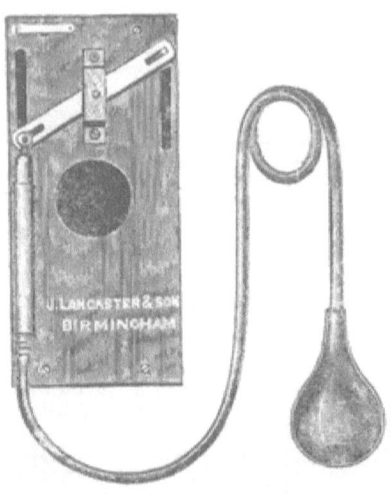

Prices—⅓ plate, 10/6 ;   ½ plate, 12/6 ;   1/1 plate, 15/-

LANCASTER'S "OVAL SEE-SAW" SHUTTER (Patent).

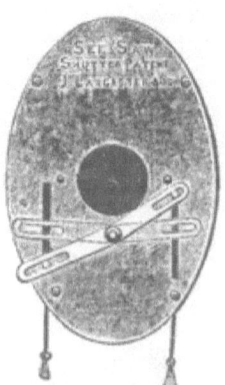
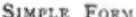
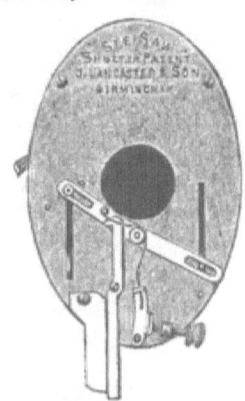

SIMPLE FORM.   BEST FORM.

Prices—¼, 5/- ; ½, 7/6 ; 1/1, 10/6.   Prices—¼, 10/6 ; ½, 12/6 ; 1/1, 15/-

The See-Saw Shutter can be used for time or instantaneous work, giving instantaneous exposures from 100th of a second.

GUERRY'S PNEUMATIC SHUTTER.
THE SINGLE-FLAP SHUTTER.

Is only suitable for the Studio. It is placed inside the Camera or upon the Lens.

¡THE DOUBLE-FLAP SHUTTER.

Has Three Transformations, and is the Shutter *par excellence* for Amateurs.
Note.—The smallest shutters being the most rapid, there is a great advantage in removing the hood and placing the shutter on the body of the lens.

SINGLE-FLAP.			DOUBLE-FLAP.		
From 1½ to 3⅜	..	£0 17 6	1½ to 3⅜	..	£1 7 6
„ 4 in.	..	1 2 6	4 in.	..	1 12 6
„ 4 to 6 in.	..	1 7 6	4 to 6½ in.	..	1 17 6

Complete with pneumatic release.

CAMERA STANDS FOR THE STUDIO.

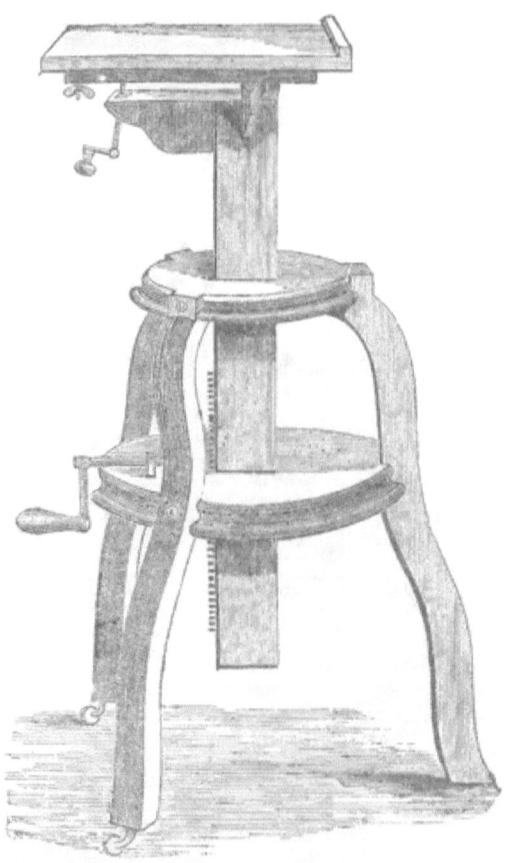

Table Stand, substantial, for the operating room :—

		£	s	d
White wood, with rising pillar, for ¼ and ½-plate camera		£0	10	6
Ditto, of ash, with rackwork, for larger camera, varnished		0	17	6
Ditto, ditto, large size, superior finish, rack adjustment, French polished		1	7	6
Ditto, Shew's Improved Archimedean, with Archimedean screw, and screw for adjusting top..		2	5	0
Ditto, ditto, ditto, large size ..		3	15	0
Ditto ditto, of extra large size, for heavy cameras, very massive, best finish, curved legs, superior fittings, the whole in polished mahogany		5	15	0

PORTABLE TRIPODS.

Folding Stand with Ash top, for ¼ and ½-plate cameras £0 7 6

Ash, folding, polished, of superior make, lock-joint, mahogany top,
  covered in cloth, with 5-in. top, 10/6 ; 6-in. ditto, 14/6 ; 8-in. ditto   0 18 6

Ditto, sliding leg, mahogany top, 4-in., 16/6 ; 6-in., 21/- ; 8-in.   ..   1 2 6

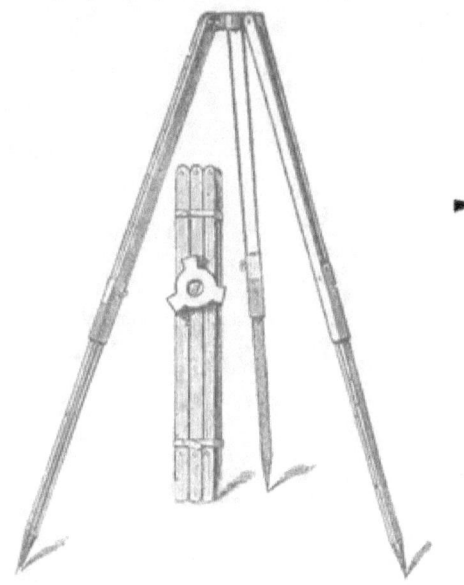

SHEW'S MODEL STAND.

Mahogany, French polished, with legs adjusting to any length, for
  working on uneven ground, and with new improved fixed screws

With 4-in top, 18/6 ; 6-in. top, 21/- ; 8-in. top, 24/- ; 10-in. top, extra
  strong 1 6 6

THE UNIVERSAL STAND.

With patent universally adjusting top, giving any position to the camera,
  with sliding legs

¼-plate, 10/6 ; ½-plate, 15/6 ; 1/1 plate   1 1 6

SHEW'S NEW THREE-FOLD STAND.

The Perfection of Steadiness.

A three-joint Folding and Sliding Stand, perfectly rigid when extended, with
bottom leg sliding in a manner that effectually prevents any sticking. Made of
Ash, French polished, with mahogany top, velvet covered.

Price, with 4-in. wood top   ..   ..   £1 1 0 each.
  ,,   6-in.   ,, ...   1 4 0   ,,
  ,,   9-in.   ,, ...   1 5 6   ,,

Cases for above from 3/6 each.

WALKING STICK STANDS.

For Eclipse or other small Cameras.

SHEW'S PATENT BAMBOO WALKING STICK TRIPOD.

WITH universal top, moving in every direction; perfectly rigid; thoroughly unobtrusive, being finished as an ordinary walking cane, varying in length from 40-in. to 48-in.

Price, £1 5 0 each.

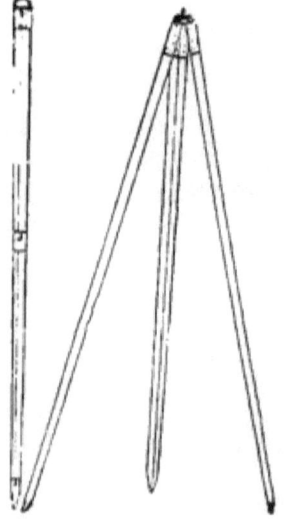

THE ALPENSTOCK TRIPOD.

FORMING when closed a round polished walnut stick or rod, without projections.

Price 17/6 and 21/-.

With ball and socket, giving universal movement to the camera, extra 7/6.

THE TOURIST STAND.

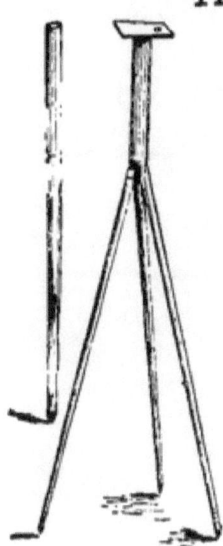

THESE Stands are constructed to supply the want of a really useful Stand that shall be rigid, and of a convenient height when opened but which will easily close and form a not too heavy walking stick. Weight, 1¾ lbs.

As will be seen from the illustration, they are made in two parts, the lower being an improved form of the usual stick stand, to which the upper portion formed of brass tubing, one-and-a-half inch in diameter, is screwed. When not in use, this is carried as a sheath on the upper part of the legs.
Price 21/- each.

THE UMBRELLA TRIPOD.

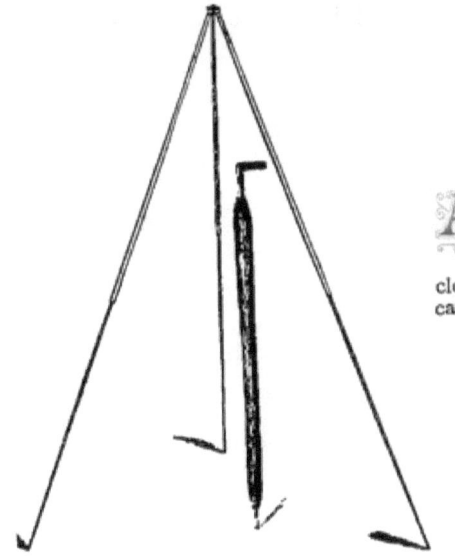

A METAL Tripod with bayonet joints, the handle being removed and reversed forms a screw to hold camera. Enclosed in American cloth umbrella case.

Price £1 1 0 each.

TURNBULL'S WALKING STICK TRIPOD.

 A METAL TELESCOPIC STAND enclosed in metal and wood case, undistinguishable from an ordinary walking stick.
Price: £1 2s

SHEW'S NEW FOUR-FOLD STAND.

 A VERY LIGHT MAHOGANY FOLDING TRIPOD, with bottom leg sliding, 5-in mahogany, velvet lined top, &c., measuring closed 18 × 2¼ × 2¼
Price: £1 1s

SHEW'S ARTISTS' STAND.
A SPECIALITY FOR HAND CAMERAS.

 A VERY LIGHT, COMPACT MAHOGANY STAND, carrying the top (of specially constructed, very portable pattern), when closed without any increase of bulk, when folded 21 × 2¼ including top. Price: 13/6.

SHEW'S POCKET CAMERA CLIP.

F OR attaching THE ECLIPSE or other SMALL CAMERAS to any support, such as a wall, gate, fence, &c., particularly useful to yachtsmen. Price: 12/6.

SHEW'S CYCLE CLIP.

F OR securely fixing the Camera to the handle bar of a Cycle, with ball and socket arrangement for instantly fixing or levelling the Apparatus on uneven ground, or in any position desired. Price: 10/6.

SHEW'S POCKET CAMERA REST (Patent).

An ingenious contrivance for fixing light Cameras to any support, easily carried in the pocket. Weight, 2½-ozs. ; size, 4½ × 2 × ¾-in. ; Price 3/-, for ½ plate, 4/-

DIRECTIONS FOR USE.

Unfold and screw (with the gimlet-pointed screw supplied) through the small bar into any gate, fence, tree, or other available support ; fix the small hinged rod on the pin at side, push this along in its groove until the top or largest bar is level, then screw the camera on. By slightly loosening the screws and turning the Camera, or the Rest as required, the Camera may be placed at any angle.

SHEW'S UNIVERSAL CAMERA CLIP.

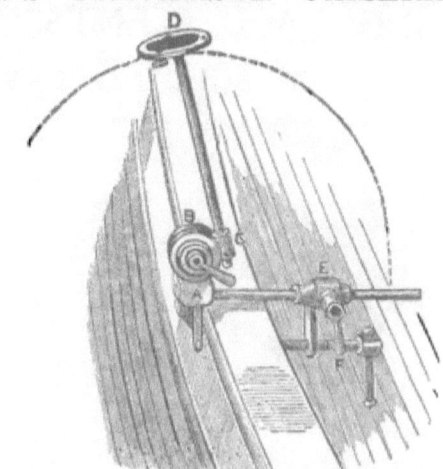

CONSISTS essentially of a clamp formed by a solid gun-metal block A, carrying a turned steel rod, about a foot long, upon which slides a movable block E, capable of being fixed in any position by the set screw shown. Through an arm projecting from this sliding piece passes a vice-screw, which, in conjunction with the block A, forms a clamp of very wide range, capable of easy and rapid adjustment to any projecting object, be it a wall, a gate, a chair-back, a tricycle seat or wheel, a window-frame or even a mantelpiece. The sliding block E permits the rough adjustment to be made rapidly, the final clamping being done with the screw F. Cast on to the block A is an adjustable hinge B, carrying the upright rod to which the camera plate D is affixed. By reversing the upright in the split boss C, in which it is tightened by the same screw that governs the hinge B, and by suitably adjusting the latter, the axis of the lens may be pointed in an upward, downward, or horizontal direction, or at any intermediate angle.

This Instrument is particularly recommended to Travellers and Yachtsmen, as it can be instantly attached to any part of the vessel where the Tripod Stand is not available.

No. 1. For Cameras 8½ × 6½ and under, 25/-
No. 2. For   ,,   12 ,, 10 and under, 37/6.

Extra deep cheeks sometimes required for gripping on large rail of Yachts etc., extra, 4/6.

Circular Motion to Nos. 1 and 2, enabling hinge B to be turned at right angles to A. extra 12/-

Gimbal Pendant for suspending Cameras in a level position from any projecting part of a vessel, 25/-

LEWIS'S PATENT ADJUSTABLE
STAND HOLDER.

For keeping Tripod steady and effectually preventing slipping.

Price, 4/- each.

LANCASTER'S CHEAP FOLDING TRIPODS.

¼-plate, 5/-; ½-plate, 7/6; 1/1 plate, 10/6.

CHANGING BAGS, TENTS, ETC.

SHEW'S PORTABLE FOLDING DRY·PLATE CHANGING BOX.

Open.   Closed.

THESE boxes will be found invaluable for tourists, and for every description of out-door photography, their extreme simplicity and portability far exceeding that of any other yet made for the purpose. They are put up in one minute, and when not in use fold into the form of a portfolio for travelling. They are very durable, and thoroughly efficient for dry-plate work. The sizes named below are our stock sizes. Any others made in one week from receipt of order. To meet the greatly increasing sale for these boxes, we have a large stock in hand. Purchasers may rely upon receiving them immediately. For extremely hot climates it is found necessary to make them throughout of leather; this increases the cost two-thirds of the prices named.

PRICES OF CHANGING BOXES.

No.	For changing Plates.	Size expanded.	Size closed.	Weight.	Price·
1.	6¼ × 4¾ and under	13 × 10 × 10	13 × 10 × 1	Under 2½ lbs.	12/6
2.	8½ ,, 6½ ,, ,,	17 ,, 13 ,, 12	17 ,, 13 ,, 1	,, 4 ,,	17/6
3.	10 ,, 8 ,, ,,	21½ ,, 14 ,, 13½	21½,, 14 ,, 1	,, 5 ,,	24/·
4.	12 ,, 10 ,, ,,	24 ,, 16 ,, 16	24 ,, 16 ,, 1	,, 6¼ ,,	34/·

THE COMPACT CHANGING BAG.

Of linen, black, lined with orange, with yellow window and elastic sleeves.

¼-plate, 5/6.   ½-plate, 7/6.   1·1 plate, 10/6.

PUMPHREY'S CHANGING BAG.

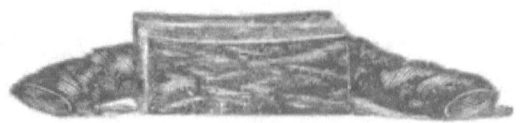

A square, easily folding box, of millboard, linen covered, with linen sleeves, taking very little room when closed flat.

¼, 8/6.   ½, 10/9.   1·1, 13/6.   10 × 8, 15/6.   12 × 10, 18/6.

THE PYRAMID CHANGING BAG.

To hang under the tripod, with elastic sleeves and rings to fasten to legs of stand!

½ plate   10/-   10 × 8   15/-

SHEW'S PORTABLE DEVELOPING BOXES

Of Ash with cistern, waste pipe, folding sink, well and strongly made

For Plates 6½ × 4¾   £2 17 6   For Plates 8½ × 6½   £3 10 0

THE UMBRELLA TENT.

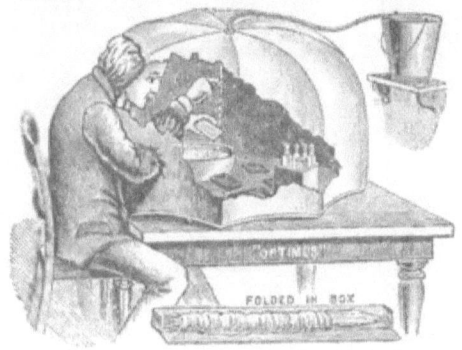

A VERY portable tent, folding into a small space as an umbrella, covered in two materials. The head and hands of the operator being introduced so to watch the developing, whilst the tent rests on the table.

For changing plates only, measuring closed 24 × 3   £1 5 0
For developing also   ,,   ,,   28½ × 3   1 15 0

THE PORTABLE FOLDING TENT.

A SIMPLE and very light contrivance for changing or developing dry plates, with a working space of 33 inches from right to left, forming a table 33-in. × 12-in.   Price £1 1 0

STANLEY'S OPERATING TENT.

For outdoor use, very strong, folding into a small compass, with tripod.

£1 15 0

Ditto, ditto, with waterbag supply pipe and stop cock, sink with waste pipe, &c.

£2 10 0

DARK ROOM FITTINGS.

CISTERNS (Galvanized Iron).

MADE to hang, and fitted with brass tap or union so that the cistern may be placed in any position by attaching a piece of india-rubber tubing.

Size.				To hold.		Price.
12 × 8 × 10	..	..	..	3½ gall.	..	7/6
15 ,, 8 ,, 12	..	..	..	5 ,,	..	10/-
20 ,, 8 ,, 12	..	..	..	7 ,,	..	12/6

Other size to order.

THE CHAMPION PORTABLE LEAD LINED DARK ROOM DEVELOPING SINK.

OPEN, VERY RIGID.

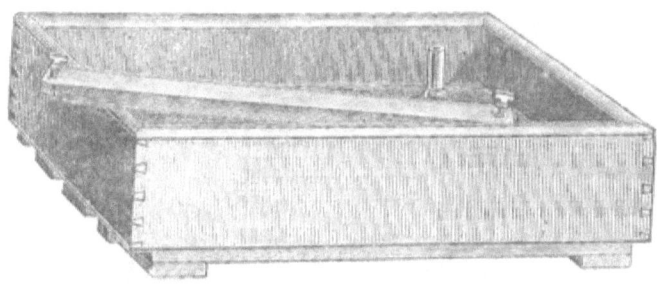

CLOSED.

Size 30½ × 19½, complete with Plug and Waste, on stand.   £2 15 0

The above, without Stand, £1 7 6

DARK ROOM FITTINGS.

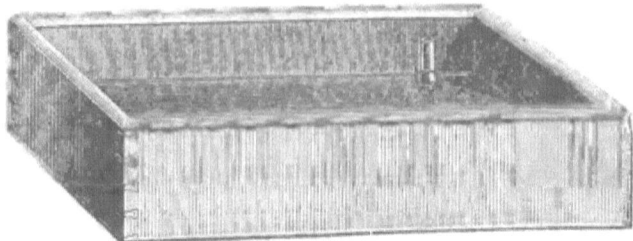

LEAD LINED SINKS.

THESE Lead Lined Sinks are much better than stoneware, and are not affected by acids. They are lighter and do not break the negatives.

Outside Dimensions

24 × 17 × 3½ ..	17/6
30 „ 19 „ 3½ ..	21/6
36 „ 25 „ 5 ..	28/-

VITRIFIED ENAMEL STONEWARE TROUGHS.

FOR Dark Room Sinks. The plug has overflow holes bored at the top, so that the water can be kept running when the sink is full. Fitted with patent trap so that any risk of unpleasant effluvia from the drain is obviated.

Inside Measurement.	Inside Depth.	Price.
21 × 15 ..	.. 4 in. ..	12/-
27 „ 21 ..	.. 4 in. ..	15/-
33 „ 27 ..	.. 4½ in. ..	20/-

ROSE TAPS.

THESE are for use over the Dark Room Sink. They are supplied complete for fixing, with arm to shut water off, as being much easier to use than ordinary tap. At the end is a finely perforated rose, producing a wide and delicate spray, thus thoroughly and careful'y washing the plates.

Price complete, in Best Brass,

BRASS ROSE TAP ONLY.

AFFIXED to Tap over Dark Room Sink by means of a piece of rubber tubing. Gentle spray for rinsing plates; most useful.

6d. and 1/- each.

SHEW'S ORIGINAL AUTOMATIC ROCKER, FOR DEVELOPING.

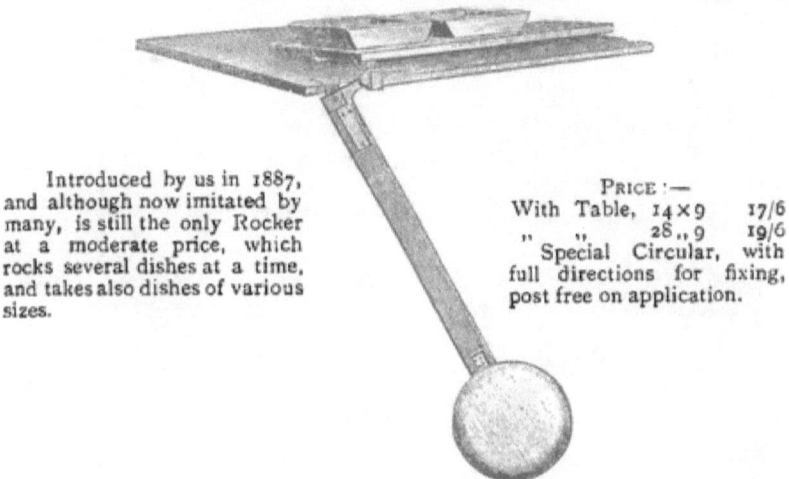

Introduced by us in 1887, and although now imitated by many, is still the only Rocker at a moderate price, which rocks several dishes at a time, and takes also dishes of various sizes.

PRICE :—
With Table, 14 × 9   17/6
   ,,   ,,   28 ,, 9   19/6
Special Circular, with full directions for fixing, post free on application.

THIS useful apparatus should form a part of every amateur or professional Photographer's developing room. It enables the operator to keep as many as six dishes in motion as long as required, thus avoiding the tedious operation of holding or shaking the dish, leaving the operator free whilst several dishes are under the action of the developer, and ensuring the necessarily prolonged development for instantaneous exposures so much in use.

By its use perfect freedom from stains is insured where long development is necessary. It is perfectly smooth and silent in action, and will be found particularly valuable in developing large plates, which, without some such help, quickly tire the arms of the operator. Development proceeds easily and rapidly ; any sized dish can be placed on the Rocker, and the plates safely left while mixing solutions, etc., etc.

The Rocker consists of three fixed and two moving parts—the Table and the Pendulum. When not in use, the Table can be easily put away for convenience.

HUNTER'S PENDULUM ROCKER.

A simple arrangement for rocking a small dish, consisting of cradle, weight, stand and rod, complete, 6/.

AUTOMATIC PLATE ROCKER.

Price for Whole Plates and under, 17/6 ; packed in box, 6d. extra.

Price for 15 × 12 and under, 25/ ; packed in box, 9d. extra.

WASHING APPARATUS.

ZINC WASHING TANKS WITH SYPHONS.

For Plates.	Grooves.	
	12	24
4¼ × 3¼	3/-	4/-
5 ,, 4	3/3	4/3
6½ ,, 4¾	3/9	4/9
7½ ,, 5	4/-	5/3
8½ ,, 6½	4/3	6/-
9 ,, 7	4/6	6/6
10 ,, 8	5/6	6/9
12 ,, 10	6/6	8/-
15 ,, 12	8/-	9/6

To take ¼, ½ and 1/1 combined, 7/- each.
To take 1/1, 10 × 8 and 12 × 10 combined,
10/- each.

THE CHAMPION.

For Dry Plates, with Removable Draining Rack and Syphon,
Enamelled White Inside.

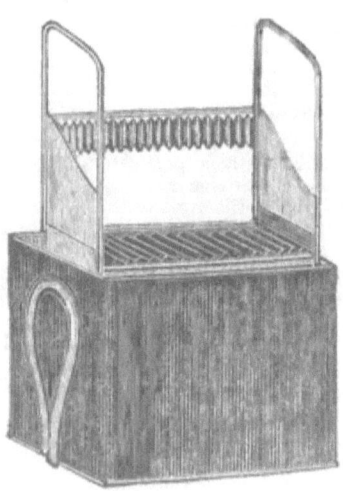

For Plates.	Grooves.	
	12	24
4¼ × 3¼	3/6	6/-
5 ,, 4	4/-	6/3
6½ ,, 4¾	4/6	7/-
7½ ,, 5	5/-	7/6
8½ ,, 6½	5/6	7/6
10 ,, 8	6/-	8/9
12 ,, 10	7/-	10/6
¼, ½ and 1/1 combined	—	9/6
8½ × 6½, 10 × 8, 12 × 10 combined	—	12/6

LEAD TANKS FOR FIXING.

Will resist Hypo. and other Chemicals

For Plates.	10 Grooves.	20 Grooves.	For Plates.	10 Grooves.	20 Grooves.
4¼ × 3¼	5/3	10/-	8½ × 6½	8/6	13/-
5 ,, 4	6/-	11/6	9 ,, 7	10/-	15/6
6½ ,, 4¾	6/3	11/9	10 ,, 8	11/6	18/-
7½ ,, 5	7/-	12/-	12 ,, 10	12/-	22/-

THE COMBINATION ZINC PLATE WASHER.

THIS Washer is fitted with a loose rack for the plates so that they may be lifted out after washing without touching the films. The rack can also be used as a drying rack.

No. 1 to take 3¼ × 3¼, 4¼ × 3¼, 5 × 4, 7½ × 5, and 8½ × 6½   5/- each.
No. 2 to take ditto   ditto   ditto   up to 10 ,, 8   7/- ,,
No. 3 to take ditto   ditto   ditto   up to 12 ,, 10   9/- ,,

The above are fitted with Syphons.

TYLAR'S WASHING APPARATUS.
TYLAR'S RIGID RACKS.

English.				Continental.	
3¼ × 3¼	1/-	8½ × 6½	2/6	9 × 12	1/6
¼-Plate	1/-	9 ,, 7	3/-	13 ,, 18	2/-
5 × 4	1/6	10 ,, 8	3/6	18 ,, 24	3/-
½-Plate	1/9	12 ,, 10	4/6	Any size to order.	
7½ × 5	2/-				

TYLAR'S TANKS, TO HOLD RACKS.

Japanned, with Tap to regulate outflow.

English.				Continental.	
3¼ × 3¼	1/3	7½ × 5	2/-	9 × 12	1/6
¼-Plate	1/3	1/1-Plate	2/6	13 ,, 18	2/-
5 × 4	1/6	10 × 8	3/6	18 ,, 24	3/6
½-Plate	1/9	12 ,, 10	4/3	Other sizes to order.	

TYLAR'S WHIRLPOOL WASHERS.

TO Amateurs who have only a few dozen prints at a time, and those generally of the smaller sizes, the apparatus figured in margin will be found the most thorough and useful washer extant.

The tank cannot run dry or overflow; and when started requires no further attention.

15 × 9   8/6 each.

DIRECTIONS.—Fill tank with water, then attach it to tap with india-rubber tube; and turn the water on.

TYLAR'S "AQUAPOISE" AUTOMATIC ROCKING CRADLE WASHER.

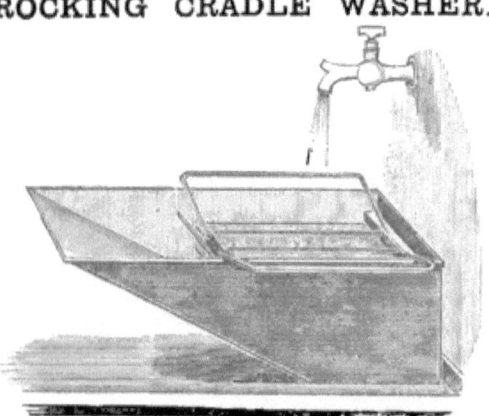

FILLING.

For Plates or Prints; entirely Automatic; requires no attention, and cannot get out of order. To hold six plates each.

3¼ × 3¼ plates	each	2/6	CONTINENTAL SIZES.		
			c. c.		
½ ,,	,,	3/-	9 × 12	each	3/6
½ ,,	,,	4/6	18 ,, 13	,,	5/-
1/1 ,,	,,	6/-	18 ,, 24	,,	7/-

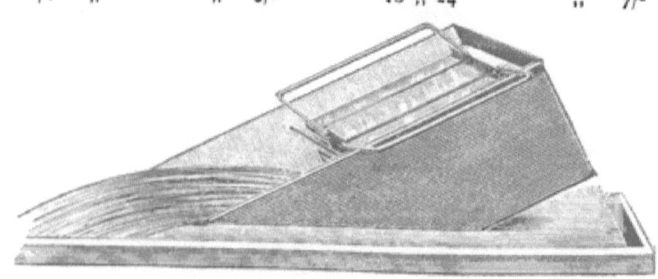

DISCHARGING.

PRINT CRADLES.

To fit these Washers.

¼-plates	10d.	½-plates	1/3	1/1-plates	2/-
Foreign Sizes	9 × 12 1/-		13 × 18 1/6		18 × 24 3/6

THE CHAMPION PLATE RACK.

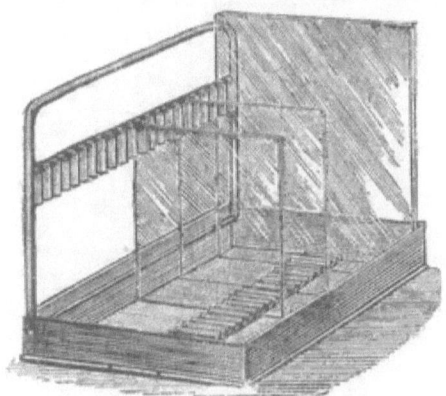

OPEN.

SHUT.

This Rack has advantages possessed by no other,

No. 1 will take ¼, 5 × 4, and 6½ × 4¾ at the same time, in all 24 plates.

The grooves being V-shaped it does not injure the film.

No. 2 will take ½-plate, 7½ × 5, and 1/1 plate.

No. 3   „   1/1   „   9 × 7, 10 × 8, and 12 × 10.

	Plain Zinc.	White Enamelled.
No. 1—24 grooves	1/-	1/10
„ 2—24 „	1/3	2/3
„ 3—24 „	2/-	3/6

JAPANNED METAL DRAINING RACKS.

	Rigid.	Folding.
¼-plate	9d.	1/3
½ „	1 3	2/-
1/1 „	1/9	2/3

RIGID NEGATIVE PLATE RACK.

WHITE ENAMELLED.

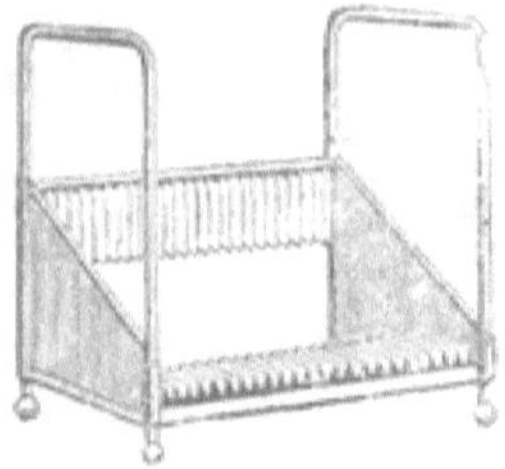

With V-shaped grooves which do not scratch the film.

For Plate.	Price.	For Plate.	Price.
4¼ × 3¼	3/-	7½ × 5	3/6
5 ,, 4	3/-	8½ ,, 6½	3/9
6½ ,, 4¾	3/6	10 ,, 8	4/-

8½ × 6½, 6½ × 4¾, and 4¼ × 3¼ combined 4/6
12 × 10 and 10 × 8 combined 6/-

SHEW'S FOLDING PLATE-WASHER AND DRAINING RACK, COMBINED.

THIS very ingenious and handy little piece of apparatus should be in the hands of every photographer. It is invaluable to the Tourist who has not the means of obtaining a large supply of water, or of carrying the usual bulky washing trough, rendering it quite easy to develop at hotels, etc., *en route*. It folds perfectly flat when not in use; and a size to contain six plates 6½ × 4¾, weighs only two-and-a-half ounces. Others in proportion. Each Rack is constructed to carry six plates, which are placed face downwards, and the Rack then placed in any convenient vessel, with sufficient water to cover the plates, then moved about in the water two or three times again and again at intervals. It will be found that the plates will be thoroughly washed in an hour or two. The Rack can then be placed in a cool place to dry. No dust will settle on the films in their inverted position during the drying.

For plates	Price.		Price.
4¼ × 3¼	9d.	8½ × 6½	1/3
5 ,, 4	9d.	10 ,, 8	2/3
6½ ,, 4¾ } 7½ ,, 5 }	1/-	12 ,, 10	2/9

PINE FOLDING RACK.

12 grooves	¼-plate	1/6	½-plate	2/-
24 ,,	,,	2/-	,,	2/6

Extra large for 1/1-plate, and 12 × 10, 3/.

THE NEW PORCELAIN FIXING BATH AND PLATE WASHER.

For plates	4¼ × 3¼	6½ × 4¾	8½ × 6½	10 × 8	12 × 10
6 grooves	3/6	4/6	7/6	10/6	15/6
12 ,,	5/-	6/-	9/6	—	—

To take ¼ and ½ plate 7/6 To take ½ and 1/1 plate 10/-
To take 1/1 plate, 10 × 8 and 12 × 10 12/6.

WOOD'S PRIZE MEDAL WASHER AND ADJUSTABLE RACK.

The Most Rapid "HYPO" Eliminator in the Market.

ADVANTAGES OF WASHER.

RAPID elimination of HYPO (plates in 15 minutes, prints 20 minutes), platinotype prints freed from Acid in 5 minutes. Non-æration of water, consequently prints and plates are not injured by being covered with air-bells.

Prints are always on the move.

An automatic shut-off so that prints and plates are never left dry if water is unexpectedly turned off. Contaminated water drawn off from bottom.

No bruising or tearing of prints during washing.

Thoroughly well made, will last a lifetime.

ADVANTAGES OF RACK.

Adjustable for all sizes of Plates. Long folding handles, for holding up to drain and dry Plates after Washing.

PRICES.

8½ × 6½ Washer	12/6	8½ × 6½ Rack (Adjustable for 9 sizes)	4/6
12 ,, 10 ,,	20/-	12 ,, 10 Rack (Adjustable for 12 sizes).	8/0

Packing Cases 6d. and 1/- extra.   Larger sizes to order.

ROCKING PRINT WASHER.

THE water running from a tap acts as motive power to revolve the welled wheel. This wheel is connected with the cradle, and causes it to rock up and down at each revolution, so keeping the prints in constant motion.

The tank is fitted with a syphon which drains off the chemically charged water, whilst the fresh supply entering, quickly cleanses the prints.

One hour of such washing will quickly remove all traces of hyposulphite.

These Washers are made in various sizes.

MEASUREMENT OF CRADLE.

5¾ × 7¾	Japanned Zinc	16/6	13 × 11	Japanned Zinc	32/-
9 ,, 7	,,	18/6	16 ,, 13	,,	39/6
11 ,, 9	,,	28/-	20 ,, 16	,,	55/-

THE GODSTONE PLATE WASHER (Patent).

(Only three plates are shown in the engraving so that the arrangement may be clearly seen).

IT is admitted by all Photographers the proper and most effectual way to thoroughly cleanse gelatine plates is to place them face downwards.

To meet that view this plate washer has been designed.

The Washer consists of two principal parts, an outer case or tank and an inner frame or cage, also a plain sheet of metal for a shifting partition.

The cage is so arranged that without the partition it will take six plates of the largest size the Plate Washer is intended for, and from ten to twenty smaller size plates, all face downwards. In the Whole-Plate size Washer and the larger sizes, when the partition is used, different sized plates, viz., $6\frac{1}{2} \times 4\frac{3}{4}$, 5×4, $4\frac{1}{4} \times 3\frac{1}{4}$ and stereo, etc., may be washed at the same time, the lower edge being always on the projecting ledges allowing the plates to lean against the partition. The ledges on the opposite side do not touch the plates.

PRICES.

For Plates.	Cage only.	Tank only.	Complete.
A, Half-plate	7/-	4/-	10/-
B, Whole-plate	8/6	5/-	12/-
C, 10 × 8	9/6	3/-	16/6

THE "GODSTONE" AUTOMATIC WASHING TRAY (PATENT).

For Washing Prints and occasionally Negatives.

A, for Prints to $\frac{1}{2}$-plate, 6,9 ; B. $\frac{1}{4}$-plate, 9/- ; C, 15 × 12, 14/6.

CIRCULAR PRINT WASHERS.

THESE Circular Print Washers are made of zinc, with a perforated bottom, cut funnel-shape, to prevent any sediment of hypo from rising in the trough. Under the bottom is a well, from which is fixed a syphon to carry off the water. Though cheap these Washers are very effective.

14 × 5 deep   9/6 each.
18 ,, 6¼ ,,   13/6 ,,
24 ,, 6½ ,,   23/6 ,,

Enamelled White Inside, 2/3, 3/3 & 4/6 extra.

SHEW'S IMPROVED WASHING TROUGHS FOR PRINTS.

Zinc circular with perforated false bottom and syphon. This useful instrument will be found the best and quickest method of effectually washing prints, as the operator can cause it to fill and empty itself continually, thereby effecting a great saving of time, and more effectually washing the prints than by any other method.
Diameter 15 in., 10/6; 18 in., 15/6; 20 in., £0 18 6

THE CHAMPION PRINT WASHER.

PRICES.

12 × 10 in.   16/-
13 ,, 11 ,,   18/6
16 ,, 13 ,,   28/6
17 ,, 20 ,,   38/-

DIRECTIONS.

A piece of tube should be attached to the water tap and then on to the inlet of apparatus. When the overflow begins to act, the prints should then be put in, when the rotary movement will thoroughly cleanse them from all Hypo.

It is only necessary to empty the apparatus occasionally, when any sediment left in the well can be run off from the tap at the bottom, which should be done at least once a week.

DARK ROOM LAMPS, ETC.
FOR OIL, GAS OR CANDLE.

THE CLIMAX.

A Square Lantern, 13 inches high, with handle on top. Glasses can easily be renewed if broken. Regulated and filled from outside.

Price   6/6 each.

Burns paraffin.

THE "OPTIMUS" LAMP.

EITHER square or round. To burn gas or oil. Fitted in front with a sheet of orange or ruby glass, and a screen of canary fabric set in metal frame, both of which are easily removable, these render the light quite safe, even for the most sensitive plates. Ventilation is well considered, as a shaft at the back of Lamp, open at bottom and top, encourages a free circulation of air.

Price ..   ..   13/- each.

A smaller size also supplied, for oil only, and fitted with one sheet ruby and one sheet orange glass, both removable.

Price ..   ..   7/9 each

CHEAP DARK ROOM LANTERN.

Japanned tin, with ruby glass front, to burn night lights. Price 10d. each.
Oil lamps to fit above with screw top, 6d. each.

PARAFFIN LAMPS.

Glass container, fitted with ruby chimney and brass top to exclude light.
Prices 4/- and 5/6 each.
Extra chimneys 4d. and 6d. each.

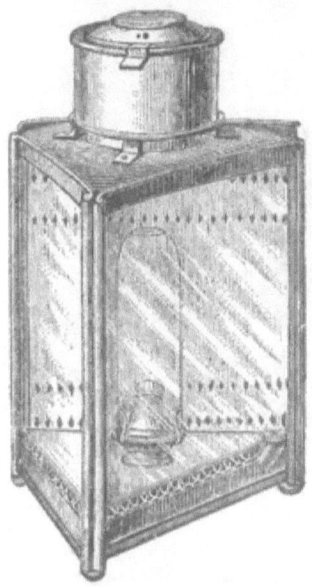

THE "GEM" LAMP.

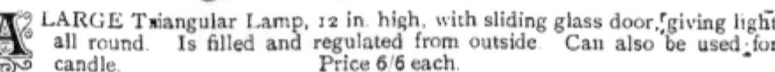

A LARGE Triangular Lamp, 12 in. high, with sliding glass door, giving light all round. Is filled and regulated from outside. Can also be used for candle. Price 6/6 each.
Also made 7½ in high, 2/6 each.

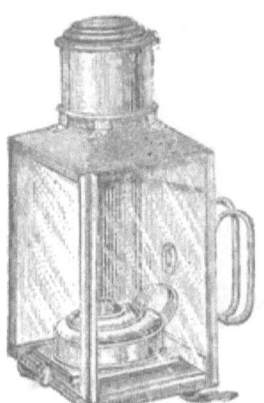

THE "MODEL" LAMP.

A square lamp, with sliding back, for colza oil.   Price 4/- each

THE "WONDER" LAMP.

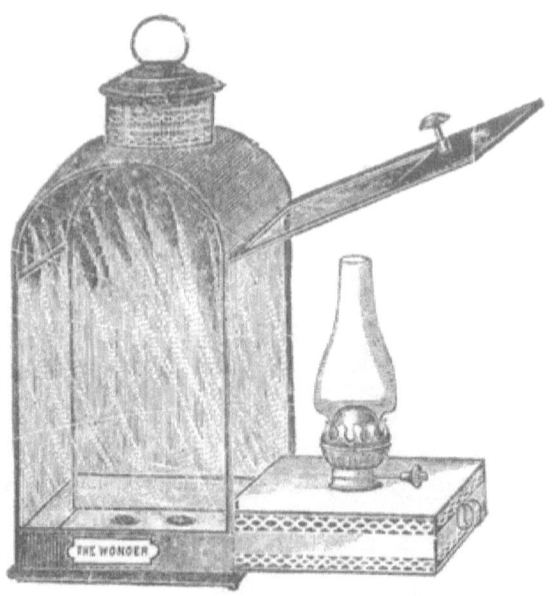

The "Wonder" (open).   Registered.

A LARGE flat ruby lamp, with four glass sides and arched top, constructed to burn oil, or when required a night light may be used instead. The lamp is removable so that it can be used outside the lantern.

Price, large size 12 inches high, **8/6** each.

This pattern is also made in a smaller size, measuring in box ready for travelling 7 × 3 × 2 inches.

Price **3/-** each.

Square Lantern, to burn a night light, glazed with non-actinic glass of best quality, **2/-**

CANDLE LAMPS.

THE "CHAMPION" DARK-ROOM SPRING CANDLE LAMP.

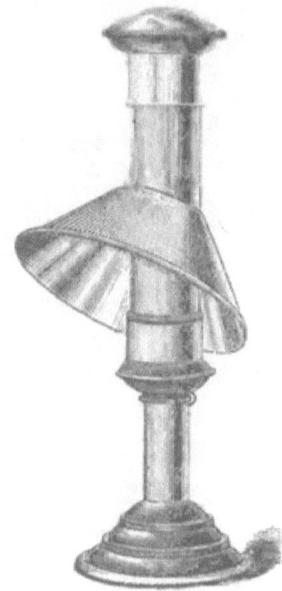

This is a very superior Dark-Room Lamp, and will also serve as a reading lamp.

ADVANTAGES :—

No danger from explosion as in paraffin lamps.
When once lit it requires no further attention.
It is very firm, therefore not easily turned over.

Price 5/6 each, complete, with ruby or yellow chimney.

Each one is fitted with a carriage lamp candle.

THE "AMATEUR" ECONOMIC DARK-ROOM LAMP.

(With Ruby Fabric Window)

A CHEAP handy lamp, to burn ordinary candles. Well ventilated and light-tight. Non-actinic medium of ruby fabric in place of glass. To light, remove body of lamp. This top will conveniently hold plates, etc. for travelling, the bottom then forming a lid to the box.

Size 6 in × 4 in. × 9 in.   Japanned Black.   1/9 each.

Gives a better diffused light than any at its price. Oil Lamps, to fit Candle Rings, 6d. each.

SQUARE LANTERN.
THE "PERFECTION" PHOTOGRAPHERS'
DARK-ROOM CANDLE LAMP.
(HAES' PATENT)

MORE Light, with less heat   Cleaner, easier to manage
than any other lamp   No smell   White light as
required. Price £1 1 0

OIL AND CANDLE LAMP.

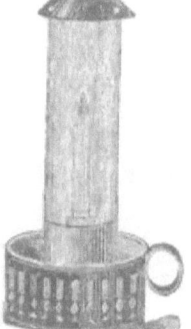

THIS Lamp can be used for either Oil or Candle   It
stands very firm and is not easily turned over.
Candlestick with Oil Lamp and Cone Top   ..   1/6
Ruby Chimneys ..   ..   9d.

THE "BOTTLE" LAMP.

A GOOD and safe lamp for amateurs.   Fitted
with socket for candle.
Price 1/- and 2/6 each.

GAS STANDARD.

With Ruby Chimney and Copper Top,

Price 7/6 each, complete.

Extra Ruby Chimneys ..   10d. each.

ARGAND BURNER.

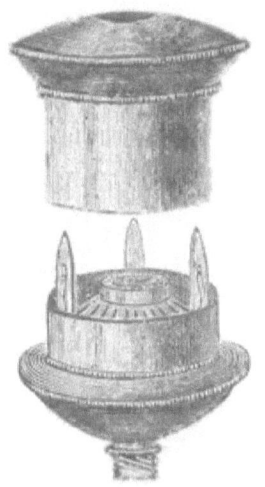

Fitted with Light-Tight Base and Copper Top.

Will fit any size Gas Bracket or Standard and is most useful for travelling, as it can be fitted on gas bracket in bedroom, and therefore avoids the danger of oil lamps, which are likely to get upset, explode, &c.

PRICES.

Burner and Copper Top	3/6
Ruby Chimney	.. 10d.
Complete	.. 4/2

KINNEAR'S PATENT SELF-LIGHTING GAS BURNER.

Darkness or light procured instantly by a touch.   No matches required
Price each 2/9, with globe holder, 4/-.

Ruby Chimneys, for gas	each 1/-
,, for paraffin lamp	,, 1/9

FOLDING
TRAVELLING LANTERNS, SCREENS, &c.

SHEW'S EXCELSIOR FOLDING LANTERN, no loose pieces, no glass, the simplest and most efficient yet made, folding quite flat for travelling, is put up in an instant, being all in one piece, and is made with orange or ruby windows, with specially prepared light, which burns without grease, smoke or smell **7/6**

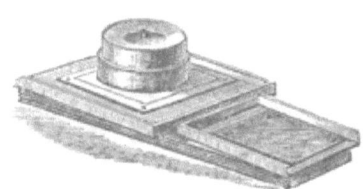

In three sizes, 4/6, 7/6, and **10/6**
Specially Prepared Lights, for ditto, per doz. 2/- and **3/-**

REDDING'S IMPROVED POCKET RUBY LANTERN.

A convenient lantern for travelling. It goes into a small box only some six inches long, four inches wide, and $\frac{3}{4}$-inch thick, so that it would take up hardly any space in a portmateau or knapsack. There is no glass about it, nothing to get out of order, and the light is obtained from night-lights.

No. 1.—Small size, in Case ($6\frac{1}{2}$ by $3\frac{1}{2}$ by $\frac{3}{4}$) complete   ..   ..   3/- each.
„   2.—Large „   „ (10 by 5 by $\frac{3}{4}$)   ..   ..   ..   6/- each.

EXTRA SPECIAL LIGHTS.

No. 1.—Small size, to burn 4 hours ..   ..   2/6 per doz.
„   2.—Large „   „   8 „   ..   ..   3/6 „

FOLDING SCREENS OR LANTERNS.

With Metal Foot and Ventilating Cap, to carry night-light or small low lamp, 8-inch high, 1/10; 12-inch, 2/3.

THE TRAVELLING LAMP.

CAN be used as Reading Lamp by inserting white glass in place of Ruby. To burn Colza Oil.

Price 3/6 each.

MAGNESIUM LAMPS FOR FLASH LIGHT.

THE NEW REPEATING FLASH LAMP.

MODE OF USING THE LAMP.

Remove the Stopper A from the Reservoir B, fill the Reservoir B with as much spirit as the sponge will absorb, replace the Metallic Gauze as well as the Stopper A to prevent evaporation.

Remove Stopper C from Reservoir D, into which pour the Magnesium powder, *which should be perfectly dry*. Replace the Stopper C to prevent loss of Powder. The Lamp may be held in the hand or stood on a table or other support. The Lamp being now ready, remove the Stopper A and light the Spirit Reservoir, waiting untill it burns well, press the Pneumatic Ball G to assure your-self that the air passes freely without extinguishing the flame. Press the Spring Tap F which will allow the Powder to enter the Tube above it and close again. Now on squeezing the Ball G the air will force the Powder through the flame and give a brilliant flash. By pressing the Tap F two or three times, more Powder can be burned, and a more intense flash may be obtained.

To create a continnous light remove the Pneumatic Ball G from the Rubber Tube at L, and blow softly with the mouth, at the same time holding open the Spring Tap F which will allow the Powder to enter the passage whilst the wind you blow into the Tube carries it through the flame.

The Screw Cap K may be removed to enable the passage to be cleansed.

Price   ..   ..   9/6.

THE HIBBARD REPEATING FLASH LAMP.

(WITH PATENT ATTACHMENTS.)

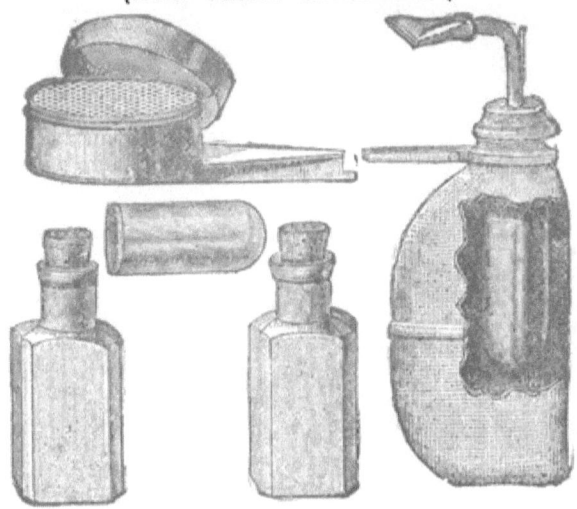

Lamp and Attachments, complete 10/6

E

"LE TISON-ECLAIR" or LIGHTNING-FUSEE FLASH LAMP.

Price of Apparatus .. 6/6.   Double .. .. 12/6.

THE LIGHTNING FUSEE CONSISTS

1st—Of the Fusee, which is lighted by rubbing it on the box, and burns for eight seconds, in spite of rain and wind.

2nd—Of Magnesium, which ignites on coming into contact with the air, and produces a bright and instantaneous flash (no explosion possible within the apparatus).

THE Fusee only should be used, because it is the only inflammable product that keeps burning without regard to weather (by this we mean the fusee-vestas obtained in every tobacconists).

The Fusee is used in preference to any other flame, because it contains chlorate of potash, which gives out a very intense heat, and consumes all the particles of magnesium.

This little apparatus has the advantage of working without the aid of spirit, as well as of being very portable, measuring only $1\frac{3}{4} \times 1\frac{1}{2} \times \frac{3}{4}$ inch.

SHEW'S FLASH LAMP.

Of Oval Shape, with reflector, giving a broad flame, and entirely consuming the powder, which is blown through the flame. Made in two sizes.

Price, including ball and long tube .. .. Small, 4/9 ; Large, 7/6.

HASTING'S FLASH LAMP.

With ball and tube .. 2/6.   With tube and mouth-piece .. 1/3

THE APTUS FLASH LAMP.

A small circular Lamp, with mouth-piece 1/6

ENGLAND'S FLASH LAMP.

With ball and tube complete .. 4/-   Without ball 2/6

THE FARLEIGH.

A very portable and effective Lamp, having three wicks through which the Magnesium is blown.

With pneumatic discharge 4/6

THE CHAMPION.

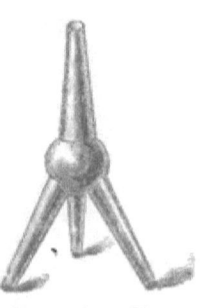

Connecting Pieces,

7d each.

Price, with I.R. tube and mouth-piece 1 6

Extra tubing, 9d. per yard.

CLOCK-WORK MAGNESIUM LAMPS

To burn Magnesium Ribbons. For Copying, Enlarging, Interior or Studio Work

THE DUPLEX MAGNESIUM LAMP.

With roller and German silver reflector to carry one or two ribbons as desired ; of best manufacture, easily regulated. On solid stand, complete, £3 3 0.

THE PERFECT CLOCK-WORK LAMP
(PATENT).

This Lamp with its latest improvement, is practically the most efficient for every purpose in the market   The ribbon burning in an enclosed chamber affords a ready means of carrying off any fumes caused, and burning steadily for one hour either one or two ribbons as required, with effective arrangements for starting and stopping the light at any moment. Price £4 15 0.

THE AUTOMATIC.

Brass body, black handle and nickelled reflector, with clock-work movement and regulator, 18/6.

E 2

BOTTLES.

COLLODION BOTTLES OR POURERS.

Capped and Stoppered (cometless).

			2 oz.	4 oz.	6 oz.	10 oz.	
Collodion Bottles, plain			2/3	2/6	3/0	3/9	each.
,,	,,	graduated	2/9	3/3	3/9	5/-	,,
,,	,,	stoppered, plain	1/-	1/6	2/-	2/6	,,
,,	,,	,, graduated	1/6	2/-	2/6	3/-	,,

COLLODION FILTERS.

4 oz. 5/-   8 oz. 6/6.   12 oz. 7/6 each.

DROPPING BOTTLES.

	1 oz.	2 oz.	4 oz.
Patent Drop Bottles, with stopper	—	6d.	9d.
Chalk's Pneumatic, with Pipette	1/-	1/3	—

ENGRAVED BOTTLES.

For dark room use to contain solutions, the following inscriptions in stock—

Hypo Solution, &c.   Hydrokinone.
Pyro   ,,   Toning Solution.
Potash   ,,   Intensifying Solution.
Reducing   ,,

20 oz. with ground-in stoppers each   2/0
10   ,,   ,,   ,,   ,,   1/6
5   ,,   ,,   ,,   ,,   1/3

BOTTLES.

White glass, narrow or wide-mouthed, plain, not stoppered, per dozen :—

1 oz.	11d.	4 oz.	1/4	10 oz.	2/6
2 ,,	1/-	6 ,,	1/6	20 ,,	3/-

Green glass, narrow or wide-mouthed, plain, not stoppered, per dozen :—

5 oz.	10d.	16 oz.	1/6	30 oz.	3/-
10 ,,	1/3	20 ,,	2/-	40 ,,	3/9

Green glass, narrow-mouthed, stoppered, per dozen :—

5 oz.	2/6	16 oz.	3/9	40 oz.	6/-
10 ,,	3/-	20 ,,	4/-	80 ,,	9/-

Green glass, wide-mouthed, stoppered, per dozen :—

5 oz.	3/9	20 oz.	6/-
10 ,,	4/6	40 ,,	7/-

White glass, direct squares, plain, per dozen :—

1 oz.	10d.	5 oz.	2/-	20 oz.	6/6
2 ,,	1/3	10 ,,	4/-		

White glass, direct squares, narrow mouth, stoppered, per dozen ;—

oz.	2/6	5 oz.	3/9	20 oz.	7/6
2 ,,	3/-	10 ,,	5/-		

Wide mouth, stoppered, one-fourth extra.

DISHES.

GERMAN GLASS.

For developing, with spout and rib at bottom, each—

For plates.	Price.	For plates.	Price.	For plates.	Price.
4¼ × 3¼	8d.	6½ × 4¾	1/3	10 × 8	2/9
5 ,, 4	9d.	8½ ,, 6½	2/2		

NEW MAKE WHITE GLASS.

Straight sides, perfectly flat at bottom, the best dish for developing paper negatives—

For plates.	Price.	For plates.	Price.	For plates.	Price.
4¼ × 3¼	8d.	6½ × 4¾	1/6	8½ × 6½	2/3
5 ,, 4	10d.	7½ ,, 5	1/9	10 ,, 8	3/3
				12 ,, 10	4/-

DISHES OF PORCELAIN.

With spout, best quality.

Size.	Shallow.	Deep.	Size.	Shallow.	Deep.
4¼ × 3¼	6d.	7d.	14 × 12	3/3	4/2
5 ,, 4	7d.	8d.	16 ,, 12	4/6	5/8
6 ,, 5	8d.	10d.	16 ,, 14	6/10	8/2
7 ,, 5	8d.	10d.	18 ,, 16	7/3	9/8
8 ,, 6	9d.	11d.	19 ,, 15	8/4	12/-
9 ,, 7	11d.	1/2	20 ,, 12	11/6	13/-
10 ,, 8	1/2	1/4	20 ,, 17	12/-	16/-
11 ,, 9	1/5	1/7	24 ,, 19	17/-	21/8
12 ,, 10	1/10	2/3	24 ,, 22	21/-	26/-
13 ,, 11	2/6	3/2	—	—	—

Ditto with ribs at bottom:—

¼ plate 7d. ½ plate 9d. 1-1 plate 1/-

Granitine Dishes at same prices as porcelain.

DISHES OF VULCANITE.

For developing dry plates:—

For Plates.	Price.	For Plates	Price.
3¼ × 3¼	5d.	7½ × 5	1/2
4¼ ,, 3¼	5d.	8½ ,, 6½	1/4
5 ,, 4	7d.	10 ,, 8	2/-
6½ ,, 4¾	8d.	12 ,, 10	3/6

DISHES OF PAPIER-MACHE, or COMPOSITION.

Deep or Shallow.

For Plates.	Price.	For Plates.	Price.
4¼ × 3¼	7d.	14 × 12	3/6
5 ,, 4	8d.	16 ,, 14	5/6
6½ ,, 4¾	1/-	21 ,, 16½	7/6
7½ ,, 5	1/2	24 ,, 20	12/-
8½ ,, 6½	1/4	27 ,, 22	13/6
10 ,, 8	2/-	30 ,, 25	21/-
12 ,, 10	2/6	34 ,, 28	22/6

PORTABLE DISHES or TRAYS,

Folding, for sinks, etc., with brass fitting for tube :—

Size.	Price.	Size.	Price.
9 × 7	2/3	15 × 12	3/9
12 ,, 10	3/-	18 ,, 16	5/3

TYLAR'S PATENT COMPRESSED PULP TRAYS (Labelled).

Per Set of 4 Trays.

Size.	Price.	Size.	Price.
¼ plates	3/6	10 × 8	12/-
5 × 4	4/-	12 ,, 10	15/-
½ plates	5/-	15 ,, 12	20/-
7½ × 5	6/6	20 ,, 16	50/-
1-1 plates	8/-	24 ,, 20	65/-
—	—	26 ,, 23	80/-

TYLAR'S PATENT FOLDING TRAYS.

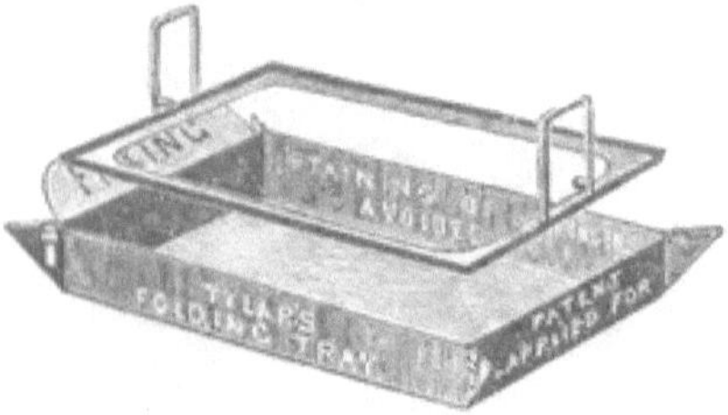

Per Set of Four.

English.		Continental.	
¼ Plate	1/-		
5×4 ,,	1/3	9×12 Plates	1/3
½ ,,	1/6		
7½×5 ,,	2/-	13×10 ,,	2/-
1/1 ,,	2/6		
10×8 ,,	3/6	18×24 ,,	3/6
2×10 ,,	4/6		

These are specially made for travelling, extremely portable, pack flat when not in use. These are also labelled as the above, and are made of Willesden waterproof paper.

TYLAR'S "MULTIPLE" TRAY.

Of compressed pulp—invaluable for plates of similar exposures, such as lantern slides, &c., &c. Divided for 4 plates.

Price for 4 3¼ × 3¼ plates	2/- each.
,, 4 4¼ × 3¼ ,,	2/6 ,,

THE NEW DEVELOPING DISH.

Glass bottom, with well at one end, which enables operator to examine plate without removing it from the dish, and entirely prevents the fingers from being stained.

¼ Plate	1/-	1/1 Plate	2/9
5/4 ,,	1/6	10×8 ,,	3/6
½ ,,	1/8	12×10 ,,	4/6
7½×5 ,,	2/-	15×12 ,,	6/-

THE NEW XYLONITE DISHES,

Unbreakable and very light in use.

3¼×3¼ Plate	4d.	7½×5 Plate	10d.
¼ ,,	5d.	1/1 ,,	1/-
5 × 4 ,,	7d.	10×8 ,,	1/4
½ ,,	9d.		

ANDERSON'S WAVELET DISH.

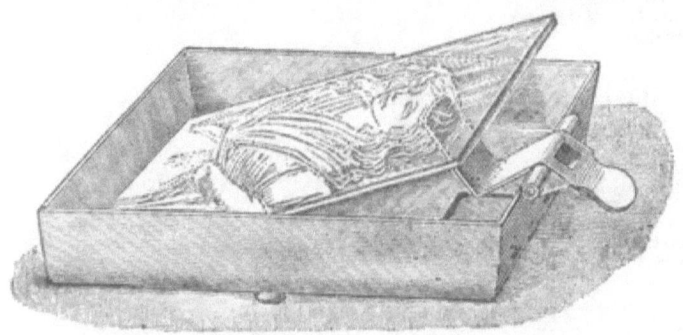

For plates	3¼ × 3¼	1/-		7½ × 5	2/6
	4¼ „ 3¼	1/3		8½ „ 6½	3/-
	6½ „ 4¾	2/-			
Also for	10 × 8 or 2 7½ × 5	5/- each.			
	8½ „ 6½ or 2 ½ plates	4/- „			

CELLULOID DISHES.

Unbreakable, in various colours, so as to be easily distinguishable in dark room.

3¼ × 3¼	9d.		7½ × 5	2/3
¼ plate	10d.		8½ „ 6½	2/9
5 × 4	1/-		10 „ 8	4/-
½ plate	1/4			

THE "ACME" DISH.

A light make of iron dish, enamelled.

¼ plate	10d.		10 × 8	2/3
½ „	1/3		12 „ 10	2/9
1-1 „	1/9			

DISHES FOR LANTERN SLIDES.

	Each.		Each.
Celluloid	9d.	Glass	8d.
Vulcanite	5d.	Tylar Multiple, for 4 plates	2/-
Glass bottom, wood sides	11d.	Xylonite	4d.

DISHES FOR ENLARGEMENTS.

New improved Wood Dishes, with glass bottoms, well made and varnished. Glass bottom easily replaced in case of breakage.

11 × 9	2/9		24 × 19	6/6
13 „ 11	3/-		27 „ 23	8/6
16 „ 13	3/9		31 „ 23	9/6

Also see Papier Mache and Porcelain Trays, large sizes, page 101.

SHEW'S AUTOMATIC ROCKER

Will be found of great service when manipulating several dishes at a time.
See page 81.

BATHS OR DIPPING TROUGHS.

FOR FIXING PLATES, &c.

To take Plates	4¼×3¼	6¼×4¾	8½×6½	10×8	12×10
White German Glass	2/-	2/6	3/6	4/6	6/6
Porcelain	1/9	3/-	3/6	7/-	12/-

DIPPERS.

Of Porcelain,	each	6d.	9d.	1/-	1/9	2/-
Of Glass	,,	5d.	7d.	9d.	10d.	1/2.

BATH STANDS.

Of Pine, for Baths   4¼×3¼, 1/-; 6½×4¾, 1/3; 8½×6½, 1/9.

FUNNELS.

Diameter.	Glass.	Papier Mache.	Diameter.	Glass.	Papier Mache.
2 in.	2d.	—	6 in.	8d.	1/-
3 ,,	3d.	—	7 ,,	1/-	1/4
4 ,,	4d.	—	8 ,,	1/2	2/-
5 ,,	6d	9d.			

GLASS GRADUATED MEASURES.

Taper or Cylinder shape, each—

1 dram	6d.	2 ounce	8d.	13 ounce	1/4
2 ,,	7d.	4 ,,	11d.	20 ,,	1/11
1 ounce	6d.	6 ,,	1/1	40 ,,	3/4.

NEW PATENT OPAQUE MEASURES.

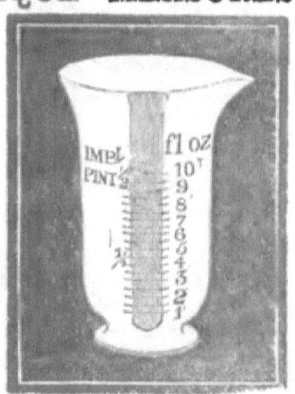

T HE advantage of these measures over those of plain glass consists in their being made of pure white enamel tubing, with a narrow opening of clear glass back and front, through which to read the liquid, and the divisions and figures being written in black and fired on the enamel are indelible, and can be read with the greatest ease in almost any light. They will be found an inestimable boon by persons of weak sight, as well as by all other users of such measures, to whom this distinct advance in medical and philosophical appurtenances means a saving of time and money.

1 dram	1/10	6 ounce	2/10
2 ,,	2/-	10 ,,	3/11
2 ounce	2/1	20 ,,	4/6
4 ,,	2/6		

NEW NESTED MEASURES.

Fitting one in another, with graduations deeply cut and whitened.
per nest of 4, 4/-
Or singly, each 1 oz. 6d.; 2 oz. 1/-; 5 oz. 1/3; 10 oz 1/9.
The small sizes are very useful as developing cups.

BOXES.

Of DEAL, for Storing Negatives.   Best make with grooves numbered.

	12 Gr.	24 Gr.	50 Gr.	100 Gr.
4¼ × 3¼	1/-	1/3	1/9	3/4
5 ,, 4	1/3	1/4	1/10	3/9
6½ ,, 4¾	1/4	1/9	2/4	4/6
7½ ,, 5	1/9	2/6	3/-	6/-
8½ ,, 6½	2/-	2/9	3/4	6/9
10 ,, 8	3/-	4/-	5/6	11/-
12 ,, 10	4/-	5/-	6/6	12/-

Ditto, of PINE, varnished, with V grooving.

4¼ × 3¼	1/8	2/-	2/9	—
5 ,, 4	2/1	2/2	3/-	—
6½ ,, 4¾	2/2	2/11	4/3	—
8½ ,, 6½	3/-	4/6	5/3	—
10 ,, 8	4/6	6/6	7/9	—
12 ,, 10	5/9	7/6	8/9	—

WOLFFS COMPACT NEGATIVE BOXES.

For the Systematic Storage of Negatives.

BY the use of these boxes the following advantages are secured :—Economy of space, ease of reference, immunity from damage, economy in price.   By the use of an Index in connection with these boxes, any particular Negative in a collection of many thousands may be at once found.   The Negatives occupy less than one-third the space required by the usual boxes.

The following sizes are kept in stock, but any size can be made to order at proportionate prices :—

For Plates.	Each.	Per doz.	For Plates.	Each.	Per doz.
4¼ × 3¼	5d.	4/6	7½ × 5	8d.	7/-
5 ,, 4	5d.	4/6	7½ ,, 6½	8d,	7/-
6½ ,, 4¾	6d.	5/-	10 ,, 8	10d.	9/-
			12 ,, 10	1/-	11/-

Each box holds one dozen Negatives.

LIGHT TIGHT BOXES.

For Unexposed Plates or Undeveloped Negatives.

SHEW's Improved Leather Light-tight Boxes, very durable, light, and will not warp or split.   Invaluable for travelling.

Size.	7 Gr.	13 Gr.	Size.	7 Gr.	13 Gr.
4¼ × 3¼	2/3	3/-	7½ × 5	4/9	5/6
5 ,, 4	3/-	3/9	8½ ,, 6½	5/-	6/-
6½ ,, 4¾	3/9	4/9	10 ,, 8	5/9	8/-
7½ ,, 4½	4/3	5/6	12 ,, 10	9/-	10/6

Boxes, Light-tight, for Dry Plates, of mahogany, slide lid, with spring pressure board.

Size.	12 Gr,	24 Gr.	Size.	12 Gr.	24 Gr.
4¼ × 3¼	3/6	4/-	7½ × 4½	5/-	5/6
5 ,, 4	3/6	4/-	7½ ,, 5	5/-	5/6
6½ ,, 4¾	4/3	5/-	8½ ,, 6½	5/6	6/-

SHEW'S NEGATIVE BOOK.

For Paper and Film Negatives.

Containing 50 leaves of Prepared Non-Absorbent Paper, to hold 100 or more Negatives.   Strongly bound and finished.   Each—

4¼ × 3¼ 2/9   6½ × 4¾ 3/6   7½ × 5 4/-   8½ × 6½ 4/6

TYLAR'S STORING CABINET FOR NEGATIVES.

Made to hold 100 Negatives in Envelopes.

	¼ plate.	½ plate.	1-1 plate.
Well-finished in wood, covered with imitation morocco, folding doors, etc.	4/6	6/-	—
In pine, stained, without doors	3/-	4/6	6/6

TYLAR'S NEGATIVE ENVELOPES.

Very strong. Manufactured of Waterlow's Indestructible paper, perfectly smooth inside, printed in such a way that a history of each Negative can be kept outside, with tag attached to each for Index number. Per 100—

¼ plate.	Lantern Size.	½ plate.	1-1 plate.
2/6	2/6	3/9	5/6

NEW LIGHT TIGHT BOXES.

For storing Cut Sensitized Paper or Prints. This box is fitted with a loose drawer and metal cover with spring attached, which has the effect of keeping the paper perfectly flat as well as air-tight.

Price each for Cut Sheets—

4¼ × 3¼	1/2	7½ × 5	1/9	12 × 10	3/9
5 ,, 4	1/4	8½ ,, 6½	1/10	15 ,, 12	5/-
6½ ,, 4¾	1/6	10 ,, 8	3/-		

THE PRESERVATIVE BOX FOR CUT SENSITIZED PAPER.

THIS Box is made after the same style as our Cut Paper Box, with one improvement. It has a perforated holder for Chloride of Calcium which will be readily appreciated by all who use Platinotype and other papers which are spoilt by damp. With one of these boxes there is no risk of spoiling, as the paper is kept quite flat, and the box is both light-tight and dry. Each—

4¼ × 3¼	1/6	7½ × 5	2/3	11 × 10	5/-
5 ,, 4	1/9	8½ ,, 6½	2/6	15 ,, 12	7/6
6½ ,, 4¾	2/-	10 ,, 8	3/9		

LANTERN SLIDE BOXES.

Cloth covered, very light, to carry 24 lantern slides, price 6d. each.

PLAIN DEAL STORING BOXES.

For 36 slides, without grooves 1/2 each.
,, 24 ,, with ,, 1/- ,,
,, 50 ,, ,, ,, 1/6 ,,
,, 100 ,, ,, ,, 2/3 ,,

WHITE WOOD BOXES.

With special hard wood, grooving, superior make.
For 24 lantern slides 2/- each.
,, 48 ,, 2/6 ,,
,, 100 ,, 3/6 ,,

EXHIBITION BOXES.

Of polished walnut with or without walnut grooves, good lock, and nickeled handle. For 42 slides, without grooving 5/6 each.
,, ,, with ,, 6/- ,,

LANTERN SLIDE BOX.

Japanned Tin, to hold 50 pictures, perforated bottom padded top, and diaphragm to stand level when the box is closed, and when in use by inverting it, marking the position of the next picture to be shown, and the place for the one last exhibited, thus replacing as first arranged.

EXPOSURE METERS.

THE WATKINS' EXPOSURE METER.

THIS instrument—the only one constructed on correct principles—calculates the proper exposure for photographic plates under every imaginable condition. It is equally applicable for Landscapes, Shutter Work, Sky Views, Sea Views, Portraits, Interiors, Architecture, Copying Enlarging, Photo-Micrographs.

This compact little instrument is a combination of a bromide of silver actinometer (most simple in use), a chain pendulum for timing the exposure, and a set of four calculating rings, each carrying a pointer, which, when set to the correct value for each factor, causes a fifth pointer to indicate the correct exposure in seconds or fractions of a second.

It is beautifully finished in brass, and measures only 2½ inches long, and 1⅞ inches in diameter.

It is not complicated in use, and the average time occupied in testing the light and adjustment of calculator is only 30 seconds.
Price, 15/- By Post, 15/3.
Rolls of Bromide Paper for refilling, post free, 7d.
Also now ready, cloth binding, for the Pocket, price 1/6, for use with above,
EXPOSURE NOTES.
Containing Instructions, further Information, and suitable Ruled Pages for Notes.

TYLAR-PICKARD EXPOSURE METER.

IN using the above, all that is needed is to place the instrument close to the eye and point it to the object to be photographed, moving the lever across the scale plate. This lever actuates a valve in such a manner as to allow a varying flood of light to fall upon a lettered screen inside the tube of the instrument. As soon as the letters on this screen become indistinct the instrument is taken from the eye, and the exposure for any given stop will be at once seen on the right hand side of the lever by referring to the scale plate and reading the exposure shown thereon. Price. 7/6.

FINDERS.

SHEW'S ECLIPSE FINDER.

Of box form, with angle mirror and shade, very light, and giving
image of good size, with plates for attachment to Camera .. £0 7 6
Extra plates for working the same Finder both ways 0 0 9
METAL BOX FINDER, of smaller size, with fixing plate, complete 0 4 9

THE APTUS FINDER.

Reversible, and easily carried in the waistcoat pocket 0 3 0

TAYLOR'S FINDER.

Of Metal, for hand or other Cameras, each 5/-   Extra fittings, 6d.

LANCASTER'S FINDER.

Can be attached to the side or to the top of the Camera, with two brackets, complete 5/-

SHEW'S PATENT FINDER.

A rectangular lens in frame, perfectly flat for the pocket 3/6

FOCUSSING EYE PIECES.

THE COMBINED FOCUSSER AND FINDER.

Fitted with stem and socket to attach it to the Camera for use as a finder
By removing the bayonetted tube which carries the ground glass it is converte
into a Focussing Eye Piece. Price complete 7/6.
Ditto, smaller size 5/3

THE REVERSING EYE PIECE.

Shewing the image now inverted on the screen glass .. 10/6.

THE ARCHIMEDEAN.

With rapidly adjusting screw and fixing ring .. 7/6.

FOCUSSING EYE PIECE.

Of Brass, with sliding adjustment, each .. 1/9, and 3/6.
Ditto, superior make, smaller size, very high power .. 2/6.

TYLAR'S FOCUSSING CHAMBER.

I T can be fitted to any make of Camera, all the fitting needed being the insertion of four small screws into the focussing screen frame. If the screen is not covered by the tailboard, the chamber affords excellent protection to the ground glass. It can be removed at a moment's notice by slot arrangement, and replaced as quickly ; both eyes can be used in focussing It is folded flat instantly, and can then be thrown with the screen on top of the Camera. When expanded it is perfectly rigid, leaving both hands and head entirely free. In windy weather it is simply invaluable, doing away with all old grievances. Well finished in morocco leather and metal fittings.

| ¼ plate | 3/6 | ½ plate | 5/6 | 1/1 plate | 7/6 |

Extra Springs, 4d. each.

LEVELS.

SHEW'S REVERSING LEVEL.

With 2 sockets for attachment to Camera, for horizontal or vertical work, 2/6.
Ditto,   ditto,   the Duplex 3/6.

TAYLOR'S LEVELS.

No. 3 is intended for the pocket. The others may be screwed to the Camera.

Nos. 1, 2, and 3 indicate correct position of both face and sides of the plate, when the bubble is central.

No. 4 indicates the two positions separately.

No. 1.	Finished Brass	..	1/6	No. 1A.	Electrum ..	..	..	1/9
No. 2.	„ „	..	2/-	No, 2A.	„ ..	..	..	2/4
No. 3.	Electrum ..	..	2/3	No. 3A.	With Morocco Pocket			
No. 4.	Finished Brass	..	4/6		Case ..	..	..	3/-
				No. 4A.	Electrum ..	..	..	5/-

THORNTON'S PLUMB INDICATORS.

Price ..   .. 1/- each.

Ditto, 1 inch square, for back of camera   1/-

BACKGROUNDS.

THE EMPIRE PHOTOGRAPHIC BACK-GROUNDS.

THE Empire Patent Cloth may be had either by the yard, in the widths stated below, or mounted on a roller with fittings complete.

Both sides are equally serviceable, and may, if desired, be of different shades of colour, so that one Background (on being reversed) will answer the purpose of two.

PRICE PER YARD, UNMOUNTED.

Width.	Single Colour.	Reversible.	Width.	Single Colour.	Reversible.
37 in.	1/7	not made.	81 in.	6/4	7/6
48 ,,	3/0	,,	90 ,,	7/4	8/9
54 ,,	3/8	,,	99 ,,	8/4	10/0
72 ,,	5/4	6/3	104 ,,	9/6	11/6

MOUNTED BACKGROUNDS.

SYSTEM A.

Mounted on a 2 inch well-seasoned pine roller (specially rabbeted), and tacked on to a lath, 2½ inches wide, with two screw eyes for hanging background up, and with cord to work same up and down on theatrical scenery system.

SYSTEM B.

Mounted on a tin barrel roller with metal flanges, iron bottom rod, strong brackets for fixing up to wall, cord and cleat-hook complete. This system is the most convenient where a large number of backgrounds are in use, and is in every respect the most satisfactory.

Size. Width.	Long.	Single Colour. System A.	System B.	Reversible. System A.	System B.
4 ft. 0 in.	6 ft.	12/-	16/6	13/6	18/0
6 ,, 0 ,,	7 ,,	21/-	28/-	23/-	29/9
6 ,, 0 ,,	8 ,,	23/-	29/6	26/-	32/6
7 ,, 6 ,,	8 ,,	29/6	37/-	33/6	41/6
8 ,, 3 ,,	9 ,,	36/-	43/6	42/6	49/6
8 ,, 6 ,,	10 ,,	43/-	56/6	49/-	61/-

SCHOLZIG'S GRADUATED BACKGROUNDS FOR PORTRAITS.

Size 48 × 40.

Complete with Frame and Fixing Rod 5/6
Wooden Stand for ditto 3/3

This can be quickly arranged, and by giving a light background to the shaded side of the portrait and making the lighted side of the face fall on to the darker parts of the graduated background, the picture is brought out into strong relief and gains immeasurably in life, as compared with portraits taken on an even coloured background.

WASHABLE CLOTH BACKGROUNDS.

The cheapest and most useful Backgrounds made in two tints, suitable for Vignette and plain portrait work. On light deal roller.

6 × 4 ft.	3/6 each.		8 × 7 ft.	9/- each.	
6 ,, 5 ,,	4/6 ,,		8 ,, 8 ,,	11/- ,,	
8 ,, 6 ,,	7/- ,,		9 ,, 8 ,,	13/- ,,	

WOOLLEN CLOTH BACKGROUNDS.

Of superfine woollen cloth, without crease or dress. Various colours, any length cut. 8 feet wide, per yard, 8/-

PAINTED BACKGROUNDS.

			s. d.
DISTEMPER.—On strong Paper, Landscape. or Interior, 8 × 5 ft. ..		£0 6 6
Ditto	ditto	8 × 6 ft.	0 9 0
Ditto, on Linen, 8 × 6 ft.		1 1 6
Ditto, do., of best quality, by first-class Artists only, 8 × 6 ft..		1 15 0
Ditto, ditto .. .. 8 × 7 ft..		2 2 6
Larger sizes to order. Photographs on application.		
Side Slips, on strong paper .. .. each		0 3 0
Ditto, on Linen .. .. ,,		0 9 6

HEAD RESTS.

Of wood, French polished, with adjusting screws, to attach to chair £0 5 6

Of metal, nickeled and well-finished, double-jointed, giving universal
movement, to clamp on the back of a chair 0 9 6

Head and Body Rest of Iron, with waist support, to stand on the
floor, rising to 6 feet, and descending low enough for children .. 1 11 6

SUNDRIES.

	s. d.
Argentometer, for testing the strength of the silver bath, in case	2 0
Test tube for ditto	0 6

Carriers for Films, (Eastman's) per dozen—

4¼ × 3¼	12/-	6½ × 4¾	16/-	8½ × 6½	21/-
5 ,, 4	15/-	7½ ,, 5	18/-	10 ,, 8	27/-

England's ditto—

4¼ × 3¼	6/-	6½ × 4¾	9/-	8½ × 6½	15/-
5 ,, 4	7/6	7½ ,, 5	12/-	10 ,, 8	18/-

Carrier Lock. Godstone's, each 1 0

Clips of Wood for suspending paper, &c., per dozen, 5d.; per gross .. 5 6

Ditto of metal, per dozen 1 6

Clips (Tylar's Film). A simple clip
for developing bromide paper or
film. Prices—

Per set of 6 ¼ plates	1/6
,, ½ ,,	2/6
,, 1/1 ,,	3/6

Cutting Wheels for glass, each .. .. 6d and 1 0

Cutting Board or Revolving Table, with glass top, for cutting prints
upon. 10 in. 3/9; 12 in. 5 6

Developing Cups of ebonite, each 9d. ; in sets of 3 .. .. .. 2 0
Ditto   of glass   ,,   4d.   ,, ... 1 0
Diamonds for cutting glass, each 12/6 and 15 0
Ditto   for writing, each 8 6
Finger Stalls of india-rubber, each 2d. ; per dozen 1 9

GLASSES.

Obscured plate for focussing Screens.

	Each.	Per doz.			Each.	Per doz.
$4\frac{1}{4} \times 3\frac{1}{4}$	3d.	2/-	10 ,, 8		10d.	8/6
5 ,, 4	4d.	2/6	10×10		1/-	10/6
$6\frac{1}{2}$,, $4\frac{3}{4}$	4d.	3/-	12 ,, 10		1/2	12/6
$7\frac{1}{2}$,, 5	5d.	3/9	12 ,, 12		1/3	13/6
$8\frac{1}{2}$,, $6\frac{1}{2}$	7d.	5/6	15 ,, 12		1/6	16/6

GLASS PLATES.

Plain uncoated plates, best selected and polished, per dozen—

$4\frac{1}{4} \times 3\frac{1}{4}$	7d.	$8\frac{1}{2} \times 6\frac{1}{2}$	2/9
5 ,, 4	1/-	10 ,, 8	3/6
$6\frac{1}{2}$,, $4\frac{3}{4}$	1/3	12 ,, 10	5/6

OPAL GLASS.

English pot metal, finely ground, matt surface, per dozen—

$4\frac{1}{4} \times 3\frac{1}{4}$	8d.	$8\frac{1}{2} \times 6\frac{1}{2}$	2/9
5 ,, 4	1/-	10 ,, 8	4/9
$6\frac{1}{2}$,, $4\frac{3}{4}$	1/6	12 ,, 10	7/-

CONVEX GLASSES.

Glasses raised or convex for the Chromo Photographs, &c., per dozen pairs—

	C.-de-V.	Cabinet.	$8\frac{1}{2} \times 6\frac{1}{2}$.
Oval or square	1/6	6/6	14/6

NON-ACTINIC GLASS.

Green for silver printing—

$\frac{1}{4}$, 3d. ; $\frac{1}{2}$, 4d.; 1/1, 6d. 10×8, 8d.; 12×10, 10d.; 15×12, 1/-
Ruby or orange for window Lamps, &c., per foot 11d.

Gloves of india-rubber, assorted sizes, per pair 7 6
Grooving of hard wood, each 3d. ; or per bundle of 6 .. .. .. 1 3
Head Covers for focussing, of black twill, 50×36 .. .. 1 0
Ditto   ditto   of black velvet, 52×44 .. .. 5 0
Ditto   ditto   of india rubber cambric, very light, folding
    into a small compass and serving also to protect the camera,
    45×30 3/6 ; 45×36 .. .. 4 6
    Or per yard run, 66 ins. wide 5 6
Labels. A book of fourteen pages of useful labels, with blanks, and also
    a page of perforated squares for negatives 0 6
Ditto Wheeler's 400 assorted, red labels for poisons, blanks, &c. .. 0 6

Plate Holders, pneumatic. for varnishing or cooling plates.

The Globe Holder, in rubber ..	4	6
The Cup Holder, in wood ..	2	9

Plate Lifters.

Tylar's, fitting on to the side of any ordinary dish	o	6
The Thimble Lifter of ebonite, each	o	3
The Curved Lifter or Vulcanite Hook per dozen	1	o

Pincers of ebonite, for lifting prints, each .. .. o 6
Ditto of box-wood, each .. .. o 3

Scales in oak box, 6 in. beam, with brass pans, weights, grains, scruples and drachms .. .. o 2 4
Ditto, superior, with glass pans, with weights complete .. o 3 3
Ditto, ditto, of larger size, with 5 in. pans, and weights from 1 gr. to 4 oz. .. .. o 12 o

Superior standard scales, moveable glass pan, on brass arm, and French polished mahogany stand, with drawer and extra weights .. .. 1 5 o
Set brass weights, grains, scruples, drachms .. .. .. o o 9
Scale pans of glass, paired and drilled, per pair .. .. o 1 6

Springs for printing frames, per dozen.
¼ plate, 9d. 5×4, 1/- ½ plate, 1/4 1/1 plate, 1/8 10×8, 3/- 12×10 4/-

Squeegees of india-rubber, flat, each

4 in.	6 in.	10 in.	12 in.	15 in.
1/.	1/3	1/8	2/-	2/6

Ditto, roller pattern, 1 in. diam.

4 in.	6 in.	8 in.	10 in.
1/4	2/-	2/8	3/4

Ditto, ditto, of superior make, 1¼ diam. full.

4 in.	6 in.	8 in.	10 in.
2/-	3/-	4/-	5/-

Ditto, Duplex   6 in. 4/-   10 in. 6/8
Ditto, Glass Roller, Patent.
A well-mounted glass roller, with polished handle, very useful for mounting, and imparting a perfectly smooth surface to the print, each, 3½ in. 2/6 ; 6 in., 5/- ; 8 in. .. .. 7 o

Squeegee Slabs of enamelled iron, size 14×10 ins., each 6d.
Ditto of vulcanite, each

7×5	9×7	12×10	13×11
9d.	1/3	1/9	2/3

Stirring Rods of glass.
6, 9, and 12 in., each 2d. 15 and 18 in., 3d.

Test Papers, or Litmus Books.
Blue or red, each 2d. .. .. per doz. 1 6

Tops for Tripod Stands. Round .. .. 1/6 to 4 o
Triangular, of brass. 4 in., 2/6 ; 6 in., 3/- ; 8 in., 5/- ; 10 in. .. .. 7 o

Twill for tents, windows, etc.
Yellow, red, or black .. .. .. per yard 1 o

PRINTING FRAMES.

Of **Teak Wood, strong make,** to take plates :—

Brass Straps.			Steel Straps.		
$4\frac{1}{4} \times 3\frac{1}{4}$	4/-		$7\frac{1}{2} \times 5$		10/6
5 ., 4	5/-		$8\frac{1}{2}$,, 6		15/-
$6\frac{1}{2}$,, $4\frac{3}{4}$	8/-		10 ,, 8		20/-
$7\frac{1}{2}$,, $4\frac{1}{2}$	10/6		12 ,, 10		25/-

Ditto, of Teak, very **superior, extra stout,** with rounded corners, brass screwed, per dozen :—

$4\frac{1}{2} \times 3\frac{1}{4}$	5/-		$8\frac{1}{2} \times 6\frac{1}{2}$		20/-
5 ,, 4	7/-		10 ,, 8		24/-
$6\frac{1}{2}$,, $4\frac{3}{4}$	10/-		12 ,, 10		30/-
$7\frac{1}{2}$,, 5	14/-		15 ,, 12		50/-

Ditto, of **Mahogany, superior make,** French polished, brass springs. Per dozen :—

$4\frac{1}{4} \times 3\frac{1}{4}$	8/-		$8\frac{1}{2} \times 6\frac{1}{2}$		30/-
5 ,, 4	10/-		10 ,, 8		40/-
$6\frac{1}{2}$,, $4\frac{3}{4}$	15/-		12 ,, 10		54/-
$7\frac{1}{2}$,, 5	19/6				

Ditto, **cheap make Mahogany,** nickeled springs.

$4\frac{1}{4} \times 3\frac{1}{4}$	6/6		$8\frac{1}{2} \times 6\frac{1}{2}$		21/-
5 ,, 4	7/9		10 ,, 8		30/-
$6\frac{1}{2}$,, $4\frac{3}{4}$	10/9		12 ,, 10		35/-
$7\frac{1}{2}$,, 5	15/-				

Of **Oak, stout plate glass,** steel springs, hinged bars, and pressure board, of best make only :—

	Each.			Each.
7×5	8/6	13×11	—
9 ,, 7	9/6	14 ,, 12	15/6
10 ,, 8	10/6	16 ,, 14	17/6
12 ,, 10	12/6		

Felt Pads for Printing Frames, per dozen :—

$4\frac{1}{4} \times 3\frac{1}{4}$	2/6	10×8	4/6
$6\frac{1}{2}$,, $4\frac{3}{4}$	2/6	12 ,, 10	6/6
$8\frac{1}{2}$,, $6\frac{1}{2}$	3/3		

TYLAR'S PERFECT PRINTING FRAME.

Best make, round corners, polished Pine.

	Each.			Each.
$4\frac{1}{4} \times 3\frac{1}{4}$	11d.	$8\frac{1}{2} \times 6\frac{1}{2}$	3/-
5 ,, 4	1/1	10 ,, 8	4/-
$6\frac{1}{2}$,, $4\frac{3}{4}$	1/8	12 ,, 10	5/-

THE SAFETY PRINTING FRAME.

With unequally divided back.

$4\frac{1}{4} \times 3\frac{1}{4}$ 8d. $6\frac{1}{2}$,, $4\frac{3}{4}$ 1/1 $8\frac{1}{2} \times 6\frac{1}{2}$ 1/9

RETOUCHING DESKS AND PENCILS

RETOUCHING DESKS.

Pine, blacked, with plate glass reflector, for plates 8½×6½ and two smaller sizes	£0 10	6
Ditto, ditto, for 12×10 and under	0 15	6
Ash, polished, well made, with drawer and plate glass reflector, to take 1-1, ½ and ¼ plate	0 15	6
Ditto, ditto, for 12×10 and under	1 2	6
Ditto, ditto, for 15×12 and under	1 15	0
Mahogany, polished, with drawer, and plate glass reflector :—½ plate	0 16	0
1-1 plate, 21/-; 10×8, 25/6; 12×10	1 10	6

Each of the above supplied with carriers for two sizes smaller.

FABER'S RETOUCHING PENCILS.

First quality pencils, in screw case .. .. each 8d

Refills for the above, in 6 degrees, per box of 6, 2/-

FABER'S PENCILS.

In 4 degrees—No. 1 soft, to No. 4 hard.

In Ever-Pointed Holders .. .. each 5d.	per doz.	4/-
Refills for ditto	,,	1/2

HARDTMUTH'S RETOUCHING PENCILS.

In 6 degrees—No. 1, very soft. to No. 6, very hard.

Ever-Pointed Holders .. .. .. large, each 4d.	small	3d.
Refills, per box of 6 .. .. ,, 6d.	,,	4d.

RETOUCHING CASE, Complete.

Containing 4 pencils, in screw cases, 24 refills, stump, rubber, etc. .. 2/-

,, 3 ,, ,, 12 ,, ,, ,, ,, .. 1/6

HARDTMUTH'S BLACK CHALK ARTISTS' PENCILS.

Prepared to match the Bromide Tone, for working up Bromide Prints, etc.

In Ever-Pointed Holders .. .. each 1/-	per doz.	10/6
Refills for the above.. .. .. per box of 6		9d.

RETOUCHING MEDIUM.

Ellis's "Paragon"	per bottle	6d.
Autotype Medium	,,	1/-

NON-ACTININE (BEALE'S PATENT.)

BY means of this new Preparation, clouds may be made on negatives ; objectionable parts blocked out; flaws hidden; portions strengthened ; and many other useful and artistic effects produced.

Thin, poor Negatives need not now be thrown away. They can be rescued from destruction, and made to give good prints by the use of BEALE'S NON-ACTININE.

Price. 6d., 1/- and 2/6 per bottle, with full instructions.

CLOUD NEGATIVES.

Perry's Grainless Cloud Negatives.

	Each.		Each.
$6\frac{1}{4} \times 4\frac{3}{4}$	1/6	10×8	3 -
$8\frac{1}{2}$,, $6\frac{1}{2}$	2/-	12 ,, 10	4/-

LUND'S WAXED PAPER CLOUD NEGATIVES.

	Each.		Each.
$4\frac{1}{4} \times 3\frac{1}{4}$	6d.	10×8	2/-
$6\frac{1}{2}$,, $4\frac{3}{4}$	1/-	12 ,, 10	3/-
$8\frac{1}{2}$,, $6\frac{1}{2}$	1/6	15 ,, 12	4/-

TRANSLUCENT PAPER.

For softening prints during printing.

This paper diffuses the light passing through the negative, and the prints gain considerably in softness and appearance by its use.

Per 100 sheets $4\frac{1}{4} \times 3\frac{1}{4}$ 6d. $6\frac{1}{2} \times 4\frac{3}{4}$ 9d.

WHEELER'S PRESERVATIVE PAPER.

For laying between negatives.

A pure vegetable paper containing nothing injurious to the negative.

Per 500 sheets	$4\frac{1}{4} \times 3\frac{1}{4}$	4d.	$7\frac{1}{2} \times 5$	1/-
,, ,,	5 ,, 4	6d.	$8\frac{1}{2}$,, $6\frac{1}{2}$	1/4
,, ,,	$6\frac{1}{2}$,, $4\frac{3}{4}$	8d.	10 ,, 8	2/-

VIGNETTING GLASSES, &c.

Of flashed orange glass, with well graduated openings.

$4\frac{1}{4} \times 3\frac{1}{4}$	7d.	$8\frac{1}{2} \times 6\frac{1}{2}$	1/8
5 ,, 4	9d.	10 ,, 8	2/6
$6\frac{1}{2}$,, $4\frac{3}{4}$	1/1	12 ,, 10	3/6

ZINC VIGNETTING SHAPES.

In boxes of 6 $\frac{1}{4}$ plate, assorted, pear-shaped openings	..	..	..	3/-
,, ,, 3 $\frac{1}{2}$,, ,, ,,	..	..	..	2/6
,, ,, 3 $\frac{1}{4}$,, ,, oval openings	..	..	..	1/6
,, ,, 3 $\frac{1}{2}$,, ,, ,,	..	..	..	2/6

FRENCH VIGNETTE GLASSES.

Pear shape for Portraits.

	Each.		Each.
C.-de-V.	6d.	$8\frac{1}{2} \times 6\frac{1}{2}$	2/-
Cabinet	1/-	10 ,, 8	2/6

WAXED PAPER VIGNETTERS.

	Each.		Each.
C.-de-V. or $\frac{1}{4}$ plate	3d.	10×8	1/6
Cabinet or $\frac{1}{2}$ plate	6d.	12 ,, 10	2/-
$8\frac{1}{2} \times 6\frac{1}{2}$	1/-	15 ,, 12	4/-

THE PARALLEL TRIMMER.
PATENT APPLIED FOR.

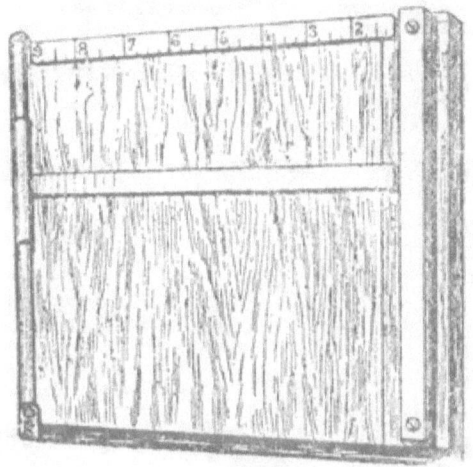

THIS Apparatus is designed to trim prints of all sizes, from the smallest to the largest the trimmer will take, with the sides parallel to the vertical lines, and of any proportion most suitable for the picture.

Price, to trim up to 8½ × 6½   £0 3 0   Ditto   ditto   12 × 10   0 10 6

SHEW'S REVOLVING CUTTING BOARD, WITH GLASS TOP.

Price, with Top 10 inches square   £0 3 9   Ditto ditto 12 ditto   0 5 6

CUTTING SHAPES.
Of Plate Glass, oval, dome, or square, each:—

C.-de-V., 6d. ; ¼-plate, 6d. ;   5 × 4, 9d. ;   Cabinet and ½-plate, 1/- ; 7 × 5, 1/3 ; 8½ × 6½, 1/9 ;   10 × 8, 2/6 ;   12 × 10, 3/3.

Ditto, ditto, with glass handle, and the surface ground to prevent slipping when cutting, each :—

C.-de-V., 8d. ;   ¼-plate, 1/- ;   Cabinet, 1/2 ;   ½-plate, 1/3 ;   7½ × 5, 2/- ; 8½ × 6½, 2/3 ;   10 × 8, 3/3 ;   12 × 10, 3/9.

CUTTING WHEEL FOR PRINTS.
THE NEW PHOTO TRIMMER.

Cuts with a perfectly clean edge, either wet or dry, and never requires sharpening.

The paper to be cut by this Trimmer must be placed on some hard substance, and glass is the best.   Price, Bronzed, 2/-.   Nickeled, 2/9.

THE PERFECT PRINT TRIMMER.

Straight Pattern 1/6 Swivel, for cutting Ovals, &c.	2/-	
Knives for trimming Prints, best Sheffield make, round end	1/-	each.
,, ,, ,, ,, pointed end	9d.	,,
,, cutting Cardboard Mounts	9d.	,,
Hard Wood Sheath for ditto, with fixing screw	2/-	,,

BURNISHERS.

The "Amateur's" Burnisher, highly finished, nickel plated, easy to use.
C -de-V., 27/-   Cabinet, 6½ in. roll, 50/-
Ditto, ditto new pattern, 6 in. roll, 36/- ; 8 in. roll, 45/-

VEVER'S CHEAP BURNISHERS.

6 in. roll   12/6   9 in.   20/-   11 in.   26/-
Lamp, 1/- extra, any size.

SHEW'S SIMPLE BURNISHER.

Cabinet   £1 5 0   12 × 10, 11 in. roll £2 17 6
1/1 plate, 7½ in. roll   1 12 0   15 ,, 12, 13   ,,   3 10 0

THE "KNOX" BURNISHER.

A THOROUGHLY serviceable and reliable burnisher, the roller of which, by removal of a pin, can be hinged back, thus allowing burnisher to be cleaned or heated without trouble. The burnisher is of specially made high-class steel — not cast iron.

Prices with Spirit Lamp—

6 in roller	18/-	10 in. roller	33/-
8 ,,	25/6	14 ,,	45/-

Other sizes to order.   Extra for Bunsen burner 1/6 and 2/6.

TYLAR'S BURNISHERS.

THE Burnishers consist of a case-hardened Steel Bar, with milled rolls, to enable cards to pass through easily, lubricators to bearings, adjustable bed carrying burnishing bar, so that different thicknesses of cards can be accommodated.

					Roll and Bar Nickel Plated Extra.
5½ in. roll	..	..	..	8/-	2/-
6½ ,, for Cabinets	..	..	..	11/-	2/6
9 ,, ..	..	..	..	14/6	3/6
11 ,, ..	..	..	..	20/-	5/-
15 ,, ..	..	..	..	35/-	7/6

Each with Lamp complete.   Larger sizes to order.

ROLLING PRESSES, &c.

Rolling Press for Carte-de-Visite, double cylinder centre pressure,
   best town made £1 4 0
Rolling Press for ½ plate and cabinet, 5 in. rolls, best town made .. 1 15 0

IMPROVED HOT ROLLING PRESS.

CONSTRUCTED so as to allow of a Gas Jet or Spirit Lamp being placed under it to heat the plate, giving a highly-glazed surface to the photograph :—

Carte-de-Visite and Stereo size with steel plate 10 × 4, on iron bed.. £8 10 0
Cabinet and ½ plate   ditto   13 × 7   ditto   4 10 0
Steel plates, highly polished, supplied separately, 8 × 4, 7/6 ;
   12 × 4, 10/6 ; 12 × 7, 15/- ; 14 × 12   ..   ..   0 18 0

TYLAR'S CARD PRESS.

No. 1.—4½ × 3¼ Bed		5/6
,, 2.—7¼ ,, 5	,,	7/6
,, 3.—9 ,, 7	,,	12/6

Effectually flattens Mounted Prints, and will be found useful for many purposes besides.

EMBOSSING PRESSES.

Die and press for embossing the cameo portraits.

C.-de-V. each 9/6

Cabinet ,, 21/-

Extra brass dies C.-de-V. 2/- Cabinet, 3/6.

MASKS AND DISCS.

C.-de:V., Cabinet, or whole plate, well assorted, per packet, 8d.

For Lantern Masks, see page 159.

NEGATIVE BAGS OR ENVELOPES.

For Plates.	Per 100.	Per 1000.
4¼ × 3¼	6d.	3/9
6½ ,, 4¾	9d.	5/6
8½ ,, 6½	1/-	8/-
10 ,, 8	1/3	10/9
12 ,, 10	1/6	15/6

BOOK POST WRAPPERS.

Of superior quality, covered both sides with white paper, with gummed laps and printed label for name and address.

	Per 100.	Per 1000.
C.-de-V.	2/6	18/-
Cabinets	3/6	31/-

MICA

for protecting Negatives.

Size.	Per doz.	Size.	Per doz.
6½ × 4¼	4/6	8½ × 6½	15/6
6½ × 4¾	5/6	10 × 8	21/-
8½ × 4¼	12/6	13 × 8	30/-
7½ × 5	12/6	12 × 10	45/-

BRUSHES.

Round Camel Hair in quill, for dusting plates or use in developing.

From 2d. to 6d. each.   s. d.

	s.	d.
Flat Camel Hair in tin cedar handle, from ½ in. to 4 ins. wide, at per in. ..	0	6
Flat Hog Hair in tin, white-wood handles, ½ in. to 4 ins. wide ,, ..	0	4
Spotting Brushes, red sable, Nos. 1 to 3, each	0	3
,, Fitch, Nos. 0 to 3, each	0	2
Camel Hair Pencils in quills, assorted sizes, per doz.	0	9
,, ,, in black handles and tin ferrules, Nos, 1, 2 and 3, each ..	0	3
or per dozen	1	3

Brown Sable Pencils, in polished handles, Albata ferrules,

each .. .. No. 1, 3d. ; No. 2, 5d. ; No. 3,	0	6
or per dozen .. .. .. ,, 2/9 ; ,, 4/- ; ,,	5	0
Round Hog Hair Brushes, for gumming, pasting, &c,, from.. .. 2d. to	0	6

COLORS.

	s.	d.
Liesegang's Spotting-out Colors, for Aristotype or any glossy surface . papers, per tube	0	8
Newman's Powder Colors, per bottle	0	9

PAPERS VARIOUS,

	s.	d.
Black Paper, for masks, &c., per quire, 1/9 ; per ream	30	0
Blotting Boards, white, extra stout, measuring 25½ × 19½. per quire ..	4	0
,, ,, ,, ,, ,, per ream..	75	0
Blotting Paper, white, per quire, 10d. ; per ream	15	0
Filtering Paper, grey, per quire, 6d. ; white, per quire	0	8

  ,,   round, in bands containing 100 each—

Diam.	Grey	White	Diam.	Grey	White	Diam.	Grey	White
6 in.	6d.	8d.	13 in.	1/2	1/6	20 in.	2/-	2/6
7½ ,,	8d.	9d.	16 ,,	1/6	1/10	32 ,,	—	—
10 ,,	10d.	11d.	18 ,,	1/8	2/1			

	s.	d.
Wheeler's Blotting Book, No. 1, 5½×4 in. each	0	4
,, ,, ,, No. 2, 8½ ,, 5¼ ,, ...	0	6
,, ,, ,, No. 3, 8½ ,, 7 ,, ...	0	9
,, ,, ,, No 4, 11 ,, 8½ ,, ...	1	0
,, ,, ,, No. 5, 17 ,, 11 ,, ...	2	0
Litmus Paper, blue or red, per book, 1½d. ; per dozen	1	3
Ruby Paper, for dark rooms, per quire, 1/- ; per ream	15	6
Yellow ,, ,, ,, 8d. ; ,, ...	10	6
Tissue ,, ,, ,, 4d. ; ,, ...	5	6

PHOTOGRAPHIC PAPERS.

SCHOLZIG'S PAPERS.

Splendid rich tones on Albumenized paper a certainty. Pure black tones on Matt Surface Paper equal to the finest Platinotypes at half the cost. See new process of printing through green glass.

READY-SENSITIZED, DOUBLE ALBUMEN-IZED, AND MATT SURFACE PAPERS.

READY CUT FOR MOUNTING.

	C.-D.-V's. or $5\frac{3}{8}\times4$—Cabs. $5\frac{3}{8}\times4$		Matt or Brilliant.	Enamel.
1 quire, containing	1008 or	360	15/-	16/6
½ " "	504 "	180	8/-	8/9
¼ " "	252 "	90	4/5	4/11
1 Sheet Packet {10 pieces, ½-plate}{25 pieces, ¼-plate} 42 "		15	1/-	1/2

	Matt or Brilliant.	Enamel.		Matt or Brilliant.	Enamel.
½-plate	2/9 per 100	3/- per 100.	10×8	7/9 per 50	8/3 per 50
½-plate	6/6 "	7/- "	12×10	13/6 "	14/6 "
7½×5	7/3 "	7/9 "	12×15	20/- "	21/- "
1-1-plate	10/6 "	11/3 "			

PRINTING UNDER GREEN GLASS.

THIS new method, which emanates from Mr. Otto Schölzig, of Binfield Road, Clapham, is applicable alike to Albumenized or Matt Surface Papers. A paper upon the subject from the pen of Mr. Edward A. Golledge, appears in "*The Camera*," for July, 1890, from which a description of the process is quoted.

In order to get the best effect it is necessary that the paper should be printed *very deep;* in fact, so deep that detail in the shadows is quite lost. Under ordinary circumstances it would appear to be much over-printed. I am of opinion that intensification of negatives will be rendered quite unnecessary if, when printing, the precaution is taken to print through the green or yellow glass. Of course the time occupied in printing is longer, but to my mind this is no drawback to the process.

The after-manipulations are much about the same as with ordinary printing, but when using Schölzig's Matt Surface Paper, the prints simply require a *rinse* in one water before placing in the toning bath. I recommend the following toning bath for *pure black* tone :—

Borax	..	..	..	..	..	1½ drm.
Uranium Nitrate	..	..	..	..	4 grs.
Gold	..	..	..	..	..	3 grs.
Water	..	..	..	..	..	24 oz.

Of course, if a number of prints are to be toned, more gold should be added, but with the bath above given, I have toned from 2½ to 3 dozen whole-plate prints on Schölzig's matt surface paper. It is necessary to replenish the bath with gold if it becomes weak, and the same solution may be used several times, provided gold has been added.

The tungstate and phosphate bath, as recommended by Mr. Schölzig, gives fine dark tones on the Matt Surface Paper. The time occupied in toning this paper is but a few minutes. I place the prints into salt and water, and fix in the usual manner.

BROMIDE PAPERS.
"ILFORD" BROMIDE PAPER.

Rough or Smooth.   Rapid or Slow.
They are characterised by a wonderful linear fineness and gradation of tone.
Colour, a rich engraving black.   Rapid for enlargements by artificial light, slow
for contact printing.

$4\frac{1}{4} \times 3\frac{1}{4}$ in.	6d. per doz. sheets.	$8\frac{1}{2}$,, $6\frac{1}{2}$ in. 2/3 per doz. sheets.
5 ,, 4 ,,	9d. ,, ,,	10 × 8 ,, 3/- ,, ,,
$6\frac{1}{2}$,, $4\frac{3}{4}$,,	1/2 ,, ,,	12 ,, $10\frac{1}{2}$,, 4/6 ,, ,,
8 ,, 5 ,,	1/9 ,, ,,	$15\frac{1}{2}$,, $12\frac{1}{2}$,, 7/- ,, ,,

18 × 15 in. 5/3 per ½ doz. sheets.
20 ,, 16 ,, 5/9 ,, ,,
23 ,, 17 ,, 6/9 ,, ,,
$24\frac{1}{2}$,, 19 ,, 7/6 ,, ,,
Roll, 10 ft. long × 24 in. wide, 8/6.

DEVELOPER.

No. 1.

Neutral Oxalate Potash,   1lb. avoir.
Warm water ..   .. 64 oz.
Bromide Ammonium ..   20 grs.

Clearing Solution.

Alum, ... 4 oz. avoir.
Citric Acid, ... 1 oz. avoir.
Warm water, ... 80 oz.

No. 2.

Sulphate Iron, .. 1lb. avoir.
Warm water   .. 48 oz.
Citric Acid   .. ½ oz. avoir.

Fixing Solution.

Hyposulphite Soda, 1lb. avoir.
Water, ... 80 oz.

"ILFORD" ALPHA PAPER.

Rough or Smooth. Unique. Warm tones, like Albumen Prints, with
greater gradation and finer detail. Any tone at will. By gaslight. Matt or
enamelled surface.

$4\frac{1}{4} \times 3\frac{1}{4}$ in.	5d. per doz. sheets.	$8\frac{1}{2} \times 6\frac{1}{2}$ in. 1/9 per doz. sheets.
5 ,, 4 ,,	8d. ,, ,,	10 ,, 8 ,, 2/6 ,, ,,
$6\frac{1}{4}$,, $4\frac{3}{4}$,,	1/- ,, ,,	12 ,, 10 ,, 3/6 ,, ,,
8 ,, 5 ,,	1/4 ,, ,,	

15 × 12 in. 5/6 per doz. sheets.
20 ,, 16 ,, 6/- per ½ doz. sheets.
24 ,, 19 ,, 6/6 ,, ,,
Roll, 10ft. long by 24in. wide, 7/-.

DEVELOPER.

No. 1.
Oxalate of Potash (Neutral) 1 lb. avoir.
Bromide Ammonium   320 grs.
Warm water ..   .. 64 oz.

No. 2.
Sulphate of Iron $4\frac{1}{2}$ ozs. avoir.
Citric Acid $\frac{1}{2}$,, ,,
Water   .. 80 ,, ,,

CLEARING SOLUTION.

Alum .. .. 4 oz. avoir.
Citric Acid .. .. 1 ,, ,,
Warm water .. .. 80 ,, ,,

TONING AND FIXING BATH.

Water .. .. 10 oz. ⎫
Hyposulphite of Soda .. .. $2\frac{1}{2}$,, ⎪
Acetate of Soda .. .. $\frac{1}{2}$,, ⎬ Avoir.
Sulphocyanide of Ammonium .. .. $\frac{1}{4}$,, ⎪
Stock Solution of Gold .. .. 4 drs. ⎭

EASTMAN PERMANENT BROMIDE PAPER.

For enlarging copying plans and direct contact printing from negatives.

We recommend the rough paper for plain enlargements and contact prints of all kinds, on account of the fine artistic effects to be obtained.

A—SMOOTH SURFACE, THIN PAPER.
B—SMOOTH SURFACE, HEAVY PAPER.
C—ROUGH SURFACE, HEAVY PAPER.

These papers may be used for positive printing or copying drawings by contact; for enlargements plain or working up in crayon, ink, water colours or oils, according as the taste or judgment of the operator may suggest.

All one price. 12 sheets in each package.

Size					Size			
$4\frac{1}{4} \times 3\frac{1}{4}$	..	..	...	-/8	10 × 8	..	..	3/6
5 ,, 4	..	..	..	-/11	12 ,, 10	..	..	5/-
$6\frac{1}{2}$,, $4\frac{3}{4}$	..	..	..	1/6	$15\frac{1}{2}$,, $12\frac{1}{2}$	..	..	7/6
$7\frac{1}{2}$,, 5	..	..	..	1/8	23 ,, 17	..	..	14/-
8 ,, 5	..	..	..	2/-	25 ,, 21	..	..	21/-
$8\frac{1}{2}$,, $6\frac{1}{2}$	..	..	..	2/6	30 ,, 25	..	..	28/6

Full directions in each package.

DEVELOPER.

A	B	C
Oxalate Potash, 1 lb.	Protosulphate Iron, 1 lb.	Bromide Potassium, 1 oz.
Hot water, 3 pints	Hot water, 1 quart.	Water, 32 oz.
Acidify with Sulphuric or Citric Acid.	Sulphuric Acid ½ drm. (or Citric Acid, ¼ oz.).	

Clearing Solution.

Acetic Acid	..	1 dram.
Water	.. ..	1 quart.

Fixing Solution.

Hyposulphite Soda, 3 oz.
Water .. .. 1 pint.

MORGAN & KIDD'S ARGENTIC GELATINO-BROMIDE PAPER.

FOR ENLARGING & PRINTING DIRECT FROM THE NEGATIVE.

Size.	6 Sheet.	12 Sheet.	Size.	6 Sheet.	12 Sheet.
$12\frac{1}{2} \times 10\frac{1}{2}$	4/6	3/-	25 × 21	18/6	10/-
$15\frac{1}{2}$,, $12\frac{1}{2}$	7/-	4/-	30 ,, 23	24/6	12/6
18 ,, 15	9/6	5/3	30 ,, 25	26/6	14/-
23 ,, 17	12/6	6/9			

In Rolls of 20 ft.—17 in. wide, 12/-; 25 in. wide, 17/6; and 30 in. wide, 21/-. The Positive Paper can also be had with a *rough* surface, same price; but in all cases, unless *rough* is specially ordered, smooth is sent.

Sample sheet, $23 \times 17\frac{1}{2}$, 1/6.

MORGAN & KIDD'S SPECIAL POSITIVE PAPER.

FOR CONTACT PRINTING.

In cut sizes, and packed flat for printing direct from the negative by artificial light; smooth or rough surface.

Two doz., $4\frac{1}{4} \times 3\frac{1}{4}$, 1/3. One doz., 8 × 5, 1/9. One doz., 10 × 8, 3/-.
One ,, $6\frac{1}{2}$,, $4\frac{3}{4}$, 1/3. ,, $8\frac{1}{2}$,, $6\frac{1}{2}$, 2/3. ,, 12 ,, 10, 4/6

DEVELOPING SOLUTIONS.

No. 1.—OXALATE SOLUTION. Potash, neutral oxalate, 1 lb.; acid, citric, 1 dr.; hot water, 50 oz.

No. 2.—IRON SOLUTION. Iron sulphate (pure), 15 oz.; acid, citric, 1 dr.; hot water, 30 oz.

No. 3.—BROMIDE SOLUTION.—Bromide of potassium, 1 oz.; water, 20 oz.
For NORMAL DEVELOPER, add to 6 oz. No. 1, 1 oz. No. 2, and 6 drops No. 3, to be mixed in order given and immediately before using.

No. 4.—CLEARING SOLUTION. Acid, acetic 1 oz.; water, 12 pints.

No. 5.—FIXING SOLUTION. Soda hyposulphite, 6 oz.; water, 40 oz.

No. 6.—CLEARING SOLUTION. Acid, sulphuric, 1 oz.; water, 80 oz.

LIESEGANG'S ARISTOTYPE PAPER.

In Packets containing 12 sheets each:—

4¼ × 3¼	9d.	6½ × 4¾	1/8	8¼ × 6¼ 3/-
5 ,, 4	1/3	7¼ ,, 4¾	2/-	10 ,, 8 4/6
6 ,, 4	1/3	7½ ,, 5	2/- 6 sheets 12 ,, 10 3/3

Toning Formula for the above.

Place the washed prints for a minute or two in a solution of 1 part of alum in 20 parts of water; with the paper as supplied presently this bath may be omitted, except perhaps in very hot climates.

Stock solutions—

A.

Water	2 oz.
Chloride of gold	2 grains.

B.

Water	2 oz.
Sulphocyanide of ammonia	30 grains.
Hyposulphite of soda	1 grain.

Mixed together by one part of A being poured into an equal part of B, in no case the reserve; dilute with water if necessary. Any good gold bath may be used for toning, provided it be not too strong.

The Acetate Toning Bath is recommended for purple tones.

OBERNETTER'S CHLORIDE OF SILVER EMULSION PAPER.

Prices per packet—

¼-plate	50	3/6	½-plate	25	2/6	10 × 8 25 9/0
5 × 4	50	4/6	7½ × 5	25	4/6	12 ,, 10 25 12/6
Cabinet	25	2/6	1-1 plate	25	6/6	

TONING.—The following *Toning Bath* has after experiment proved to give very fine brown (or black) tones, and is therefore recommended.

The prints are first washed in cold water, and toned in the following bath—

(1.)   1 ounce recrystallised Acetate of Soda in 25 ounces distilled water, to which add 8 ounces of a 1 per cent. solution (1 grain of gold in 100 min. of water) or approx. 1 Tube. (15 grs.) gold in 3 ounces of water.

(2.)   2 drams. Sulpho Cyanide of Ammonia in 8 ounces distilled water to which add 2 ounces of gold solution (as above.)

N.B.—For reddish brown tones add to No. 2 10 to 15 grains Hyposulphite of Soda.

SCHÜTZE & NOACK'S COLLODIO CHLORIDE OF SILVER EMULSION PAPER.

12 sheets 4¼ × 3¼	1/-	12 sheets 6½ × 4½ 1/8
12 ,, 6 ,, 4	1/3	12 ,, 8¼ ,, 6¼ 3/-

This paper is much more sensitive than albumenized paper, consequently greater care must be taken in exposing to other than subdued light.

Formula for the Combined Toning and Fixing Bath.

Distilled Water	1 pint.
Hyposulphite of Soda	4¼ oz.
Citric Acid	1 drachm.
Pure Acetate of Lead	1½ ,,
Sulphocyanide of Ammonium	1½ ,,
Powdered Alum	1 ,,
Solution of Chloride of Gold	1 oz.

½ sheet of Emulsion Paper.

THE PLATINOTYPE PROCESS.
SENSITIZED PAPER.

The following qualities of Sensitized Paper are manufactured :—

QUALITIES.		DESCRIPTION.
A. For the Hot-Bath Process	}	Smooth paper. Medium thickness. More used of this quality than of any other.
X. For the Cold-Bath Process		
B. For the Hot-Bath Process	{	Smooth paper. Thick and very strong. Suitable for large prints.
C. For the Hot-Bath Process	{	Rough-surfaced paper. Thick and very strong. Suitable for large work, where a rough surface is preferred.
S. For the Hot-Bath Process	{	Smooth paper. To give rich Sepia colour. Requires addition of "Special Solution" to the developer.

These papers will be supplied in Sealed Tin Tubes, either in whole sheets (measuring 26in. × 20in.), or cut to photographic sizes.

The Prices are as follows:—	Hot-Bath Process. Quality A. s. d.	Cold-Bath Process. Quality X. s. d.
4¼ × 3¼, 24 pieces in tube	1 6	0 11
5 ,, 4, 24 ,,	2 3	1 3
6½ ,, 4¾, 24 ,,	3 6	1 11
7½ ,, 5, 24 ,,	4 6	2 6
	Quality A, B, C or S.	Quality X.
8½ ,, 6½, 24 ,,	£0 6 0	£0 3 3
10 ,, 8, 24 ,,	0 8 6	0 4 10
12 ,, 10, 12 ,,	0 6 6	0 3 9
15 ,, 12, 12 ,,	0 9 6	0 5 6
3 sheets 26 × 20, in tube	0 6 6	0 3 9
6 ,, 26 ,, 20, ,,	0 12 6	0 7 0
12 ,, 26 ,, 20, ,,	1 4 0	0 12 6
24 ,, 26 ,, 20, ,,	2 8 0	1 4 6

The C paper can be had *to order*, larger in either dimension than 26 × 20, at rate of 8d. per square foot.

PRICE OF CHEMICALS FOR DEVELOPING.

For Hot-Bath Process { Neutral Oxalate Potash, per lb. 9d. Special Solution to be added to the developer, for the Sepia Papers, Price 1/6.

For Hot or Cold Process. Developing Salts, in ¼lb. packets, 1/3 per ¼lb.

For Cold-Bath Process { Platinum Salt, 60 grains, in bottle, 6/-. ,,   1 oz., in bottle, 45/-.

For Clearing, either Hydrochloric or Citric Acid can be used.

JACOBY'S PLATINUM PAPER.

Prices per packet of 12 :—

¼ Plate	1/-	7½ × 5	2/6	12 × 10	10/-
Cabinets	1/6	1-1 Plate	3/6	15 ,, 12	12/-
½ Plate	2/-	10 × 8	6/6		

Full Sheets, 26 × 19, 2/6 each.

The above is fixed with two Hydrochloric Baths. The First consisting of one part acid to 75 parts of water. The Second, one part acid to 50 parts of water.

HESEKIEL'S THULA PLATINUM PAPER.

Prices per packet of 25 :—

¼ Plate	1/3	7½ × 5	3/3	12 × 10	10/6
Cabinet	2/3	1-1 Plate	3/6	15 ,, 12	15/-
½ Plate	2/6	10 × 8	6/6		

Full Sheet, 26 × 19, 1/6 each.

Concentrated Toning Solution sufficient for about 70 cabinets **2/6** per bottle, or any old weak gold bath will answer the purpose.

LIESEGANG'S PLATINUM PAPER.

Prices per packet of 12 :—

¼ Plate	-/9	7½ × 5	2/-
½ ,,	1/6	1/1 Plate	2/9

This is fixed in a Hydrochloric Bath, composed of 80 parts of water to one part of acid.

THE KALLITYPE PROCESS.

A New Printing Process yielding prints of a beautiful black tone on a mat surface.

24 pieces, 4¼ × 3¼	-/9	3 Sheets, 26 × 20	2/6		
24 ,, 5 ,, 4	1/-	6 ,, 26 ,, 20	4/9		
24 ,, 6½ ,, 4¾	1/6	12 ,, 26 ,, 20	9/-		
24 ,, 7½ ,, 5	2/-	24 ,, 26 ,, 20	18/-		
24 ,, 8½ ,, 6½	2/6				
24 ,, 10 ,, 8	3/6				
12 ,, 12 ,, 10	2/9				

Developing Salts, sufficient for 10 ozs. of Solution, 1/3.

Citrate of Soda, 3/- per lb.

SHEW'S PRESERVATIVE SENSITIZED PAPER.

The still rapidly increasing sale proves the superiority of this paper over all others in the market. It is always uniform, gives brilliant prints, and will keep for months without deterioration; no fuming required. White, pink, and mauve always in stock :—

1 sheet, 10d.; 3 sheets, 2/3; 6 sheets, 3/9; ½-quire, 7/-; 1 quire ... 0 13 6
On roller, post free, 1/-, 2/6, 4/-, 7/3, and 0 14 0

SHEW & Co.'s ALBUMENIZED PAPERS, best Rives or Saxe (Steinbach), white or tinted, per quire, 5/6 ... ... per ream 4 17 6
On roller, post free, ½-quire, 3/- ... ... 1 quire 0 5 6

SHEW & Co.'s CELEBRATED STAR PAPER, universally acknowledged to be the best Albumenized Paper yet produced. Every sheet carefully selected both before and after albumenizing, and bearing the annexed trade mark, stamped in the corner. Rives or Saxe, white or tinted ... ... per quire, 6/-,
per ream, ... 5 10 0
On roller, post free ... ... ½-quire, 3/6; one quire 0 6 6
One sheet, as sample, of both the above papers, post free 0 1 0

MOUNTS.

CARTE-DE-VISITE.

Of first quality only, rounded corners, without printing.

	Per 100.	Per 1000.
Bristol, cream, white, cream, pink, salmon, or grey	10d.	7/6
,, with red marginal line ditto	11d.	8/-
,, with red rand ditto	1/-	9/6
,, with gilt edges ditto	1/3	11/6

The above supplied of a second quality at about 15 per cent. less to order only, in quantities of not less than 1000 of each kind.

THE NEW REGISTERED MOUNTS.

Of superfine Bristol, toned, with ornamented backs, with chaste designs for letterpress printing of name and address.   Per 100, 1/4; 1000, 11/6.

ENAMELLED ROUNDED CORNERS.

	Per 100.	Per 1000.
Tinted cream, pink, salmon, or grey	1/-	8/9
With red line ditto	1/1	10/-
With red rand ,, ...	1/2	10/6
With gilt rand ,, ...	1/3	11/-
Black, chocolate, olive, maroon..	1/2	10/6

CABINET MOUNTS.

Rounded Corners, without printing.

	Per 100.	Per 1000.
Bristol, white, cream, pink, salmon, and grey ..	2/6	25/-
,, with red line, ditto	3/-	28/6
,, with red rand	3/3	30/-
,, with gilt rand	4/-	32/-
,, with red line and scroll, " Cabinet Portrait "		28/6

The above supplied in second quality at 5/- per 1000 reduction in quantities of not less than 1000.

	Per 100.	Per 1000.
Enamelled white, cream, pink, or grey	3/-	27/6
,, with red line	3/6	33/-
,, with gilt rand	3/9	35/-
,, with gilt edges	4/-	37/-
,, chocolate, black, or olive green	3/4	31/-
,, with gilt rand	4/-	37/6

THE NEW REGISTERED MOUNTS.

	Per 100.	Per 1000.
Similar to C.-de-V. above	4/-	35/-

REAL GOLD BEVELLED EDGE MOUNTS.

MIDGET MOUNTS.

	Per 100.	Per 1000.
Black, olive-green, and chocolate enamel, 2¾ × 1½..	2/-	18/-

PROMENADE MIDGET MOUNTS.

	Per 100.	Per 1000.
Tints as above, 3¼ × 1⅝	2/3	21/-

CARTE-DE-VISITE.

Enamelled black, chocolate, olive-green, and cream—

Dozen.	100	250	500	1000
6d	2/10	6/3	12/-	23/-

Bristol, cream, grey, pink, and blue—

| 5d | 2/6 | 5/6 | 10/9 | 21/- |

CABINET.

$6\frac{3}{4} \times 4\frac{1}{4}$

Enamelled black, chocolate, olive-green—

Dozen.	100	250	500.	1000.
10d.	5/6	13/-	25/6	50/-

Bristol, cream, rose, blue, or grey—

8d.	4/9	11/9	22/9	45/-

MALVERN.

$6\frac{1}{2} \times 3\frac{1}{2}$

Enamelled black, chocolate, olive-green, and cream—

Dozen.	100	250	500
9d.	5/-	12/-	22/6

BOUDOIR.

$8\frac{1}{2} \times 5\frac{1}{2}$

Enamelled black, chocolate, olive-green and cream—

Dozen.	50	100	200	500
1/8	6/-	11/6	21/-	50/

PROMENADE.

$8\frac{1}{4} \times 4$

Enamelled black, chocolate, olive-green, and cream—

Dozen.	100	250	500	1000
1/4	9/-	21/-	45/-	85/-

IMPERIAL.

$10 \times 6\frac{7}{8}$

Enamelled black, chocolate, olive-green, and cream—

Dozen.	50	100	200	250
2/3	9/-	16/6	32/-	40/-

PANELS.

$13 \times 7\frac{1}{2}$

Enamelled black, chocolate, olive-green, or cream—

Each.	Dozen.	25	50	100
8d.	5/6	11/6	22/6	40/-

LARGE PANEL.

$17 \times 10\frac{1}{2}$

Enamelled black, chocolate, green or cream—

Each.	Dozen.	25	50	100
10d.	10/-	18/-	35/6	70/-

GRAND PANEL,

$23 \times 13\frac{3}{4}$

Enamelled black, chocolate, green, or cream—

Each.	Dozen.	25	50	100
1/8	3/-	35/6	72/6	140/-

VIEW MOUNTS.

SPECIAL SIZES FOR VIEWS.

Of first quality. All rounded corners.

$4\frac{1}{4} \times 3\frac{1}{4}$.—6 Sheet.

	Per dozen	100	500	1000
Bristol, various tints, plain ..	3d.	1/4	5/6	11/-
,, with marginal line ..	4d.	2/3	10/-	19/6
Enamelled black, green, chocolate	4d.	1/6	—	13/6

5×4—6 Sheet.

Bristol, various tints, plain ..	4d.	2/-	9/-	17/6
,, with marginal line ..	5d.	2/8	12/6	24/6
Enamelled black, green, chocolate	5d.	2/6	—	20/-

$6\frac{1}{2} \times 4\frac{3}{4}$—6 Sheet.

Bristol, various tints, plain ..	6d.	3/3	15/-	28/-
,, with marginal line ..	6d.	3/8	17/6	35/-
Enamelled black, green, chocolate	7d.	3/9	—	34/-

$7\frac{1}{2} \times 5$—8 Sheet.

Bristol, various tints, plain ..	9d.	5/-	24/-	45/-
,, with marginal line ..	1/-	7/6	—	—
Enamelled black, green, chocolate	1/-	6/6	—	—

$8\frac{1}{2} \times 6\frac{1}{2}$—8 Sheet.

Bristol, various tints, plain ..	1/-	6/6	27/6	52/6
,, with marginal line ..	1/2	8/6	—	—
Enamelled black, green, chocolate	1/3	9/-	—	—

10×8—8 Sheet.

Bristol, various tints, plain ..	1/6	10/-	45/-	80/-
,, with marginal line ..	1/8	12/-	—	—
Enamelled black, green, chocolate	2/-	12/6	—	—

12×10.

Bristol, various tints, plain ..	2/-	14/-	—	—
,, with marginal line ..	2/3	18/-	—	—
Enamelled black, green, chocolate	2/6	17/-	—	—

THE NEW ANTIQUE MOUNTS.

With plate sunk centres.

Size of Board.	Plate Sunk Mark.	Per doz.	Per 100.
$8\frac{1}{2} \times 6\frac{1}{2}$	$5\frac{1}{2} \times 4\frac{1}{2}$	10d.	6/6
10 ,, 8	8 ,, 6	1/-	9/6
12 ,, 9	$8\frac{1}{2}$,, $6\frac{1}{2}$	1/3	11/6
12 ,, 10	10 ,, 8	1/6	12/9

ANTIQUE GOLD BEVEL MOUNTS.

With plate sunk centres.

Size of Board.	Plate Sunk Mark.	Per Dozen.	Per 100.
$8\frac{1}{2} \times 6\frac{1}{2}$	$5\frac{1}{2} \times 4\frac{1}{2}$	1/8	12/6
10 ,, 8	8 ,, 6	2/2	16/-
12 ,, 9	$8\frac{1}{2}$,, $6\frac{1}{2}$	2/9	21/6
12 ,, 10	10 ,, 8	3/3	23/6

F

REAL GOLD BEVELLED EDGE MOUNTS.

Special sizes for Views. · Of first quality only

Size 4¼ × 3¼

		Doz.	50	100	1000
Bristol Cream,	blue, grey, pink	7d.	2/-	3/9	35/-
Enamelled ,,	black, chocolate, olive, maroon	8d	2/2	4/-	37/6

Size 5 × 4.

Bristol Cream,	blue, grey, pink	8d.	2/4	4/8	44/-
Enamelled ,,	black, chocolate, olive, maroon	9d.	2/8	5/-	47/6

Size 6½ × 4¾

Bristol Cream,	blue, grey, pink	10d.	3/2	6/-	58/-
Enamelled ,,	black, chocolate, olive, maroon	1/-	3/5	7/-	63/-

Size 7½ × 5.

Bristol Cream,	blue, grey, pink	1/4	5/-	9/-	85/-
Enamelled ,,	black, chocolate, olive, maroon	1/6	5/6	10/-	95/-

Size 8½ × 6½

Bristol Cream,	blue, pink, grey	1/8	6/6	12/-	110/-
Enamelled ,,	chocolate, black, olive, maroon	1/9	6/8	14/-	120/-

Size 10 × 8.

Bristol Cream,	blue, pink grey	2/6	9/6	18/-	170/-
Enamelled ,,	chocolate, black, olive, maroon	2/9	10/6	22/-	190/-

Size 12 × 10

Bristol Cream,	blue, pink, grey	4/-	15/6	30/-	280/-
Enamelled ,,	cholocate, black, olive, maroon	4/6	16/6	32/-	300/-

TONED BOARDS WITH OXFORD LINE.

Superfine quality, extra stout.

Size of Board.	Size of Oxford Line.	Per dozen.	Per 100.
7 × 5	5¼ × 3½	8d.	4/6
10 ,, 8	6 ,, 5	9d.	5/-
11½ ,, 9¼	7 ,, 5	1/-	7/9
13¼ ,, 10¾	9½ ,, 7½	1/6	11/-
17 ,, 14½	11½ ,, 9½	2/9	21/-
21 ,, 16	13½ ,, 11½	3/9	27/6

OXFORD LINE MOUNTS.

Second quality.

Board.	Line.	Per 100.
7 × 5	4¼ × 3¼	3/-
8 ,, 6	5 ,, 4	3/6
8½ ,, 6½	6 ,, 4½	3/6
10 ,, 8	6¾ ,, 5	4/3
12 ,, 9	8½ ,, 6½	5/9
12 ,, 10	9½ ,, 7½	5/9
14½ ,, 10½	10 ,, 8	8/6
16 ,, 12¼	10¼ ,, 8¼	11/-
18 ,, 14½	12 ,, 10	15/6
20 ,, 15½	13 ,, 11	17/9
24 ,, 19	16 ,, 13	22/6

NEW OXFORD LINE MOUNTS.

In Bristol Cream—Red Lines.

Size of Board	Size of Oxford Line.	Per dozen.	Per 100.
8 × 6	5¼ × 3¾	7d.	3/9
8½ ,, 6½	6 ,, 4¼	9d.	4/-
10 ,, 8	7½ ,, 5½	10d.	5/6
12 ,, 9	8 ,, 6	1/-	8/-
12 ,, 10	8½ ,, 6½	1/2	9/-
14 ,, 11½	10 ,, 8	1/8	12/-
18 ,, 14	12 ,, 10	2/6	18/-

MOUNTING BOARDS.

Plain, White or Tinted, superfine quality.

			4-sheet.	6-sheet.
8 ,, 6	White or tinted	per dozen	6d.	7d.
10 ,, 8	,, ,,	,,	8d.	9d.
12 ,, 9¾	,, ,,	,,	10d.	1/-
15 ,, 11	,, ,,	,,	1/3	1/9
18 ,, 14	,, ,,	,,	2/3	2/9
25 ,, 20	,, ,,	,,	2/6	3/-
32 × 22	,, ,,	,,	4/-	5/-

WOLFF'S PATENT ADHESIVE MOUNTS.

Eight-sheet Boards with gold bevelled edge, olive green, chocolate, black, plum, or cream.

								EXTRA STOUT.	
Price	C.deV.	4⅛x3⅛	4⅞x3⅞	Cabinet	6⅜x4⅝	7⅜x4⅞	8⅜x6⅜	7⅞x9⅞	9⅞x11⅞
Per doz.	8d.	10d.	1/-	1/2	1/4	2/4	2/9	5/6	7/6
Per 100	4/6	6/-	7/-	8/6	9/6	15/-	18/6	36/-	50/-

Stout toned Boards with rounded corners.

								EXTRA STOUT.	
Price	C.deV.	4⅛x3⅛	4⅞x3⅞	Cabinet	6⅜x4⅝	7⅜x4⅞	8⅜x6⅜	7⅞x9⅞	9⅞x11⅞
Per doz.	4d.	6d.	8d.	9d.	11d.	1/6	2/-	3/6	5/6
Per 100	2/-	3/-	4/-	4/6	6/-	9/6	12/-	20/-	34/-

Any other size cut to order at proportionate rates.

N.B.—The mounts are made ⅛ in. smaller than the plate, so that when trimmed the prints may be mounted with as small a margin as possible.

BLOCKS FOR SHOW MOUNTS.

Every Photographer having these can arrange effective Show Mounts for himself.

Black enamelled, 30 sheets thick, with gold bevelled edges.

	C.-de-V.	Cabinet.	Promenade.	Boudoir.	Imperial.	Panels
Each	3d.	5d.	6d.	8d.	10d.	1/-
Per Dozen	1/9	3/6	4/6	5/6	8/-	9/6

INDIA TINTED MOUNTS.

White Bristol board, with neutral grey tint.

Size of Board.	Size of Tint.	Per dozen.	Per 100.
8 × 6	5¼ × 3¾	7d.	3/9
8½ ,, 6½	6 ,, 4¼	8d.	4/-
9½ ,, 8	6½ ,, 5¼	9d.	5/-
10 ,, 8	7½ ,, 5½	10d.	5/6
12 ,, 9	8 ,, 6	1/-	8/-
12 ,, 10	9 ,, 7	1/2	9/-
12 ,, 10	9½ ,, 7½	1/2	9/-
14½ ,, 10½	10 ,, 8	1/8	13/-
17½ ,, 13½	12 ,, 10	2/6	18/-
20 ,, 15	14 ,, 11	4/-	30/-

PLATE SUNK INDIA TINTED MOUNTS.

The Tint, impressed on the card itself. Specially adapted for Platinotype and Bromide Prints.

Size of Board.	Size of Tint.	Per dozen.	Per 100.
8 × 6	5¼ × 3¾	10d.	£0 5 9
8½ ,, 6½	5 ,, 4	1/-	0 6 0
8½ ,, 6½	6 ,, 4¼	1/-	0 6 0
9½ ,, 8	6½ ,, 5¼	1/2	0 8 0
10 ,, 8	7 ,, 5	1/2	0 8 6
10 ,, 8	7½ ,, 5½	1/2	0 8 6
12 ,, 9	8 ,, 6	1/9	0 12 0
12 ,, 10	8½ ,, 6½	1/10	0 13 0
12 ,, 10	9 ,, 7	1/10	0 13 0
12 ,, 10	9½ ,, 7½	1/10	0 13 0
14 ,, 11½	10 ,, 8	2/6	0 18 0
15 ,, 12	10½ ,, 8¼	2/8	0 19 0
18 ,, 14	12 ,, 10	3/6	1 4 0
20 ,, 16	14 ,, 11	4/6	1 13 0
21½ ,, 17½	15 ,, 12	6/6	2 8 0
25 ,, 19	18 ,, 14	7/6	2 16 0

Plate mark ½ inch larger than the Tint all round.

SUPERIOR PLATE MARK MOUNTS.

Of various Tints with centres laid on. Of first quality only.

Size of Board.	Size of Tint.	Per dozen.	Per 100.
8½ × 6½	6 × 4¼	1/3	9/6
10 ,, 8	7 ,, 5	1/9	11/-
12 ,, 9	8 ,, 6	2/3	17/6
12 ,, 10	9 ,, 7	2/6	18/6
16 ,, 12	10¼ ,, 8¼	4/3	36/-
18 ,, 14	12 ,, 10	6/3	48/6
20 ,, 15½	13 ,, 11	6/6	50/-

PLATE MARK MOUNTS WITH CENTRES LAID ON.

Second quality.

Board.	Tint.	Per 100.
8½ × 6½	6 × 4¼	7/-
10 ,, 8	7 ,, 5	9/-
12 ,, 9	8 ,, 6	11/-
12 ,, 10	8½ ,, 6½	11/6
16½ ,, 10½	9½ ,, 7½	17/6
18 ,, 14½	12 ,, 10	28/6
20 ,, 15½	13 ,, 11	30/-
24 ,, 19	16 ,, 13	37/6
29 ,, 21	21 ,, 17	57/6

MOUNTS—BEVELLED AND BLOCKED.

Bevelled and Blocked in Pure Gold.

	Per 100.	500.	1,000.	2,500.
C.-D.-V.	5/9	22/6	35/6	85/6
Cabinet	8/6	36/-	60/-	155/-
Promenade	11/6	55/-		
Boudoir	13/9	63/6		
Imperial	18/6	90/-		
Panel	45/-			

No charge for dies on 1,000 or more, for less than 1,000, dies are charged 2d. and 3d. per letter.

CARTES-DE-VISITE MOUNTS.

With Name and Address Printed.

	Per 1,000.			2,500.			5,000.		
	£	s.	d.	£	s.	d.	£	s.	d.
Superfine Bristol, white or tinted rounded corners—									
Printed one side	0	11	6	1	7	6	2	12	6
,, both sides	0	13	6	1	13	6	2	17	6
Superfine enamelled, various tints, rounded corners—									
Printed one side	0	12	6	1	8	6	2	12	6
,, both sides	0	15	6	1	15	6	3	2	6
Superfine enamelled, various tints, rounded corners, and marginal line—									
Printed one side	0	15	6	0	17	6	3	12	6
,, both sides	1	0	6	2	9	9	4	5	0

	Per 1,000.
Extra for printing in gold, one side	1/-
,, ,, ,, both sides	2/-
,, gilt edges	6/6
,, extra thickness	1/6

The prices above quoted are exclusive of engraving, which is charged extra on the first order, according to the amount of work required.

CABINET MOUNTS.

With Name and Address Printed.

	Per 500.			1,000.			2,500.		
Extra superfine Bristol, extra thickness, white or tinted—									
Printed one side	£1	2	6	1	13	6	3	17	6
,, both sides	1	4	6	1	18	6	4	10	0
Enamelled plain, extra thickness, white or tinted—									
Printed one side	1	3	6	1	17	6	4	5	0
,, both sides	1	7	6	2	0	0	4	15	0
6 Sheet thickness		per 1,000 extra					0	3	0
Colored line, and printing of cabinet portrait on face							0	7	6
Waterproof colored rands							0	7	6
Gilt edges, in 5 or 6 sheet							0	12	6
Gilt printing on one side							0	2	0
,, both sides							0	4	0

ALBUMS FOR PHOTOGRAPHS.
UPRIGHT AND OBLONG.

No. 1.—For cutting and slipping in at corners the unmounted photograph. 60 stout cartridge leaves bound in imitation morocco, cloth sides, gilt lines.
10 × 7½, 2/8.   12 × 9½, 3/9.   15 × 11, 5/3.   17 × 12½, 9/-.

No. 2.—With 30 stout cardboard leaves, linen joints, opening out perfectly flat; bound half-roan, gilt lines :—
10 × 7½, 3/6.   12 × 9½, 5/3.   15 × 11, 7/6.   17 × 12½, 11/6.
With gilt edges to leaves—one third of the above prices extra.

No. 3.—With 38 stout superfine cardboard leaves, whole bound in morocco, gilt lined, linen joints, gilt edges to leaves :—
10 × 7½, 6/9.   12 × 9½, 9/-.   15 × 11, 12/-.   17 × 12½, 19/6.

No. 4.—With 38 stout superfine cardboard leaves, whole bound in English russia leather, extra gilt finish, gilt edges :—
10 × 7½, 16/6.   12 × 9½, 24/6.   15 × 11, 35/-.   17 × 12½, 45/-.

SKETCH ALBUMS.

For slipping in photographs for the pocket.
For ¼-plate photos, 5 × 3½, 1/-.   For 5 × 4, 6¼ × 4½, 2/-.
For ½-plate, 7½ × 5½, 2/9.

SNAP SHOTS.

A neat little album, bound in cloth, containing 24 leaves, linen jointed :—
5¾ × 4¼, 1/-.

PORTFOLIOS.

For collections of mounted or unmounted photographs.

Of best quality, half-roan, cloth sides with leather joints and stiff flaps :—
9×7, 1/3 ; 12×9, 1/6 ; 16×11, 2/6 ; 19×12¾, 3/9 ; 20×15½, 5/-.

Of best quality, half-roan, cloth sides with leather joints (without flaps) :—
9×7, 1/- ; 12×9, 1/3 ; 16×11, 2/- ; 19×12½, 3/- ; 20×15½, 3/6.

WOLFF'S BOX ALBUMS.

The "Box Album" is not so bulky as the ordinary Album, and can be placed in any book shelf. They may be lettered in gold on back, at small cost, to suit customers.

Size.	¼-pl. or C. de V.	½-pl. or Cab.	7½×5.	8½×6½.	10×8.	12×10.
Price each.	1/3	1/6	2/4	2/9	3/6	5/-

PHOTOGRAPHIC PUBLICATIONS.

British Journal of Photography	.. ..	Weekly		2d.
Photographic News	.. ..	,,		2d.
Amateur Photographer..	.. ..	,,		2d.

Thirteen Numbers of the above, free by Post, 2/9, payable in advance.

Photography	.. ..	Weekly		1d.
The Camera	.. ..	Monthly		3d.
Photographic Reporter ..	.. ..	,,	1s.	0d.
Magic Lantern Journal..	.. ..	,,		1d.
Photographic Quarterly	.. ..	Quarterly	1s.	6d.
British Journal Almanack	.. .. Annual 9d. ;	Cloth	1s.	6d.
Year Book of Photography	.. .. 9d.			

Amateur Annual .. .. Annual 1/-; Cloth	1s. 6d.
Photography Annual .. .. .. "	2s. od.
Anthony's Bulletin .. .. Published June 1st	2s. od.
American Annual	2s. od.
Art and Practice of Interior Photography. By F. W. MILLS ..	7s. 6d.
Burton's Modern Photography. By Professor W. K. BURTON, C.E.	10d.
Collotype and Photo-Lithography. By Dr. JULIUS SCHNAUS ..	4s. 6d.
Casket of Photographic Gems. By W. INGLIS ROGERS.	10d.
Dictionary of Photography. By E. J. WALL	2s. od.
Development. By LYONEL CLARK..	10d.
Enamelling and Re-Touching. By P. PIQUEPE	2s. 2d.
Æsthetics of Photography. Hints on Lighting and Posing the Sitter. By HEIGHWAY	1s. od.
Elementary Treatise on Photographic Chemistry. By ARNOLD SPILLER	6d.
Handbook of Photographic Terms. By HEIGHWAY	2s. 2d.
Instruction in Photography. By Captain ABNEY, C.B., R.E., F.R.S.	3s od.
Lantern Slides: How to make them. By A. R. DRESSER ..	6d.
Optics for Photographers. By Professor W. K. BURTON, C.E. ..	1s. od.
Platinum Toning. By LYONEL CLARK	10d.
Photographic Chemistry. By HARDWICK & TAYLOR..	7s. 6d
Photography in a Nutshell. By THE KERNEL	1s. od.
Photographic Printer's Assistant. By HEIGHWAY	10½d.
Practical Portrait Photography. By HEIGHWAY	10½d.
Pictorial Effect in Photography. By H. P. ROBINSON	2s. 2d.
Photomicrography. By J. H. JENNINGS. Also a Chapter on Preparing Bacteria. By Dr. R. MADDOX	3s. od.
Photography for All. By W. JEROME HARRISON, F.G.S.	10d.
The Book of the Lantern. By T. C. HEPWORTH	3s. 6d.
The Amateur's First Hand Book. By ELLERBECK	6d.
The Art and Practice of Silver Printing. By Captain ABNEY and H. P. ROBINSON	2s. 2d.
The Photographer's Indispensable Handbook. By WALTER D. WELFORD	2s. 6d.
Vever's Practical Amateur Photography	6d.

NOTE BOOKS, ETC.

Burton's Note Book .. .. Paper, 9d.; Cloth,	1s. od.
Exposure Notes, for Use with Watkins' Exposure Meter ..	1s. 6d.
Practical Index of Photographic Exposure. By WORMALD ..	1s. 6d.
The Photographer's Systematic Exposure Note Book .. Cloth	1s. od
" " " .. Leather	1s. 6d.
Wheeler's Exposure Register and Tables Cloth, 1s.; Leather	1s. 6d
Wheeler's Bromide Printing Register	1s. od.
Wheeler's Book of Gummed Chemical Labels	6d.

GELATINE DRY PLATES.

SHEW'S "ECLIPSE" DRY PLATE.

Specially prepared for us by Mr. England for Instantaneous Work.

$4\frac{1}{4} \times 3\frac{1}{4}$	5×4	$6\frac{1}{2} \times 4\frac{3}{4}$	$7\frac{1}{2} \times 5$	$8\frac{1}{2} \times 6\frac{1}{2}$	10×8	12×10
1/6	2/3	3/6	5/-	6/-	10/6	13/6

DEVELOPER, PYRO, AND POTASH.

PYRO SOLUTION.

Hot distilled water .. .. 4 ozs.
Sulphite of Soda (chem. pure) 3½ ,,
    Dissolve and then add
Sulphurous Acid .. .. 4 ,,
Pyrogallic ,, ... 1 ,,

POTASH SOLUTION.

Water.. .. .. .. 9 ozs.
Sulphite of Soda (chem. pure) 2 ,,
Carbonate of Potash
    (chem. pure) 3 ,,
Dissolve separately in hot water
    and mix when cold.

ENGLAND'S PLATES.

Size of Plate.	Ordinary.	Extra Rapid.	Size of Plate.	Ordinary.	Extra Rapid.	Size of Plate.	Ordinary.	Extra Rapid.
$4\frac{1}{4} \times 3\frac{1}{4}$	1/-	1/3	$6\frac{1}{2} \times 4\frac{3}{4}$	2/3	3/-	$8\frac{1}{2} \times 6\frac{1}{2}$	4/3	5/6
5×4	1/7	2/-	$7\frac{1}{2} \times 5$	3/5	4/6	10×8	7/3	9/6

Developer as above

EDWARDS' XL PLATES.

Including special patent light-tight grooved Plate Boxes

Size of Plate.				Price.	Size of Plate.				Price.
$4\frac{1}{4} \times 3\frac{1}{4}$	..	..	..	2/-	$8\frac{1}{2} \times 6\frac{1}{2}$	..	..	..	7/-
5 ,, 4	..	..	..	2/8	10 ,, 8	..	..	..	10/-
$6\frac{1}{2}$,, $4\frac{3}{4}$	..	..	..	4/-	12 ,,10	..	..	..	16/8
$7\frac{1}{2}$,, 5	..	..	..	5/-	15 ,,12	..	..	..	24/-

EDWARDS' ISOCHROMATIC PLATES.

Size of Plate.				Price.	Size of Plate.				Price.
$4\frac{1}{4} \times 3\frac{1}{4}$	..	..	..	2/-	$8\frac{1}{2} \times 6\frac{1}{2}$	..	..	..	7/-
5 ,, 4	..	..	..	2/8	10 ,, 8	..	..	..	10/-
$6\frac{1}{2}$,, $4\frac{3}{4}$	..	..	..	4/-	12 ,, 10	..	..	..	16/8
$7\frac{1}{2}$,, 5	..	..	..	5/-					

ANY good Developer may be used with these plates. With the Isochromatic Plates especial care must be taken in the dark room to avoid fogging during development. Only ruby light must be used.

ILFORD PLATES.

Inches.	ORDINARY, Yellow Label. Sensitometer No. 18.				RAPID, White Label. Sensitometer No. 19.				SPECIAL RAPID, Red Label. Sensitometer No. 24.			
	£	s.	d.		£	s.	d.		£	s.	d.	
$4\frac{1}{4} \times 3\frac{1}{4}$	..	0	1	0	..	0	1	3	..	0	1	6
5 ,, 4	..	0	1	7	..	0	2	0	..	0	2	6
$6\frac{1}{2}$,, $4\frac{1}{4}$	..	0	2	2	..	0	2	9	..	0	3	3
$6\frac{1}{2}$,, $4\frac{3}{4}$	..	0	2	3	..	0	3	0	..	0	3	8
$7\frac{1}{4}$,, $4\frac{1}{4}$	..	0	2	10	..	0	3	8	..	0	4	6
$8\frac{1}{2}$,, $4\frac{1}{4}$	..	0	3	2	..	0	4	2	..	0	5	0
$7\frac{1}{2}$,, 5	..	0	3	5	..	0	4	6	..	0	5	3
$8\frac{1}{2}$,, $6\frac{1}{2}$	..	0	4	3	..	0	5	6	..	0	6	6
9 ,, 7	..	0	5	0	..	0	6	6	..	0	7	6
10 ,, 8	..	0	7	3	..	0	9	6	..	0	11	0
12 ,, 10	..	0	10	6	..	0	13	0	..	0	16	0

ILFORD DEVELOPERS.
No. 1 Stock Solution.

Pyrogallic Acid .. .. 1 ounce.
Bromide Ammonium .. .. 600 grains.
Make up to 6 ounces with water and when dissolved add *exactly* 20 *drops*
Nitric Acid.

No. 2 Solution.

Liquor Ammonia ·880 .. .. 3 drams.
Water.. .. .. 1 pint.

No. 3. Solution.

Of No 1 .. .. 1 ounce.
Water .. .. 19 ounces.
The Solutions No. 1 and 2 will keep for a considerable time, if well stoppered;
No. 3 a few hours only.
To develop take equal portions of Nos. 2 and 3.

HYDROKINONE.
No. 1 Solution.

Hydrokinone.. .. .. .. 160 grains.
Bromide Potassium .. .. 30 ,,
Sulphate Soda .. .. 2 ounces avoirdupois.
Water .. .. .. to 20 ounces.

No. 2 Solution.

Soda Hydrate .. .. 100 grains.
Water .. .. 20 ounces.
To use, take equal portions of each.

THE LUMIERE DRY PLATE.

These Plates are found to produce more brilliant pictures with Instantaneous
exposure than any Extra Rapid Plate in the market.

Size of Plate.	Per doz.	Size of Plate.	Per doz.	Size of Plate.	Per doz.
$4\frac{1}{4} \times 3\frac{1}{4}$	1/6	$7\frac{1}{4} \times 5$	4/6	10×8	10/-
$5 ,, 8\frac{1}{2}$	2/3	$8\frac{1}{2} ,, 6\frac{1}{2}$	6/6	$12 ,, 10$	15/-
$6\frac{1}{2} ,, 4\frac{3}{4}$	3/4				

DEVELOPERS.
Oxalate and Iron Developer.

Dissolve the following :—

A { Distilled Water .. .. 53 ozs.
{ Neutral Oxalate of Potass .. .. 16 ,,

B { Distilled Water .. .. 17 ozs.
{ Sulphate of Iron .. .. 5 ,,
{ Tartaric Acid .. .. $7\frac{1}{2}$ grs.

To develope a plate $6\frac{1}{2}$-in. by $4\frac{3}{4}$-in.

Take .. .. { A .. .. 12 drams.
{ B .. .. 4 ,,

To develop instantaneous work, add to Solution A 6 per cent. of a solution
of Hyposulphite of Soda at 1000th.

Pyrogallic Acid Developer.

Dissolve the following :—

A { Water .. .. $10\frac{1}{2}$ ozs.
{ Pyro-Gallic Acid .. .. 5 drams.
{ Sulphite of Soda .. .. 2 ozs.

B { Water .. .. $10\frac{1}{2}$ ozs.
{ Carbonate of Soda (Crystals) .. .. 2 ,,
{ Sulphite of Soda .. .. 2 ,,

To develop a plate $6\frac{1}{2}$-in. by $4\frac{3}{4}$-in.

Take .. .. { Water .. .. 2 ozs
{ A .. .. $1\frac{1}{2}$ to $2\frac{1}{2}$ drams.
{ B .. .. $1\frac{1}{2}$ to $2\frac{1}{2}$,,

Increase the quantity of B drop by drop during the development if the
negative should be under-exposed.

THE MAWSON PLATE.

Size of Plate.	Per doz.	Size of Plate.	Per doz.	Size of Plate.	Per doz.
3¼ × 3¼	1/3	6½ × 4¾	3/6	10 × 8	12/-
4¼ ,, 3¼	1/6	7½ ,, 5	5/-	12 ,, 10	16/-
5 ,, 4	2/3	8½ ,, 6½	6/6		

DEVELOPER.

No. 1 Solution.

Pyrogallic Acid	1 ounce.
Water	10 ounces.

No. 2 Solution.

Liquor Ammonia ·880	1 dram.
Bromide Ammonium	1 ,,
Water	10 ounces.

For use take equal portions of each.

PAGET PRIZE PLATES.

Size.		Phœnix.	XXX.	XXXXX.
4¼ × 3¼	.. .. ..	1/-	1/3	1/6
5 ,, 4	.. .. ..	1/7	2/-	2/6
6½ ,, 4¾	.. .. ..	2/3	3/-	3/8
7½ ,, 5	.. .. ..	3/5	4/6	5/3
8½ ,, 6½	.. .. ..	4/3	5/6	6/6
10 ,, 8	.. .. ..	7/3	9/6	11/-
12 ,, 10	.. .. ..	10/6	13/-	16/-
15 ,, 12	.. .. ..	18/-	23/-	28/-

DEVELOPER.

No. 1.

Pyrogallic Acid	1 ounce.
Citric Acid	60 grains.
Soda Sulphite, pure	2¼ ounces.
Distilled Water	to 20 ,,

No. 2.

Liquor Ammonia (·880)	1 ounce.
Bromide Ammonium	80 grains.
Distilled Water	to 20 ounces.

For use take equal parts of each and add ten parts water.

DR. SCHLEUSSNER'S PLATES.

4¼ × 3¼	1/6	6½ × 4¾	3/6	8½ × 6½	6/

DEVELOPER.

Hydrokinone	1 ounce.
Soda Sulphite	6 ounces.
Water	30 ,,

Dissolve then add—

Carbonate of Potash, chem. pure	5 ounce

To develop take equal parts of Developer and Water.

THOMAS'S "PALL MALL" PLATES.

Size.				Extra Rapid.	Thickly coated. Extra Rapid.	Thickly coated. Landscape.
4¼ × 3¼	..	..	..	1/-	1/6	1/6
5 ,, 4	..	..	..	1/7	2/4	2/4
6½ ,, 4¾	..	..	..	2/3	3/6	3/6
7½ ,, 5	..	..	..	3/6	4/6	4/6
8½ ,, 6½	..	..	..	4/3	6/6	6/6
10 ,, 8	..	..	..	7/3	10/-	10/-
12 ,, 10	..	..	..	10/6	14/6	14/6

DEVELOPER.

STOCK SOLUTION No. 1.

Pyrogallic Acid ..	..	..	..	..	..	..	1 ounce.
Sulphite Soda ..	..	..	..	..	..	..	2 ounces.
Citric Acid	..	..	..	..	..	..	¼ ounce.
Distilled Water to	..	..	..	..	..	..	10 ounces.

STOCK SOLUTION No. 2.

Liquor Ammonia (·880)	..	..	..	..	..	1 ounce.
Sulphite Soda ..	..	..	..	..	..	2 ounces.
Water to	..	..	..	..	..	..	10 ,,

STOCK SOLUTION No 3.

Bromide Potassium	..	..	..	..	..	1 ounce.
Water to ..	..	..	..	..	..	10 ounces.

No 4 SOLUTION.

Solution No. 1 ..	..	..	..	..	..	1 ounce.
Water to..	..	..	..	..	..	20 ounces.

No 5 SOLUTION.

Solution No. 2 ..	..	..	..	..	..	1 ounce.
Solution No. 3 ..	..	..	..	..	..	1 ,,
Water to..	..	..	..	..	..	20 ounces.

To develope take equal parts of 4 and 5, and when image is well up ad 10 minims of No. 2.

WRATTEN'S "LONDON" DRY PLATES.

Size				Ordinary.	Instantaneous.	Drop-Shutter Special.
4¼ × 3¼	..	..	..	1/9	2/-	2/3
5 ,, 4	..	..	..	2/9	3/-	3/4
6½ ,, 4¾	..	..	..	3/9	4/3	4/9
7½ ,, 5	..	..	..	5/3	6/-	6/9
8½ ,, 6½	..	..	..	7/3	8/-	8/9
10 ,, 8	..	..	..	10/9	12/-	13/3
12 ,, 10	..	..	..	17/3	19/-	21/-

DEVELOPER.

No. 1 SOLUTION.

Pyrogallic Acid ..	..	..	..	..	1 ounce.
Citric or Sulphurous Acid	..	..	..	½ dram.
Water	..	..	..	..	..	10 ounces.

No. 2 SOLUTION.

Liquor Ammonia ·880	..	..	..	..	1 ounce.
Bromide Potassium	..	..	..	..	100 grains.
Water	..	..	..	..	..	2 ounces.

To develop take 1 dram No. 1 and ¼ dram No. 2 and add 2 ounces water.

LANTERN PLATES.

EDWARD'S SPECIAL TRANSPARENCY PLATES.

FOR LANTERN SLIDES.

WITH these Plates perfectly clear and splendid toned Lantern Slides can be made by the most inexperienced, with ease and certainty, either by contact printing by artificial light, or by Camera printing from larger or smaller negatives.

Price (with Instructions), per dozen, $3\frac{1}{4} \times 3\frac{1}{4}$, 1/6.

THE HALF-GUINEA LANTERN SLIDE-BOX, for Amateurs, contains three dozen special transparency plates (or three dozen gelatino-chloride plates)—developer for above two bottles in case, ditto intensifier, clearing solution, one ebonite developing tray, three dozen special thin covering glasses cut to size), three dozen round or cushion-shaped mats, strips for binding edges of slides, sample lantern slide as pattern, and instructions for making lantern slides ..   ..   Price 10/6.

EDWARD'S GELATINO-CHLORIDE DRY PLATES.

$3\frac{1}{4} \times 3\frac{1}{4}$	..	..	1/6	$6\frac{1}{2} \times 4\frac{3}{4}$	..	..	.. 4/6
$4\frac{1}{4} ,, 3\frac{1}{4}$	..	..	2/3	$8\frac{1}{2} ,, 6\frac{1}{2}$	..	..	8/-

DEVELOPER.

SOLUTION No. 1.		SOLUTION No. 2.	
Oxalate of Potash ..	.. 2 ozs.	Sulphate Iron ..	4 drams.
Chloride Ammonium	.. 40 grs.	Citric Acid	2 ,,
Distilled Water ..	.. 20 ozs.	Alum	90 grains.
		Distilled Water ..	20 ozs.

For use take equal parts of each.

ENGLAND'S CHLORIDE PLATES.

Size.		Per doz.	Size.		Per doz.
$4\frac{1}{4} \times 3\frac{1}{4}$ or $3\frac{1}{4} \times 3\frac{1}{4}$	..	1/-	$7\frac{1}{2} \times 5$		3/5
$5 ,, 4$	.. .. ..	1/7	$8\frac{1}{2} ,, 6\frac{1}{2}$		4/3
$6\frac{1}{2} ,, 4\frac{3}{4}$	.. .. ..	2/3	$10 ,, 8$		7/3

DEVELOPERS.
FERROUS-OXALATE or HYDROKINONE.
FERROUS-OXALATE.

SOLUTION No. 1.		SOLUTION No. 2.	
Oxalate of Potash	.. 13 ozs.	Sulphate of Iron ..	5 ozs.
Distilled Water ..	.. 50 ,,	Sulphuric Acid ..	.. 15 drops.
		Distilled Water ..	.. 15 ozs.

To develop, pour one part No. 2 into four parts No. 1—not vice versa, or a precipitate will be formed.

HYDROKINONE.

SOLUTION No. 1.		SOLUTION No. 2.	
Hydrokinone ..	150 grains.	Carbonate Soda ..	2 ozs.
Sulphate Soda ..	1 oz.	Carbonate Potash ..	2 ,,
Bromide Potassium	20 grains.	Water to	20 ,,
Water to	20 ozs.		

To develope, take equal parts of each. This developer can be used several times.

FRY'S LANTERN PLATES.

$3\frac{1}{4} \times 3\frac{1}{4}$ or $4\frac{1}{4} \times 3\frac{1}{4}$	1/- per doz.	$7\frac{1}{2} \times 5$ ..	..	..	3/5
$5 ,, 4$	1/7 ,,	$8\frac{1}{2} ,, 6\frac{1}{2}$ ..	..	..	4/3
$6\frac{1}{2} ,, 4\frac{3}{4}$	2/3 ,,	$10 ,, 8$ ..	..	..	7/3

Developers—Pyro and Ammonia, Ferrous Oxalate or Hydrokinone.

ILFORD LANTERN PLATES.

ALPHA LANTERN PLATES.

$3\frac{1}{4} \times 3\frac{1}{4}$ .. .. 1/- doz.

All other sizes at prices of yellow label plates.

THE "SPECIAL" LANTERN PLATES.

For Black Tones.

In all Sizes at Yellow Label prices.

DEVELOPER.

SOLUTION No. 1.		SOLUTION No. 2.	
Hydrokinone ..	80 grains.	Soda Hydrate ..	30 grains.
Bromide Potassium	15 ,,	Water	20 oz.
Sulphite Soda ..	1 oz.		
Water to	20 ,,		

To develop, take equal parts of each.

MAWSON'S LANTERN PLATES.

In all Sizes, at Yellow Label Prices.

DEVELOPER.

SOLUTION No. 1.		SOLUTION No. 2	
Pyrogallic Acid ..	40 grains	Liquor Ammonia ..	2½ drams.
Metabisulphite Potassium	120 ,,	Water	20 ozs.
Bromide Ammonium ..	40 ,,		
Distilled Water ..	20 ozs.		

For use take equal parts of each.

THOMAS'S PALL MALL TRANSPARENCY PLATES.

$3\frac{1}{4} \times 3\frac{1}{4}$ or $4\frac{1}{4} \times 3\frac{1}{4}$ ..	.. 1/- per doz.	$7\frac{1}{2} \times 5$ ..	.. 3/5 per doz.
5 ,, 4	.. 1/7 ,,	$8\frac{1}{2}$,, $6\frac{1}{2}$ ..	.. 4/3 ,,
$6\frac{1}{2}$,, $4\frac{3}{4}$	.. 2/3 ,,	10 ,, 8 ..	.. 7/3 ,,

DEVELOPERS

PYRO AND AMMONIA.

SOLUTION No. 1.		SOLUTION No. 2.	
Pyrogallic Acid ..	.. 1 oz.	Bromide Ammonium ..	.. 1 oz.
Sulphite Soda ..	.. 3 ozs.	Water to	.. 10
Citric Acid	.. ¼ oz.		
Water to	.. 10 ozs.		

SOLUTION No. 3.		SOLUTION No. 4.	
Liquid Ammonia ·880 ..	1 oz	Carbonate Ammonia ..	1 oz.
Water to	10 ozs.	Water to	10 ozs.

To use, take 30 minims each Nos. 1, 3 & 4, 60 minims No. 2, and make up 2 ozs. with water.

HYDROKINONE.

SOLUTION No. 1.		SOLUTION No 2.	
Hydrokinone.. ..	.. 160 grs.	Carbonate Potash ..	.. 2 ozs.
Sulphite Soda ..	.. 2 ozs.	Carbonate Soda ..	.. 2 ozs.
Citric Acid	.. 60 grs.	Water to	.. 20 ozs.
Bromide Ammonium ..	20 grs.		
Water to	.. 20 ozs.		

To develop, take equal parts of each

These plates can also be had coated upon fine ground glass.

OPAL PLATES.
"ILFORD" BROMIDE OPALS

Are prepared with the same emulsion as the Bromide Papers, and are supplied
either rapid or slow, both at the same price.

4¼ × 3¼	..	2/6 per half doz.	10 × 8 ..	8/6 per half doz.
5 ,, 4	..	3/3 ,, ,,	12 ,, 10 ..	13/- ,, ,,
6½ ,, 4¾	..	4/- ,, ,,	15 ,, 12 ..	20/- ,, ,,
8½ ,, 6½		6/6 ,, ,,	20 ,, 16 ..	34/- ,, ,,
	24 × 18	46/- per half doz.		

A piece of Bromide Paper enclosed in each box as a test for exposure.
NOTE.—When ordering Bromide Paper or Opals, please state whether the Rapid
or Slow kind is required.

DEVELOPER.

No. 1.	No. 2.
Neutral Oxalate Potash, 1 lb., avoirdupois.	Sulphate Iron, 1 lb., avoirdupois.
Warm Water .. 64 ounces	Warm Water 48 ounces
Bromide Ammonium 20 grains	Citric Acid ½ oz., avoirdupois.
Filter.	Filter.

For use add 1 ounce of No 2 to 5 ounces of No. 1.   Do not add No. 1 to
No. 2; this would cause a precipitate.   After development, *and without washing*,
immerse the plates in the following clearing solution for a few minutes:—

Alum .. 4 ounces, avoirdupois   Warm Water .. 80 ounces
Citric Acid 1 ounce ,,

This solution must be changed for every few plates.   Then rinse in three or
four changes of water, and fix in fresh Hypo. solution.

Hyposulphite of Soda .. 1 lb., avoirdupois   Water .. 80 ounces

MORGAN'S ARGENTIC BROMIDE MATT
SURFACE OPAL PLATES.

For Enlarging or Printing direct from the Negative.   Including a small sheet of
Argentic Paper for trial exposure with every plate.

Size of Plate.	6 in Box.	3 in Box.	Size of Plate.	6 in Box.	3 in Box.
4¼ × 3¼	2/6	—	10 × 8	8/6	4/10
6½ ,, 4¾	4/-	2/3	12 ,, 10	13/-	7/-
8½ ,, 6½	6/10	4/-	15 ,, 12	20/-	11/-

FOR USE WITH ABOVE.

MORGAN & KIDD'S FERROUS OXALATE DEVELOPER.
25 ozs. in two solutions, 2/-; 50 ozs., 3/·; 100 ozs., 5/-.

SPECIAL DEVELOPERS.
ECLIPSE DEVELOPER
FOR INSTANTANEOUS PLATES.

In two bottles of equal quantities of each concentrated solution, with directions for use.   4-oz. sample, 1/-; ½-pt., 1/9; per pt., 3/-; per qt., 5/6.

EASTMAN PYRO DEVELOPER.

For Bromide Paper, etc.   5-oz., 1/6; 10-oz., 2/6; 20-oz., 4/-

EASTMAN FERROUS OXALATE DEVELOPER,

For Eastman Negative Paper-Bromide.
Enlarging and contact printing paper, etc.   In two solutions:—
10-oz., 1/-; 20-oz., 1/9; 40-oz., 3/-

BEACH'S POTASH DEVELOPER.

Price: ½-pt., 1/9; per pt., 3/-; per qt., 5/6.   In two bottles of equal quantities of
each solution.

EDWARDS'S PYRO AND GLYCERINE DEVELOPER.

(Improved Formula.)

THIS Developer is supplied in a concentrated form in two solutions. It is always ready for use, and will keep for years in any climate. It is very economical, and is largely used by professional and amateur Photographers at home and abroad. For export it is preferred to dry pyro on account of its superior keeping qualities.

"The best of all alkaline developers."—Vide *Photographic News.*

Price: Two 8-oz. bottles in case, 3/- net, to make 13 pints of Developer; Free by post, 3/6; Half-pound ditto, 2/-

EDWARDS'S XL POTASH AND PYRO DEVELOPER.

IS made in concentrated form from the purest chemicals, and will keep in good condition any length of time. It combines all the advantages obtained by the use of fixed Alkaline Salts in combination with Pyrogallic Acid, and will be found invaluable for quick portraits of children and instantaneous views, for producing the most perfect portrait or landscape negatives without risk of failure.

Price: Two 8-oz. bottles in case, 2/- net, sufficient to make 6½ pints of Developer. Free by parcels post, 2/6.

EDWARD'S HYDROKINONE DEVELOPER.

FOR NEGATIVE WORK.

THIS Developer is supplied in two concentrated solutions. It does not stain the fingers or fog the plate, it will suit any plate, and will keep its good qualities for any length of time. The mixed Developer may be used for several plates. Price: Two 8-oz. bottles in case, 2/6; free by post, 3/-; Half-pound ditto, 1/6; post free, 2/-.

EDWARDS'S XL IRON DEVELOPER.

For Dry-Plate Negatives and Gelatino-Chloride Transparencies.

THE above is acknowledged to be the best and most reliable form of Ferrous Oxalate Developer for Negatives, and by simply diluting with water it produces the most exquisite Tones on Chloride Plates for Lantern Slides and Transparencies.

Price: Two 8-oz. bottles in case, 1/6 net; Free by post, 2/-.

EDWARDS'S XL INTENSIFIER.

(New Formula.)
For Gelatine Negatives and Transparencies.

BY means of the above the thinnest negatives can be readily brought to full printing density. It is also the best Intensifier for Transparencies and Lantern Slides on Gelatino-Chloride and special Transparency Plates. The results have been proved to be absolutely permanent.

Price: Two 8-oz. bottles in case, 2/6 net, post free, 3/-; Half-size, 1/6, post free, 2/-.

EDWARDS'S XL CLEARING SOLUTION.

For Pyro-developed Negatives and Gelatino-Chloride Transparencies.

THIS new preparation will be found an invaluable aid in producing brilliant and permanent negatives and transparent positives. It instantly and completely clears away the yellow stain in alkaline Pyro development, and entirely prevents any subsequent deterioration in colour or density.

Price: Two 8-oz. bottles in case, 1/6 net; post free, 2/-.

EDWARDS'S PYRO RE-DEVELOPER.

For Intensifying Gelatine Negatives before Fixing.

BY the use of this new Re-Developer the latitude allowable in exposure is enormously increased. Good Printing Negatives may be made from Plates which have received eight or ten times the correct exposure.
Price (with instructions for use) Two 8-oz. bottles in case, 2/6 net ; post free 3/- ; Half-size, 1/6 ; post free, 2/-

EDWARD'S XL SPECIAL TRANSPARENCY DEVELOPER.

FOR LANTERN SLIDES AND TRANSPARENCIES.

BY means of this new developer the most Perfect Transparencies can be obtained on suitable dry plates with the greatest facility. It is the only Developer yet discovered which will produce (on rapid gelatine plates) lantern slides of the highest class, with rich warm tones and perfectly clear glass in the highest lights.
Price (with Instructions for use) : Two 8-oz. bottles in case, 2/6 net ; post free, 3/-; Half size, 1/6 ; post free, 2/-

EDWARDS'S HYDROKINONE TRANSPARENCY DEVELOPER.

FOR LANTERN SLIDES, TRANSPARENCIES, AND REPRODUCTIONS IN BLACK AND WHITE.

BY the use of this Developer and our Special Transparency Plates, splendid Lantern slides with engraving black tones and absolute bare glass in the high lights may be obtained with the greatest ease. It is the only Developer which will give on Dry Plates suitable negatives for Photo-Lithography.
Price : Two 8-oz. Bottles in case, 2/6 ; post free, 3/- Half-pound Bottle in case, 1/6 ; post free, 2/-

ILFORD DEVELOPERS.

For Alpha Paper or Plates,
,, Bromide ,,
Universal Hydrokinone.

LOCKYER'S CONCENTRATED HYDRO-QUINONE DEVELOPER.

THIS new Developer will be found to give a decided black and white negative, without any yellow tinge, often found when "Pyro" has been used. The plates do not require to be soaked in water before development, neither is the alum bath required afterwards. For transparencies it is especially adapted. It will suit any kind of plate, and will be found invaluable in case of under exposure. It is very economical, as one portion will develop five or six plates without discolouration. Full directions are given for either under or over exposure. Bromide Paper, Films, and Opals, may be developed in the same way as plates.
Sold in Bottles, 1/3 and 2/-.   2/- size, post free, 2/6.

THOMAS'S HYDROKINONE SODA DEVELOPER.

IN two solutions, used as supplied for under exposures, or when at a temperature of 60° F. When warmer, or for over exposure, dilute with equal quantity of water.
Full instructions with each box.
Price, 2 pint Bottles in case, 3/-.

DEVELOPERS FOR TOURISTS.

DEVELOPER TONDEUR.

Concentrated Hydrokinone and Eosine, supplied in Packets sufficient to make a quart.

PRICE WITH INSTRUCTIONS, 3/-

MODE OF USING.

To prepare the Developer take an empty bottle which will hold a quart (40 ozs.) and put into it :—

1st.—The Carbonate (rose).
2nd.—The Sulphite (white).
3rd.—The Hydrokinone contained in the small box.
4th.—Fill with distilled water.

Shake for several minutes until completely dissolved. The Developer is ready for use not requiring any addition, and it will keep some months without alteration.

OLD DEVELOPER.

Do not return the used Developer into the bottle containing that which has not been used, but take a second bottle and preserve it for future use as indicated; in using the Developer composed of part old and part new, the best results are secured; the following may give a good idea.

TAKE FOR
- *Over-exposed negatives* . The old Developer only.
- *Instantaneous* .. .. Three-parts new and one old.
- *Under exposure* .. .. Half of each old and new
- *Unknown* .. .. .. Take the old Developer, but if the details are slow in appearing, continue to develop with the new solution alone.

GRAPHOL DEVELOPER.

An eikonogen Developer supplied in tins sufficient for 35 ozs. of solution, price 3/- per tin.

This Developer can also be made up as required for immediate use only, the proportion being 6 parts Graphol to 100 of water. The rapidity with which the image appears is dependent upon the proportion of powder to the water. See *British Journal of Photography*, 19th December, 1890.

THE advantages of Developing Powders of the above natures, more especially to the tourist or travelling photographer, need not be descanted on, as they are sufficiently obvious.

PLATINOTYPE CO.'S SOLUTIONS, &c.

SULPHO-PYROGALLOL
2/2.

PERFECT INTENSIFIER
3/6.

PERFECT REDUCER
2/6.

CELLULOID FILMS.

EASTMAN'S TRANSPARENT FILMS.

PATENTS APPLIED FOR.

CUT SHEETS.

Size.			Per Pkg.	Size.			Per Pkg.
3¼ × 4¼—2 dozen package	..	3/9		6½ × 8½—2 dozen package	..	15/-
4 ,, 5	,,	,,	.. 5/6	8 ,, 10	,,	,,	.. 22/6
4¾ ,, 6½	,,	,,	.. 8/6	FRENCH and GERMAN SIZES.
5 ,, 7	,,	,,	.. 10/-	9 × 12cm —2 dozen package	4/6
5 ,, 7½	,,	,,	.. 11/-	13 ,, 18 ,,	,,	,,	10/-
5 ,, 8	,,	,,	.. 11/6	18 ,, 24 ,,	,,	,,	18/6

PATENT *SPOOLS*, TO FIT THE EASTMAN-WALKER ROLL HOLDER.

Size.					Price.
3¼-inch, for 24 3¼ × 4¼ Exposures ..	..	..	..	..	4/-
4 ,, ,, 4 ,, 5 ,,	..	..	..	..	6/6
4½ ,, ,, 4½ ,, 6½ ,,	..	..	..	..	8/6
4¾ ,, ,, 4¾ ,, 6½ ,,	..	..	..	..	9/6
5 ,, ,, 5 ,, 8 ,, (or 26·5 × 7½)	..	..	..	12/6
6½ ,, ,, 6½ ,, 8½ ,,	..	..	..	..	16/6
8 ,, ,, 8 ,, 10 ,,	..	..	..	..	25/-

SPOOLS FOR FRENCH AND GERMAN SIZES.

Size.					Price.
9-cm., for 24 Exposures, 9 × 12-cm.	..	..	..	..	5/-
13 ,, ,, 27 ,, 13 ,, 18 ,,	..	..	..	..	12/6
18 ,, ,, 24 ,, 18 ,, 24 ,,	..	..	..	..	20/-

Spools of 48 Exposures at double the above prices.

Eastman's Developer Powders per package of 12 (sufficient for 48 ounces of developer), 2/6.

DIRECTIONS FOR DEVELOPING EASTMAN'S TRANSPARENT FILMS.

NOTICE—No STRIPPING.—These Films are to be developed, fixed and washed in precisely the same manner as a glass plate.

FORMULA.

PYROGALLIC ACID SOLUTION.		SODA SOLUTION.	
Pyrogallic Acid	½ oz.	Sulphite of Soda (crystals)	6 ozs.
Nitrous or Sulphuric Acid	20 min.	Carbonate of Soda ,,	4 ,,
Water	32 ozs.	Water	32 ,,

To Develop, take—

Pyro Solution 1 oz.   Soda Solution 1 oz.   Water .. 2 ozs.

Other approved developer formulæ will work with these Films, but the above is recommended as reliable.

Two Films can be developed at one time by keeping them back to back in the developer.

EASTMAN'S DEVELOPER POWDERS.—One package containing 12 powders, sufficient for three pints of Developer—can be substituted for the above. Price 2/6 per packet.

If any difficulty is met with in development with other formulæ, always try the above before complaining to the manufacturers.

RESTRAINER.

Bromide of Potash   ..   1 oz.   Water   ..   ..   .. 6 ozs
Restrainer is to be used only in case of over-exposure.

As soon as developed, rinse slightly, and transfer to a saturated solution of common Alum for two minutes, then rinse again and fix.

FIXING SOLUTION.

Hyposulphite Soda   ..   4 ozs.   Water   ..   ..   .. 16 ozs.

If a number of Films are fixed together in one tray, they should be put in *face down*, to avoid scratching or cutting the sensitive side by contact of the sharp corners.

After fixing, *wash thoroughly;* then immerse for one minute in the

SOAKING SOLUTION.

Methylated Spirit 16 ozs.   Water   ..   16 ozs.   Glycerine   ..   ½ oz.

Remove from the Soaking Solution, and pin up each Film by the corners to dry spontaneously.

A good way to dry these negatives is to pin them by two corners to the edge of a shelf and then to pin the lower corners to a light strip of wood.   Any tear drops of the Soaking Solution should be removed with a bit of blotting paper or absorbent cotton.   When the negative is thoroughly dry, *wipe off the back with a soft cloth*.

The object of the Soaking Solution is to prevent the Film from curling when dry.   The negative must *not* be rinsed after the Soaking Solution.

Always keep finished negatives flat—*do not roll them up*.

CARBUTT'S FLEXIBLE NEGATIVE FILMS.

"B" Landscape, Sen. 16.   Orthochromatic, Sen. 23.   "Special," 23 to 25 Sen.   "Eclipse," Sen. 27

3¼ × 4¼	..	..	..	5½ × 7	..	..	..
4 ,, 5	..	..	..	5 ,, 8	..	..	..
4¼ ,, 6½	..	..	..	6½ ,, 8½	..	..	..
4¾ ,, 6½	..	..	..	8 ,, 10	..	..	..
5 ,, 7	..	..	..	10 ,, 12	..	..	..
5 ,, 7½	..	..	..	11 ,, 14	..	..	..

DEVELOPER.

No. 1 PYRO STOCK SOLUTION.

Distilled or Ice Water   ..   ..   10 OZ.
Sulphuric Acid..   ..   ..   1 dr.
Sulphite of Soda, Crystals   ..   ..   4 oz.
Then add Schering's Pyro 1 ounce, and Water to make 16 fluid ounces.

No. 2 STOCK SODA SOLUTION.

Water   ..   ..   10 OZ.
Soda Sulphite Crystals   ..   ..   2 ,,
Soda Carbonate Crystals (or. dry gran. 1 oz.)   ..   ..   2 ,,
Potash Carbonate   ..   ..   1 ,,
Dissolve and add water to make measure 16 fluid ounces.

No. 3 BROMIDE SOLUTION.

Bromide of Sodium or Potassium ½ ounce ; Water, 5 ounces.

FOR USE.—Dilute 1 ounce of Stock No. 2 with 7 ounces of water for cold weather, and 10 to 12 of water in Summer.   To three ounces of dilute No. 2 add 1½ to 2½ dracmhms of No. 1.

ENGLAND'S FILMS.

$4\frac{1}{4} \times 3\frac{1}{4}$	..	..	1/10	$7\frac{1}{2} \times 5$	..	..	6/-
5 ,, 4		..	3/-	$8\frac{1}{2}$,, $6\frac{1}{2}$	..	..	7/6
$6\frac{1}{2}$,, $4\frac{3}{4}$	..	..	4/-	10 ,, 8	..	..	11/6

Developer as for Plates.   Hydroquinone will also give perfect results with
hese Films.

FITCH'S IMPROVED XYLONITE FILMS.

NEGATIVE FILMS. Any rapidity:—

		$\frac{1}{4}$	5×4	$\frac{1}{2}$	$7\frac{1}{2} \times 5$	$8\frac{1}{2} \times 6\frac{1}{2}$	10×8	
Thin	..	1/9	3/-	4/-	6/-	7/-	12/-	per Dozen.
Thick	..	3/6	4/6	8/-	12/-	14/-	18/-	,,

PYRO DEVELOPER.

Water ..	..	..	..	..	..	..	10 ozs.
Bromide Ammonium ..	..	..	..	..	..	30 grs.
Ammonia ·880 ..	..	..	..	..	..	60 mins.

To each ounce of above add for use 1 or 2 grains dry Pyro.

Usual fresh Hypo fixing.

FITCH'S IMPROVED POSITIVE IVORY FILMS.

MATT AND POLISHED SURFACES.

For Printing out by development. An advance on Opal Plates. Flexible,
unbreakable, and giving superb results, equal to Ivory miniatures. Expose 6 to
10 seconds 4 feet from gas flame.

PRICE—White or Colored.

		$\frac{1}{4}$	$3\frac{3}{4} \times 4\frac{3}{4}$	$\frac{1}{2}$	$1\frac{1}{2} \times 6\frac{1}{2}$	10×8.	
Thick	..	..	3/-	3/6	6/6	12/-	17/-	per Dozen.
Thin	..	..	2/3	2/6	5/-	7/6	14/6	,,

(White only)

IRON DEVELOPER.

NO. 1 SATURATED SOLUTION.	NO. 2 SATURATED SOLUTION.
Oxalate Potash,	Proto Sulphate of Iron,
Acetic Acid sufficient to make the	Acetic Acid sufficient to make the
Solution Acid to Litmus Paper.	Solution Acid to Litmus Paper.

Use Eight parts No. 1 to One part No. 2, and add 3 or 4 drops of a 10 per
cent. Solution of Bromide of Potassium to each ounce. Usual fresh Hypo
fixing.

ALSO

HYDROKINONE DEVELOPER.

Suitable for both negative and positive Films.

Hydrokinone ..	..	..	..	..	..	..	5 grains
Carbonate of Potash, pure Anhydrous	..	..	..	15 ,,
Sulphite of Soda	..	..	..	..	..	20 ,,
Distilled Water	..	..	..	..	..	1 oz.

Add to each oz. of above 3 to 4 drops 10 per cent. Solution Bromide o
Potassium. Usual fresh Hypo fixing. Film carriers for cut sizes.

PURE PHOTOGRAPHIC CHEMICALS
AND PREPARATIONS.

		£	s.	d.
Acid, acetic glacial, solid at 50° (variable) .. .. oz., 2d. ; lb.		0	1	0
In Winchester quarts containing 6lbs., 11d. per lb.				
Ditto, citric, pure (variable) .. .. oz., 3d. ; lb.		0	2	3
Ditto, hydrochloric, pure (sp. gr. 1·195) .. .. oz., 1d. ; lb.		0	0	6
Ditto, nitric (sp. gr. 1·450) .. .. oz., 1d. ; lb.		0	1	0
Ditto. pyrogallic, Schering's finest resublimed, 1 oz. bottles, 1/ ;				
1 dozen		0	11	6
Ditto, sulphuric, pure .. .. oz., 1d. ; lb.		0	0	6
Ditto, sulphurous .. .. oz., 1d. ; lb.		0	0	4
Ditto, tannic, pure, soluble, clear solution .. .. oz., 3d. ; lb.		0	2	6
Alcohol, pure, (sp. gr. ·830) .. .. oz., 3d. ; pint		0	3	6
Ditto, absolute (sp. gr. ·795) .. .. .. oz., 4d. ; pint		0	4	6
Ditto, methylated, 62 o.p. .. .. per pint, 6d. ; per gallon		0	3	0
Alum, powdered .. .. per lb, 2d. ; 7 lbs.		0	1	0
Ditto, chrome, pure, recrystallized .. .. .. oz., 1d ; lb.		0	0	6
Ammonia, liquid (sp. gr. ·880', pure .. .. oz., 1d. ; pint		0	0	7
Ammonium, bichromate .. .. oz., 4d. ; lb.		0	3	9
Ditto, bromide .. .. oz., 3d. ; lb.		0	2	9
Ditto, carbonate .. .. oz., 2d. ; lb.		0	1	0
Ditto, chloride, pure .. .. oz., 2d. ; lb.		0	1	0
Ditto, iodide, pure .. .. oz., 1/6 ; lb.		1	1	0
Ditto, nitrate .. .. oz., 2d. ; lb.		0	1	3
Ditto, sulphocyanide, pure .. .. .. oz., 3d. ; lb.		0	2	9
Barium, chloride, pure .. .. oz., 1d. ; lb.		0	0	6
Baryta, nitrate, pure .. .. oz., 1d. ; lb.		0	0	7
Ditto, sulphate .. .. oz., 1d. ; lb.		0	0	4
Benzole, pure, rectified, No. 1 .. .. .. oz., 3d. ; pint		0	2	0
Borax (powdered) .. .. oz., 2d. ; lb.		0	1	0
Calcium, chloride, pure .. .. oz., 1d. ; lb.		0	0	7
Camphor .. .. oz., 4d. ; lb.		0	3	6
Chalk, precipitated .. .. oz., 1d. ; lb.		0	0	8
Clearing Solution, for entirely destroying all traces of Hypo left in the film, a great saving of time in washing, is also very useful for reducing the intensity of negatives :—				
In Bottles, with directions, 6d. and 1/- ; ½-pints, 2/6 ; pints		0	4	0
Collodions in bottle—				
Mawson's .. .. 2-oz., 10d. ; 5-oz.		0	2	6
Iodizer separate .. .. 10-oz., 3/8 ; 20-oz.		0	6	8
Mawson's Enamel ditto, for giving a glass-like surface to photographs .. .. 3-oz., 1/- ; ½-pint, 1/9 ; pint		0	3	0
Collodion, plain .. .. per oz.		0	0	4
Copper Nitrate, pure.. .. .. oz., 2d. ; lb.		0	1	6
Copper, sulphate, pure recrystallized .. .. oz., 1d. ; lb.		0	0	6
Cotton Wool, fine, for polishing, filtering, etc. .. oz., 3d. ; lb.		0	2	3
Developers, various				
Dextrine, best, for mounting photographs, etc. .. oz., 1d, ; lb.		0	0	8

	£	s	d
Eikonogen, Dr. Andresen's .. .. 1/3 per oz.; per $\frac{1}{10}$ kilo ..	0	3	0
Encaustic Cerate, or Diamond Paste, for giving an enamel-like surface to photos, with directions .. .. per pot	0	1	0
Ether, sulphuric, methylated (sp. gr. ·785) .. oz., 2d.; pint	0	1	6
Ferrous Oxalate .. .. oz., 2d.; lb.	0	1	9
Gelatine, French, best .. .. oz., 2d.; lb.	0	1	0
Ditto, Nelson's .. .. .. No. 1, per oz., 4d.; 1-lb. packet	0	4	6
„ „ .. .. .. No. 2, „ 3d.; „	0	4	0
Ditto, Coignet's gold label .. .. oz., 3d.; lb.	0	3	9
Ditto. Heinrich's .. .. oz., 4d.; lb.	0	4	0
Ditto. Simeon's .. .. per lb.	0	5	0
Glycerine, pure (sp. gr. 1·250) .. $\frac{1}{2}$-lb. bottle, 1/-; 1-lb. ditto	0	1	6
Gold, chloride, in sealed capsules (Johnson's only), containing one-half pure metal, the purest article that can be manufactured : –			
7$\frac{1}{2}$ grains, 1/-; 15 grains, 1/9; 30 grains, 3/6; 60 grains	0	7	0
Per doz., 15 grains, 19/6; 30 grains, 39/-; 60 grains	3	18	0
Ditto, chloride (Shew's) .. 8 grains, in solution, in 1 oz. bottles	0	1	0
Gold Toning Bath, alkaline, 1-pint bottle ready prepared, containing sufficient chloride of gold to tone 8 sheets of paper, 1/6; $\frac{1}{2}$-pint	0	1	0
Gun Cotton .. .. per oz.	0	1	4
Hydrokinone, pure .. .. 1-oz. bottles, 1/1 4-oz., 3/6; 8-oz.	0	6	9
India Rubber Solution .. .. per bottle	0	1	0
Iron. perchloride .. .. per oz.	0	0	3
Ditto, sulphate, pure .. .. 1-lb., 2d.; 7-lb.	0	1	0
Labels, plain, gummed .. .. per 100	0	0	6
Ditto, books of .. .. 6d. and	0	1	0
Lead, acetate of .. .. oz., 2d.; lb.	0	1	0
Lime, chloride of, pure .. .. oz., 1d.; lb.	0	0	6
Ditto, carbonate, pure .. .. oz., 1d.; lb.	0	0	6
Magnesium Ribbon .. .. .. oz., 2/-; $\frac{1}{2}$-lb., 15/-; lb.	1	8	6
Magnesium Powder .. .. .. oz., 1/6; $\frac{1}{2}$-lb., 11/6; lb.	1	1	0
Mounting Medium (Shew's), warranted not to cockle or warp the mount, in bottles, with directions for use, 6d. and 1/-; pint bottle	0	2	0
Non Actinine (Beale's patent), for adding clouds, blocking out portions and strengthening negatives in parts, with full directions per bottle, 6d., 1/- and	0	2	6
Paraffin, solid white .. .. oz., 2d.; lb.	0	1	9
Platinum, chloride of, for the French toning; the 15-grain capsule	0	1	0
Potash, bichromate, pure .. .. oz., 1d.; lb.	0	0	9
Ditto, carbonate .. .. oz., 1d.; lb.	0	0	8
Ditto, ditto, chemically pure .. in bottle, per $\frac{1}{2}$-lb. 1/6; lb.	0	2	9
Ditto, chlorate, pure .. .. oz., 1d.; lb.	0	0	8
Ditto, caustic sticks .. .. oz., 2d.; lb.	0	1	6
Ditto, metabisulphite .. .. oz., 3d.; lb.	0	3	6
Ditto, nitrate, best .. .. oz., 2d.; lb.	0	0	9
Ditto, oxalate, neutral .. .. oz., 1d.; lb.	0	0	9
Potassium, bromide .. .. oz., 3d.; lb.	0	2	0
Ditto, chloride, pure .. .. oz., 2d.; lb.	0	1	0
Ditto, citrate .. .. oz., 3d.; lb.	0	3	6
Ditto, hydrate .. .. oz., 2d.; lb.	0	1	6
Ditto, iodide, pure .. .. oz., 1/2; lb.	0	15	0
Ditto, sulphide, in small pieces .. .. .. $\frac{1}{2}$-lb., 8d., 1-lb.	0	1	6

Ruby Liquid, for coating dark room windows, etc.	per bottle	0	1	0
Schleppes Salts	oz., 6d.; lb.	0	5	0
Silver Nitrate of, pure, recrystallized, 10-oz. at 2/10	per oz.	0	3	0
Ditto, triple crystallized, in amber coloured, stoppered bottles	2-oz., 8/-; 4-oz.,	0	16	0
Soda, Acetate, pure, recrystallized	oz., 1d.; lb.	0	0	7
Ditto, carbonate, crystal	oz., 1d.; lb.	0	0	5
Ditto, bi-carbonate, chemically pure	½-lb., 7d.; lb. bottle	0	1	0
Ditto, caustic, pure, hydrate sticks	oz., 2d.; lb.	0	1	6
Ditto, hyposulphite, in cask containing 1 cwt.		0	8	6
Ditto, ditto, pure English, selected quality	1 cwt.	0	10	6
	28-lbs, 2/9; 14-lbs., 1/6; 7-lbs,, 10d.; 1-lb.	0	0	2
Ditto, nitrate, pure	oz., 2d.; lb.	0	1	0
Ditto, phosphate	oz., 2d.; lb.	0	1	0
Ditto, sulphate	oz., 1d.; lb.	0	0	4
Ditto, sulphite, pure, recrystallized	oz., 2d.; lb.	0	1	3
Ditto, tungstate	oz., 2d.; lb.	0	1	0
Sodium, chloride, pure	oz., 1d.; lb.	0	1	4
Talc in fine powder, for retouching, etc.	oz., 1d.; lb.	0	0	8
Varnish Collodion	5-oz. bottle, 1/-; ½-pint, 1/9; 1-pint	0	3	0
Varnish, crystal or benzole, drying without heat, bottles, 6d. and		0	1	0
	½-pint bottle, 2/-; 1-pint ditto	0	3	6
Ditto, Mawson's Dry Plate Varnish	per bot., 1/-; ½-pt., 1/4; pt.	0	2	6
Ditto, Mawson's hard	per bottle, 1/-; pint	0	3	0
Ditto, Mawson's Orange Varnish, for blocking out actinic light, backing dry plates, etc., etc.	per bottle, 1/- and	0	2	6
Ditto, Mawson's Matt	per bottle, 1/- and	0	2	6
Ditto, Bate's dead black	in bottles, 5d. and	0	0	10

The preceding prices are for Chemicals of the purest quality only, and are subject to the fluctuations of the market.

FITTINGS FOR CAMERAS.

CAMERA BELLOWS.

PARALLEL.

Outside Size of Back.	Pull Inches.	Leather.	Cloth.	Outside. Size of Back.	Pull Inches.	Leather.	Cloth.
5 × 5	8	3/-	2/3	9¾ × 9¾	22	10/-	7/-
7¼ ,, 5¾	10	4/-	3/-	11¾ ,, 11¾	17	11/9	6/9
7¾ ,, 7¾	12	9/-	3/9	11¾ ,, 11¾	24	12/6	7/9
7¾ ,, 7¾	18	7/-	4/6	13¾ ,, 13¾	19	12/9	8/9
9¾ ,, 9¾	15	8/6	5/-	13¾ ,, 13¾	28	18/-	12/-
9¾ ,, 9¾	18	9/-	5/6	16¾ ,, 16¾	32	28/-	20/-

CONICAL.

Size of Plate.	Outside Size of Back.	Outside Size of Front.	Pull Inches.	Price in Leather.	Price in Cloth.
¼ plate	5 × 5	3 × 3	6½	3/6	2/6
½ ,,	7¾ ,, 7¾	3½ ,, 3½	9	6/-	4/6
½ ,,	7¾ ,, 7¾	4 ,, 4	14	9/-	5/6
½ ,,	7¾ ,, 7¾	4 ,, 4	16	9/-	5/9
Whole plate	9¾ ,, 9¾	5 ,, 5	15	10/6	6/-
,, ,,	9¾ ,, 9¾	5 ,, 5	18	11/6	6/6
10 × 8	11¾ , 11¾	6 ,, 6	17	13/6	8/6
10 ,, 8	11¾ ,, 11¾	6 ,, 6	24	16/-	10/-
12 ,, 10	13¾ ,, 13¾	7 ,, 7	19	15/6	9/6
12 ,, 10	13¾ ,, 13¾	7 ,, 7	28	20/-	14/-
15 ,, 12	16½ ,, 16½	7½ ,, 7½	32	30/-	22/-

CAMERA FITTINGS.

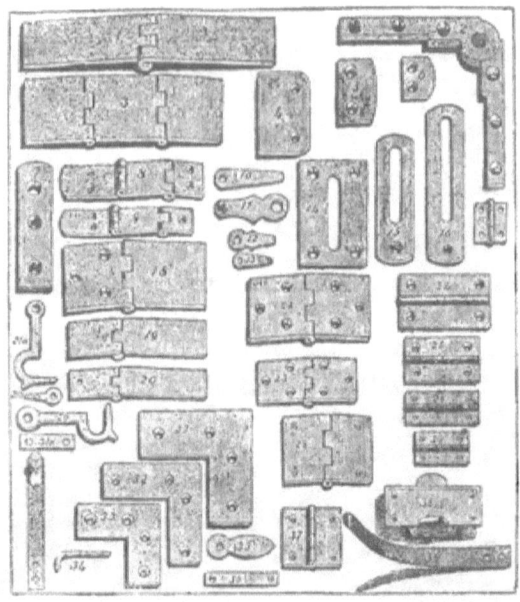

	Per Pair.	Each.
No. 1 Stout, Strong Hinge, for Base Board	6d.	
1A Very Strong and Stout	9d.	
1B ,, ,, ...	1/-	
2 Rule Joint for side of Base Board of Long Focus Cameras	10d.	
2A Hand-made, very neat	1/-	
3 Double Hinge, for Focussing Screen, 12 × 10, 10 × 8 ditto		
No. 1 Joint to Join, 1 in , No. 1A Joint to Join, 1½ in ...	Unfinished 8d.	
1B ,, 1⅜ in. 1C ,, 1¹¹⁄₁₆ in...		
4 Stop Plates, for Reversible Frames, &c.	1½d	
5 ,, 1d. per pair. 6 ditto 1d. per pair.		
7 Eyes for Tripod Legs	2d	
8 Double Hinges for Focussing Screen, 8½ × 6½ Cameras	9d. (finished)	
9 ,, ,, , 6¼ × 4¾ ,,	9d.	
10 Turn Button, light burnished	1½d.	
11 ,, Stout ,, ...	1½d.	
12 ,, ,, Small	1¼d.	
13 ,, Light ,, for Dark Slides ..	1d.	
14 Slot Plates for Rising Fronts, in rough	2d. finished 4d:	
15 ,, Swing Back, highly finished ..	4d.	
16 ,, ,, ,, ..	5d.	
17 Hinge for Small Dark Slides	1d.	
18 Bank Back Flap for Focussing Screen, rough ..	2d.	

CAMERA FITTINGS.

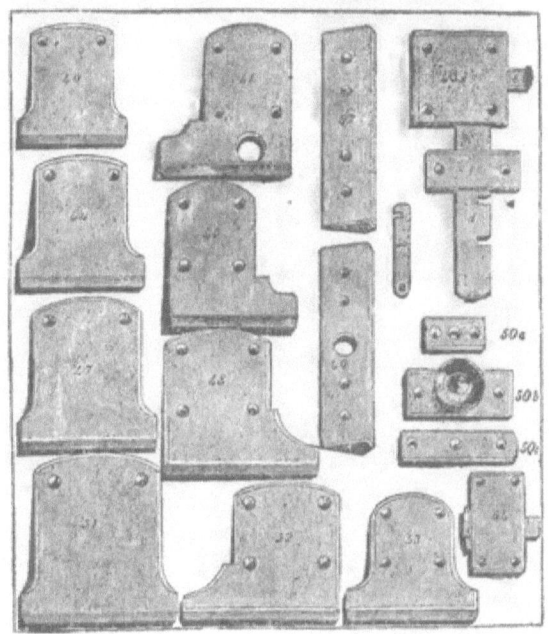

No.		Per Pair	Each.
18A 1 in. one side of Knuckle, and 2 in. the other (burnished) 8d			
19 Clips for Binding Double Dark Slides ,, ..		2d	
20 ,, Small ,, ...		2d	
21A 21B Hooks and Eye for Plate Boxes		1d	
22 Back Flap for Wing of Camera		2½d.	
23 ,, for Shutters of Dark Slides		2d	
24 1¼ Butt Hinge, burnished		2½d.	
25 1 in Butt Hinge for Bottom of Double Slide ..		1d	
26 Hook and Eye		1d.	
27 Angle for Brass Binding		3½d	
28 Wide Butt Hinge		1½d.	
29 Narrow Polished Butt		2d	
30 ,, Dipped		1d	
31A 31B Steel Spring Catch for Shutters of Dark Slides and Plate		8d	
32 Angle for Brass Binding Corners of Slides ..			1½d.
33 ,, ,, ,, ,, ..			1½d.
33A Much Narrower ,, ...		1½d	
34 Turn Pin for holding Shutters in Slide, Improved shape		1½d.	
35 Turn Button		1d.	
36 Plate for fixing Focussing Glass in Frame ..		2d	
37 ¾ Butt Dipped..		1d	

CAMERA FITTINGS.

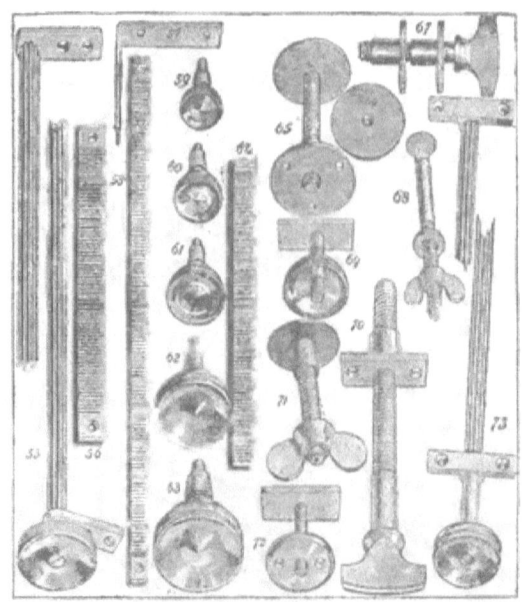

No.								Per Pair.	Each
38	Spring Catch, highly finished		..	..	..		•		1/-
39	Spring for Single Dark Slide		..	..	..				1½d
40	Guide Plate for Travelling Part of Camera, bevelled edges, highly finished				..	..			10d.
41	,, ,, shaped, bevelled edges, highly finished							1/-	
42	,, ,, for Double Swing Back				,,			10d.	
ABC 43	Slide Swing Set, bevelled edges				,,				2/3
43A	With Rack Work both Sides of Camera, per set 6/6								
43B	Complete Set with 4 No. 16, 4 Plates, 4 No. 59, which gives double swing to Camera Complete 4/3								
44	As No. 40, highly finished	..	..	..	..			9d.	
45	As No. 41	,,	..	..	..	..		1/-	
46	Small Finished Turn Hook ..		..	..	..				2½d.
47	As No. 40, bevelled edges	..	..	..	..			10d.	
48	,, 41	,,	..	..	..	..		1/2	
49	,, 42	,,	..	..	..	..		10d.	
ABC 50	Wing Screw, complete, 9d., 10d., and 1/- each.								
51	As No. 40, bevelled edges	..	..	..	..			1/2	
52	,, 48	,,	..	..	..	..		1/2	
53	,, 40	,,	..	..	..	..		9d.	
54	,, 38, narrow bolt, bevelled edges		..	..					1/

CAMERA FITTINGS.

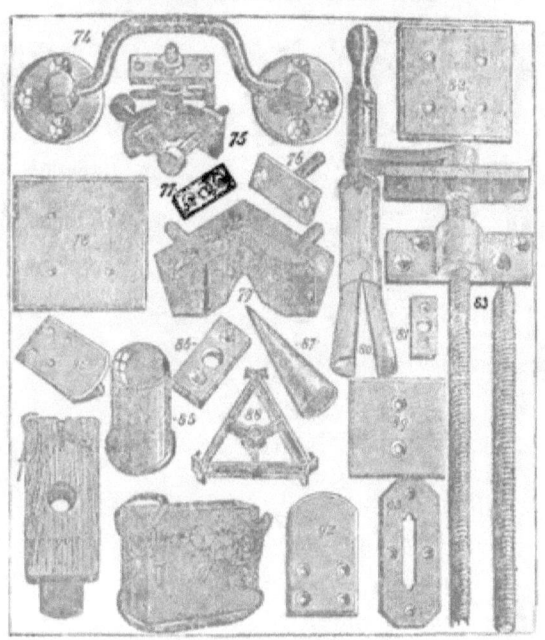

No.		Per Pair.	Each.
55 Pinion with End Bearings, for 1/1 Camera Pinion 9½, Rack 13 inch		6/6	
,, for ½ plate, Pinion 7½ in., Rack 11 in.		5/-	
,, for ¼ ,, ,, 6 ,, ,, 9½ ,,		4/-	
56 Machine Cut Rack, 1/6 per foot (single)			
57 Corner for Brass Binding Cameras			2d.
57A, 2d. ; 57B, 2½d. ; 57C, 3d. each			
59 Front Screws and Nuts, ½ in.			4d.
60 ,, ,, ⅝ ,,			4d.
61 ,, ,, ¾ ,,			5d
62 ,, ,, 1 ,,			6d.
63 Fronts Screws and Nuts 1⅛ ,,			8d.
64 As 56			
65 Bolt and Nut for Clamping Double Swing			1/-
66 Washer..			1d.
67 T Bolt and 2 Nuts for Wing and Base Board			9d.
67A ,, 1 ,, ,, ,,			6d.
68 Bolt Washer and Fly Nut for Sliding Stands, 2¼ in.			3½d.
68A ,, ,, ,, 2¾ in.			4½d.
69 Bolt and Milled Head			4d.
70 Large T Bolt and Nut for Studio Stand			1/4
71 Bolt and Nut for Tripod Head			8d.
72 As 65			10d.
73 Same Prices as 55			

CAMERA FITTINGS.

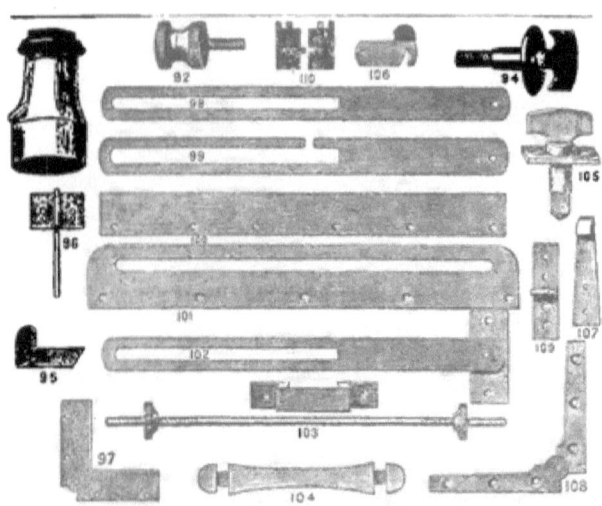

No.		Per Pair.	Each.
74	Handle for Bath Cases, &c., 4d., 8d., 10d. and 1/-		
75	Small Metal Head and Nut for Camera Bottom ..		2/6
76 & 77	Centre and Plate for Large Back Swing Camera	5d.	
78	Plate for Sliding Stand, bevelled and finished ...		4d.
79	Plate and Pins for Fixing to under side of Table Stand, per set of 3		2/6
80	Water Clip for Developing Tent		1/-
81 & 84	Outside Centre and Plate for Swing Back, best finish	1/2	
82	As 78		3½d.
83	Winch Screw Nut and Plate, and Folding Handle 1/- per in. complete		
84	As 81	1/6	
85	Lense for Finder or Focussing Eye Piece ..		9d.
88	Triangle Heads & Bolts		

Ins. 4   5   6   8   10   12
88 Triangle Heads & Bolts 2/6 2/9 3/- 5/- 7/- 13/-

89	As 78		3d.
90	Small Drop Shutter, from		3/-
93	Spirit Level and Plate, 4d. per inch. ..		
86 & 92	As 81	1/6	
97	Iron Toe for Tripod Legs		1½d.

LANTERN SLIDE REQUISITES.

BINDING MATERIALS.

HUGHES' PATENT METALLIC BINDINGS.

Of metal, forming a binder and preserver in one, per gross 18/, per doz,   1/6

,, ,, of paper, black, well gummed, of the same shape as above, cleanly cut, per 100 1/6, per dozen   ..   ..   3d.

Hughes' Patent Clamping Frame for holding the slides, and pressing up the above bindings to the sides, enabling the operator to turn over the edges neatly and with ease, each..   ..   ..   5/6

Flattening Irons for metal binders, each 1/6

Cement for ditto, per bottle 1/-

MAT AND PRESERVER COMBINED,

For Magic Lantern Sides.

Price 12/- per gross, or 1/2 per dozen.

A Mat and Preserver combined.   No black paper mat required.   No breakage at the corners.   The apertures, round or cushion, are always in the centre of the glass.

PRESSING TOOL.

Fig. —.

Price 1/3 each.

The Pressing Tool and Cement are necessary to the production of good work.   One 1/-
bottle of Cement will, with care, do one gross o
frames.   Full directions on each box,

SPECIAL METALLIC CEMENT,

In Bottles, 6d. and 1/- each.

CLAMPS OF METAL.

For Lantern Slides.
to hold them firmly
whilst binding.

Each 1/-

Ditto, ditto, with
revolving disc, en-
abling the operator
to bind all round
the slide without
removing it from
the clamp.

Each 1/6.

Boxes for Storing and for Carrying, see page 107.

Dishes for Developing, &c., see page 103.

Eclipse Lantern Carriers, suitable for all single lanterns, sub-
   stituting one slide for another, without the slightest movement of
   the picture or the screen being observed, each £0 5 3

Frames for Transparencies, 3¼ × 3¼, plain gilt, with burnished edge
   and ring to hang, per dozen 0 1 9

Frames for Exhibition, well-made, of selected walnut, polished, with
   light moulding, for divisions, either upright or oblong form with
   side support for placing the pictures at an angle.   To contain
   6 slides each 0 6 9

   12 ,,   ,,   0 9 6

Glasses for Covering, our Speciality, colorless and very thin, free free from blemishes, per gross 8/6, per dozen	0	0	9
,, ,, best quality selected crown, extra thin, per gross 5/6, per dozen	0	0	6
,, ,, second quality crown, per gross 3/6, per dozen	0	0	4
Gummed Strips for Binding, of thin pliable paper, well coated with good adhesive gum, per box of strips sufficient to bind 50 slides	0	0	6
,, ,, Vever's of various colors, per box ..	0	0	6
Index Numbers or Circular Labels for Slides, per box of 300	0	0	6

TYLAR'S LANTERNESCOPE

(Registered)

This instrument will be found very desirable to those who wish to exhibit a few slides without the trouble of preparing the lantern for use. It is always ready and can be inclined at any angle to suit the light available.

No. 1 Papier-mache Body, with floral design, on turned wood stand, with nickel-plated fittings,
£1 1 0.

No. 2 Mahogany, best quality, on mahogany stand,
£1 5 0.

MASKS.

SHEW'S LANTERN MASKS.

Hand-cut, 100 in a box, 1/-

No. 1 Square.		No. 5 Oval.
,, 2 Circular.		,, 6 Arch Top.
,, 3 Dome.		,, 7 Assorted Shapes.
,, 4 Cushion		,, 8 Reductions, assorted. Cushion.

PHOTOGRAPHIC WORK.

FREE LESSONS

Given to Purchasers of a Complete Set of Apparatus.

LESSONS IN DEVELOPING.

Printing by the various processes, &c., &c., of one hour each, 5/-

LESSONS IN ENLARGING.

By Day, or by Artificial Light, one hour, 5/-

THE USE OF THE DARK ROOM.

We have Dark Rooms on the first floor, for the use of which
we charge as follows :—

DEVELOPING ROOMS, for one hour **2/6**

ENLARGING ROOMS, with use of Lantern, &c., &c., for
one hour **4/-**

Developers are charged extra.

FILLING ROLL HOLDERS

Or Changing Plates   ...   **1/-**

For Prices of Developing Plates or Films, Printing,
Mounting, Enlarging, and Framing, see the following pages.

DEVELOPING EXPOSED PLATES OR TRANSPARENT FILMS
(NON-STRIPPING.)

THE greatest care is taken in developing to obtain the best possible printing negatives, and customers will greatly oblige by describing the conditions under which the exposures were made, and by stating the particular make of plate or film used.

SIZE.	PRICE.	SIZE.	PRICE.
4¼ × 3¼ ..	.. 3/- per doz.	8½ × 6½ ..	.. 6/- per doz.
5 ,, 4 ..	.. 3/6 ,,	10 ,, 8 ..	.. 8/- ,,
6½ ,, 4¾ ..	.. 4/- ,,	12 ,, 10 ..	.. 12/- ,,
7½ ,, 5 ..	.. 5/- ,,	15 ,, 12 ..	.. 15/- ,,

DEVELOPING "KODAK" SPOOLS.

		per Spool of 100 (T.F.) Exposures.	For quantities of less than 50,	2/- per doz.
No. I. "KODAK"	12/6	100	,,	,,
No. II. ,,	20/-	100	,,	50, 2/6
No. III. ,,	20/.	100	,,	50, 3/-
No. III ,,	—	60	,,	40, 3/-
No. IV. ,,	30/-	100	,,	50, 3/6
No. IV. ,,	—	48	,,	48, 3/6
No. V. ,,	—	54	,,	54, 5/-
No. V. ,,	—	32	,,	32, 5/-

G

ADDITIONAL WORK TO NEGATIVES.

		C. de V. and 4¼ by 3¼.	5 by 4.	Cabinet and 6½ by 4¾.	7½ by 4½ and 7 by 5	8½ by 6½ and 8 by 5.	10 by 8 and 9 by 7.	Panel.	12 by 10 and 11 by 9.	15 by 12.
		s. d.	s. d.	s. d.	s. d.	s. d.	s. d.	s. d.	s. d.	s. d.
Intensifying	each	0 6	0 6	0 6	0 7	0 8	0 9	1 0	1 0	1 6
Reducing	,,	0 6	0 6	0 6	0 7	0 8	0 9	1 0	1 0	1 6
Varnishing	dozen	2 0	2 0	2 0	2 6	2 6	3 0	3 6	4 0	5 0
Toning	,,	0 6	0 6	1 0	1 0	2 0	2 6	2 6	3 6	5 0
Retouching ..	each	¼in. head 6d.	½in. head 8d.	¾in. head 9d.	1in. head 1/-	1¼in. head 1/2	1½in. head 1/3	1¾in. head 1/6	2in. head 1/9	2¼in. head 2/6

Blocking and Spotting to Negatives charged according to time consumed.

NOTE. Developing, Intensifying and Reducing are undertaken at the owner's risk only. The risk in Developing is reduced to a minimum by sending full details as to exposure, lens and light. Reducing is sometimes necessary to expedite orders for large numbers from dense or over developed negatives. The most extreme care is taken of negatives, &c. &c., entrusted to us, but we cannot accept any responsibility in case of accidents. Increased safety in transit may be secured by insuring parcels at the Post Office, the fee being only One Penny.

PRINTING FROM NEGATIVES.

SIZE.	SILVER & SALTED. Bright or Matt Surface. PLAIN. Less than 6.	PLAIN. per doz.	VIGNET. per doz.	ARISTOTYPE. Squeegeed. Matt or Plain. Bright.	per doz.	PLATINOTYPE. Less than 6.	per doz.	BROMIDE. Less than 6.	per doz.	CARBON. Plain per doz.	Vignette per doz.
CARTE DE VISITE ..	2d. each	1/3	1/6	2/3	3/6	3d. each	2/6	3d. each	2/-	4/6	5/-
4¼ × 3¼ ..	2d. "	1/6	1/9	2/6	3/6	3d. "	2/6	3d. "	2/3	4/6	5/-
5 " 4 ..	3d. "	1/8	2/0	3/3	4/6	4d. "	3/9	4d. "	2/9	5/6	6/-
CABINET ..	3d. "	2/0	2/6	4/6	5/6	6d. "	4/10	6d. "	4/0	6/-	7/-
6½ " 4¾ ..	4d. "	2/6	2/9	5/-	7/-	6d. "	5/0	6d. "	4/6	7/-	8/-
7½ " 5 ..	5d. "	3/6	4/0	6/9	8/6	7d. "	6/3	7d. "	5/6	8/6	9/6
8½ " 6½ ..	7d. "	5/-	5/6	8/9	11/6	9d. "	8/9	9d. "	7/6	10/-	12/-
10 " 8 ..	10d. "	7/-	7/6	13/6	15/6	1/4 "	12/6	1/2 "	9/-	12/-	14/-
12 " 10 ..	1/3 "	10/6	12/-	24/-	27/-	2/- "	18/9	1/4 "	12/-	20/-	24/-
15 " 12 ..	1/8 "	14/-	16/-	30/-	35/-	3/- "	27/6	2/6 "	20/-	30/-	35/-

"KODAK" SILVER PRINTS.

Size.	Unmounted.	Mounted. On Stout Boards.	Unmounted. For less than 50	Mounted. For less than 50.
No. I.	15/- per 100.	20/- per 100.	2/- per doz.	2/6 per doz.
No. II.	20/- per 100.	25/- per 100.	3/- per doz.	3/6 per doz.

G 2

MOUNTING.

SIZE.	On Plain Toned Mounts. per doz.	On Gold B.E. India Tint or Oxford Mounts. per doz.	On Plate Sunk India Tint. per doz.	Aristotype or Emulsion Paper Prints. Matt Surface, exclusive of Mounts. per doz.	Bright Surface, exclusive of Mounts. per doz.
C.-D.-V.	.. -/8	1/3	1/9	-/9	1/6
4¼ × 3¼ ..	.. -/8	1/3	1/9	-/9	1/6
5 ,, 4 ..	.. 1/3	1/6	2/3	-/9	2/-
5¾ ,, 4 (Cabinet)	.. 2/-	2/-	2/9	1/-	2/-
6½ ,, 4	.. 2/3	2/3	3/-	1/6	2/3
7½ ,, 5	.. 2/6	3/-	4/-	1/9	3/-
8½ ,, 6½	.. 2/6	4/-	4/6	2/6	3/6
10 ,, 8	.. 3/6	7/6	5/6	3/-	4/6
12 ,, 10	.. 5/6	9/-	7/6	4/6	6/6

BURNISHING MOUNTED PHOTOS.

Per doz. .. 4¼ × 3¼ 4d.   5 × 4 6d.   6½ × 4¾ 8d.   7½ × 5 8d.   8½ × 6½ 1/-   10 × 8 1/3

ENLARGEMENTS.

BROMIDE ENLARGEMENTS ON PAPER.

Size.	Plain Enlargement.		Spotting and Mounting Extra.		Mounting in Best Quality Cut Mounts Extra.		Finished in Black and White, Extra.						Framed in Gilt Slips. Extra.		Best Gilt Frames. Extra.	
							Good.		Better.		Best.					
	s.	d.	s.	d.	s.	d.	s.	d.	s.	d.	s.	d.	s.	d.	s.	d.
10 × 8 & 12 × 10	2	6	0	6	1	0	5	0	10	0	15	0	3	6	4	0
15 „ 12	3	6	0	9	1	0	6	0	12	0	18	0	4	6	5	6
18 „ 15	5	0	1	0	1	3	7	0	14	0	21	0	5	6	6	6
23 „ 17	6	0	1	3	1	3	7	6	15	0	22	6	6	6	7	6
24 „ 20	7	9	1	6	2	0	10	0	20	0	30	0	8	6	10	0
30 „ 22	10	6	1	9	2	6	12	6	25	0	37	6	10	6	15	0
30 „ 25	12	6	2	6	3	6	15	0	30	0	45	0	15	0	17	6

BROMIDE ENLARGEMENTS ON OPAL.

Size	Enlargement.		Spotting. Extra.		Finished in Black and White, Extra.						Plush Frames, with Flat Glass and Gold sunk bevelled matt		Black and Gold Frames, with Flat Glass and Gold sunk bevelled matt.	
					Good.		Better.		Best.					
	s.	d.	s.	d.	s.	d.	s.	d.	s.	d.	s.	d.	s.	d.
8½ × 6½	4	6	0	6	5	0	10	0	20	0	7	6	5	0
10 „ 8	5	0	0	9	6	6	12	0	24	0	8	6	7	6
12 „ 7½	5	6	1	0	7	6	15	0	30	0	12	6	10	6
12 „ 10	8	0	1	3	7	6	15	0	30	0	12	6	10	6
15 „ 12	9	6	1	3	10	0	20	0	35	0	17	6	12	6
17 „ 10½	11	6	1	6	10	0	20	0	35	0	17	6	13	0
16 „ 13	15	6	1	9	11	0	21	0	36	0	21	0	15	6
18 „ 15	20	6	2	0	14	0	25	0	40	0	23	0	17	6
20 „ 16	25	6			16	0	27	0	42	0	26	0	20	0
24 „ 18					20	0	30	0	45	0	30	0	21	0

AUTOTYPE ENLARGEMENTS ON PAPER.

With Ordinary or Matt Surface.

Can be had in either of four permanent colours, viz., Standard Brown, Engraving Black, Red Chalk, and Sepia.

Sizes in Inches.	From Negatives. Printed full.	From Negatives. Vignetted.	From Paper Prints, &c. Printed full.	From Paper Prints, &c. Vignetted.	From Paper Prints, &c. Mounted on Card and Spotted.
Cabinet and under	5/6	6/-	5/6	6/-	-/4
Whole Plate	6/6	7/-	6/6	7/-	-/5
10 × 8	7/-	8/-	9/6	10/6	-/8
12 ,, 10	7/6	8/6	10/6	11/6	-/9
Panel	8/6	9/6	11/6	12/6	-/9
15 × 12	10/6	11/6	13/6	15/-	1/-
16 × 13	12/-	13/-	15/6	17/-	1/-
18 ,, 15	14/-	15/-	17/6	19/-	1/3
20 ,, 16	15/6	16/6	18/6	21/-	1/3
24 ,, 18	17/-	19/-	21/-	23/6	1/3
30 ,, 24	35/-	37/6	22/6	25/6	1/9
36 ,, 28	38/6	—	27/6	30/6	2/3

SUBSEQUENT COPIES.

Sizes.	Cabnt.	W. Plate.	10 × 8	12 × 10	Panel	15 × 12	16 × 13	18 × 15	20 × 16	24 × 18	24 × 20	26 × 21	28 × 22	30 × 24	36 × 28
Printed full	-/6	-/9	-/10	1/3	1/6	1/9	2/-	2/6	3/6	4/-	4/6	6/6	8/6	10/-	14/6
Vignette	-/9	1/-	1/1	1/6	1/9	2/-	2/3	2/9	3/10	4/6	5/3	7/9	9/9	11/-	16/-

ENLARGED OR REDUCED NEGATIVES,

from Photos, or from Prints, including one proof from same :—

Size.	Negative and one Proof.	Extra Proofs, each.
C.-de-V.	2/6	-/3
6¼ × 4¾	3/6	-/6
8½ ,, 6½	4/6	-/8

Size.	Negative and one Proof.	Extra Proofs, each.
10 × 8	5/6	-/10
12 ,, 10	7/-	1/-
15 ,, 12	8/6	1/8

Size.	Negative and one Proof.	Extra Proofs, each.
20 × 16	15/-	2/-
21 ,, 17	17/6	2/6

E have now completed the following novelties in Hand Cameras, of which we shall shortly issue a special circular.

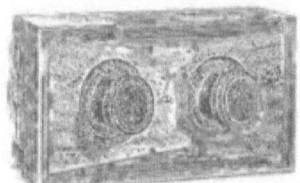

THE STEREOSCOPIC ECLIPSE.

PATENTS, Nos. 4,102 and 1,1150

THE most compact Stereoscopic Camera for time or hand exposures ever yet introduced.

THE LONG RANGE ECLIPSE.

PATENTS Nos. 4,102 and 11394.

HAVING successfully made our Eclipse Lens of increasing sizes up to 9¼ inches focus, we have been requested to adapt this lens to the ½-plate sized camera, and have now made the above special model for the purpose, which enables the operator to use the two lenses, the usual mid-angle supplied with the ½-plate camera and the latest (9¼in.) lens, which produces on this sized plate a very narrow angle.

THE INTERCHANGEABLE.

A new form of folding Hand Camera, suitable for the Eclipse or other lenses, carrying-roll holders or double backs for films or for glass, interchange-able, and entirely covered during exposure ; equally suitable for hand or time exposures, and giving good range for focussing work as well as for "fixed focus."

SHEW'S PATENT FOCUSSING FLANGE.

WE would draw attention to the exceptional success which has attended our introduction of the above, a simple device which, whilst in no way increasing bulk, gives the means of readily shifting the focus to the several scaled distances for hand work, most in use, and beyond this, of fine focussing between any of the distances scaled, converting the camera in fact into a focussing camera at will, retaining at the same time all the advantages in compactness and simplicity, of the Hand Camera.

We are fitting this Flange to any existing cameras. Orders are executed in rotation, but we cannot at present supply in less than 14 days from the receipt of the order.

SEE

The Eclipse Pamphlet, in English or French, free on application to

J. F. SHEW & CO.,

87 and 88, NEWMAN STREET

(Four Doors from Oxford Street),

LONDON, W.

www.ingramcontent.com/pod-product-compliance
Lightning Source LLC
Chambersburg PA
CBHW031115020726
47495CB00007B/2206